Praise for *The Greedy Three*

"Tense, darkly funny, and deeply entertaining, with quirky characters that are wholly original. Katchur's clever crime thriller surprised me in all the best ways and kept me riveted till the very last page."

—Laura McHugh, award-winning author
of *What's Done in Darkness*

"A darkly funny mystery with a cast of quirky characters, a scintillating premise, and a beating heart. It's the perfect book for fans of the Coen brothers and Tarantino films."

—Robyn Harding, bestselling author of *The Perfect Family*

Additional Praise for Karen Katchur

"Karen Katchur is a master at writing into the dark spaces of our intimate family relationships."

—Mindy Mejia, author of *Everything You Want Me to Be*

"I'm entranced by Karen Katchur's direct, well-crafted prose, artful plotting, and characters that leap from the page."

—Marissa Stapley, bestselling
author of *Things to Do When It's Raining*

"Karen Katchur knows how to write and write well about ordinary people stretched to their limits."

—David Bell, bestselling author of *The Forgotten Girl*

THE
GREEDY
THREE

ALSO BY KAREN KATCHUR

THE
GREEDY
THREE

a thriller

KAREN KATCHUR

Podium

Copyright © 2023 by Karen Katchur

Cover design by Podium Publishing

ISBN: 978-1-0394-1630-7

Published in 2023 by Podium Publishing, ULC
www.podiumaudio.com

To Bigfoot

THE
GREEDY
THREE

"To be clever enough to get all that money, one must be stupid enough to want it."

—G. K. CHESTERTON

CHAPTER
ONE

In the backwoods of upstate New York, Noah Weber waits for his contact. A bag full of money lies on the ground at his feet, and a .44 Magnum presses against his kidney. In the near distance, thunder rumbles across a blackened sky. It's not long before the rain starts, pattering the leaves of the tall trees.

Well, that's just great, he thinks.

A part of him wants to turn around and walk away, forget he was ever here. But this is his job. He shouldn't have to remind himself it's how he makes his money, and yet, it's always in these moments right before contact that he must. If all goes as planned, he'll pull in a whopping half a million dollars. He focuses on that.

Somewhere to his right he hears voices and the sound of feet stomping through the brush.

"Psst."

"Over here," Noah says.

Shot steps out from behind a tree. For a scrawny guy, he sure makes a lot of noise. A girl stands off to Shot's side, slightly behind him, with a bundle in her arms. The shadows make it difficult to see them clearly, but a sudden flash of heat lightning gives Noah a better view of who he's dealing with. Shot's face is sharp and pointy. The girl is a tiny thing, young and overly thin.

Noah expects Shot will want to take the lead. In his experience, the men he deals with always want to know about the money first. No matter what he's buying for his clients, whether it's stolen art, banned products, or simply information, the characters are all the same. Although Shot could be different, since Noah has never worked with him before or smuggled a baby across the border. Who knows? Maybe Shot will surprise him and ask how he's doing, or maybe he'll comment about the weather. It might make the circumstances they find themselves in a little more tolerable. Wouldn't that be something?

All right. Noah's going to stay positive, hoping that it will be different this time. Then Shot opens his mouth.

"You got the money?"

Aw, too bad, Noah thinks. So disappointing. So predictable. "Yeah, I got the money. Is she gonna give me any trouble?"

"Who? Her? Nah, she won't give you any trouble." Shot pushes the button on the switchblade that he must've been hiding in his palm this entire time. "She knows what happens if she does." His arm goes up, and the girl flinches. He laughs, as if he's only messing around with her, then in one swift motion he swipes the knife across her forehead, slicing it wide open.

"What the fuck did you do that for?" Noah asks.

Shot waves the knife under Noah's nose. "You got a problem with it?"

It takes all of a second for Noah to make the decision not to shoot him. He can't go around killing all of his contacts. It's not good for business. Instead, he throat punches him.

"Yeah, I got a problem with it."

Shot drops to his knees, clutching his neck.

Noah turns to help the girl. He doesn't see the rock in her raised fist until it's too late. "Son of a—"

CHAPTER
TWO

Hester has just sat down to work on a puzzle when the lights flicker. Thunder rattles the windows and at the same time a strong updraft carries the rain to freezing heights, then tosses it back at the cottage as hail. It's eleven o'clock at night. She can't remember a summer when they've had so many storms.

"We're going to set records with this weather."

She gets up from the card table, releasing a cacophony of creaks and pops from her joints. Reaching under the sink, setting off another round of crackling in her bones, she collects the lantern she bought with her iPad. It's not just any lantern but the camping kind. When used on low power, it can last up to forty-five days.

As she straightens, her lumbar spine sighs, letting her know what it thinks of all this unexpected bending at this time of night. Subconsciously, she rubs her lower back and stares out the kitchen window. The hail has stopped and is once again replaced by rain. The water hits the glass, and the tiny liquid snakes it makes slither onto the ledge. The night creeps in. Its inky shadow covers her fingers and slowly drifts up her arms, her shoulders, her neck, until it rolls over her head and swallows her whole.

She is trapped here, she thinks.

The lights flicker again, bringing her back from the dark place she desperately tries to avoid. Most days she's able to sidestep the longing buried deep inside her chest. It's funny how the heart tries to hide itself from the very person it beats for.

She sits in front of the puzzle again, places the lantern next to it, turns it on when the electricity goes out. The wind howls through the chimney.

The trick to puzzles is to start with the edges first. You frame it out and go from there, working your way in. She's been looking forward to starting this new one all day. The edges are already separated from the other pieces, and she picks up a corner piece, holding it close to the lantern to see it clearly. Then she looks at the box, searching the beach scene on the lid to find which corner it matches. While she tries to decide where it goes, she considers making some tea on the gas stove. Does she want tea? Does she feel like getting up again? She's restless, and she's not sure why. The corner belongs here, at the bottom right with the seashells.

The rain seems to be getting angrier. The water rushes through the downspout, pouring into the small yard at the side of the cottage. Thank goodness she cleaned the gutters at the start of summer. It had taken her all day, lugging the ladder out of the toolshed, leaning it against the stone walls, climbing up and down. Most accidents around the home happen from people falling off ladders. It's a dangerous thing to have to do by yourself, but she's used to doing things alone. There's no one around to help her, anyway. She pulled out leaves and debris, throwing handfuls to the ground. Then she walked around the yard and raked up the mess, which reminded her to buy new work gloves. She hates blisters.

Something bangs against the door. It's probably the wind, so she ignores it, picks up another puzzle piece, and studies it under the light. She takes her time. She has nothing else to do. But there it is again: a hammering noise. Putting the puzzle piece down, she turns toward the sound. Could someone be knocking? Is she hearing things? Is it simply wishful thinking? It's hard to discern what it could be over the sound of the wind and rain, and yet, there it is a third time: Someone's palm slapping the wood frame.

Getting up from the card table, she grabs the .22 that hangs on the mounts that have been screwed into the family room wall long before she moved into the cottage almost ten years ago. It's hard to believe she's lived here that long. It seems like just yesterday she bought the place with the little money her mother had left her after she'd passed. Hester had been surprised when she'd gotten a call from a lawyer here in town that her mother had a will. She'd been estranged from her parents for more than three decades. Looking back, she supposed it was the least her mother could do.

She'd met with a Realtor minutes after cashing the check. The woman wore too much makeup for Hester's taste. What was she hiding underneath that thick layer of foundation? Even so, there was something pretty about her. Maybe it was her confidence or her enthusiasm at showing the old stone cottage to a potential buyer. It had sat empty for several long years. It was in a state of decay, but there was something about it: the cold stone walls, the wooden floors that creaked when you stepped on them, the relic of a gas stove and cast-iron sink. These things spoke to Hester, told her the cottage had strong bones.

As they were leaving to fill out the paperwork at the office, driving along the dirt road through the woods that was over a mile long, the Realtor had said jokingly, "Be careful not to disappear back here."

She wasn't kidding, Hester thinks. It's exactly what has happened.

Hester holds the rifle with one hand, her finger on the trigger. With her other hand, she unlocks the door and turns the knob ever so slowly, listening for any sound coming from the other side. It's quiet except for the wind and rain. Maybe she's imagined the knocking. She'll never get any sleep unless she knows for sure. Throwing the door open, she raises the rifle. She doesn't see anyone, but she can sense she's not alone.

"Who's there?"

A young woman steps out of the shadow and onto the porch. She's soaking wet. Her hair is matted to her cheeks. Blood drips from her forehead, running down her face. Her shirt is torn. A pink bag hangs from her shoulder, and a baby cries in her arms.

"Please. Help me."

Hester keeps the rifle raised, the barrel pointed toward the yard, away from the woman and child. "Who's with you?"

"No one."

Hester doesn't believe her, but still she says, "Get inside." What other choice does she have? Hester is not a heartless woman, although the teenagers in town would say differently. They call her a witch—the crazy old witch, to be exact—who chases them out of the woods. They egg her house at Halloween, shine flashlights in her windows, paint dirty words on her canoe.

The young woman and baby slip around her and into the house. Hester points the rifle into the small yard, sweeping it left and right, trying to see through the rain that's blowing sideways. A loud crack, almost like an explosion, startles her. For a confused second, she doesn't know what has happened, and then a large branch crashes to the ground. A bolt of lightning has struck a nearby tree. Not far from the broken limb, Hester sees movement. She aims her rifle in the general area of the limb, but quickly realizes it's only the shadow figure.

She's seen this figure before: an ethereal image moving with the wind. Whatever the shadow is, it's brought this young woman and child to Hester's home, knowing she'll protect them.

Hester backs up slowly, keeping the rifle aimed at the damaged tree until she's back inside the house. She slams the door closed with her foot and turns around, lowers the gun. The young woman is standing in the middle of the living room, clinging to the baby, dripping watered-down blood onto the floor. There's fear in the young woman's eyes.

"She's cold," the woman says about the baby.

Hester steps closer to them, the rifle at her side. She stops herself from reaching out and touching them. She's been alone so long she doesn't trust what she's seeing.

"Please." The young woman falls to her knees. The pink bag slips from her shoulder. It's a diaper bag. The baby's cries pitch higher.

Hester worked in a hospital in housekeeping for many years. She might've been the invisible lady who emptied garbage cans, mopped floors, cleaned bathrooms, but she learned a thing or two. Like a ball of sticky tape rolling in and out of patients' rooms, she picked up bits and pieces of information by observing and listening to the doctors and nurses who ignored her. She knows all about sickness, disease, and diagnosing symptoms. Death. And this young woman in front of her is suffering from some kind of psychological shock from whatever has brought her here to Hester's door.

The young woman removes the wet blanket from around the baby and lets it fall to the floor. Then she takes off the baby's onesie and soiled diaper and holds the little girl close to her chest. She's trying to keep the baby warm with her body heat, but the young woman is also soaked from the rain, and she's shivering.

"Let me get you some dry blankets." So many questions swarm Hester's mind, but now's not the time to think but to act. She returns with an afghan and a small bath towel. She leans the rifle against the wall by her side. "There are some sweatshirts and sweatpants in the top drawer of the dresser in the back bedroom. Second door on the right. Take the lantern with you and get into some dry clothes, and here, wrap this around you." She holds out the afghan for the young woman to take. "Now give me the child. My body heat will get the job done faster."

The young woman clutches the baby to her chest.

"She's going to catch pneumonia if you don't give her to me." Hester holds her arms out. By the expression on the young woman's face, it's clear she's trying to decide if she can trust Hester. Hester realizes she must look a mess. She hasn't considered her appearance in some time. She can't remember the last time she's combed her hair, wearing it tied and knotted at the base of her neck: the white, frizzy mane she hasn't cut in years.

The baby cries harder. Her lips are blue. The young woman glances down at the bundle in her arms.

"She's freezing," Hester says, arms outstretched.

Reluctantly, the woman hands the baby over and takes the afghan in return, before picking up the lantern and stumbling down the hall to the bedroom.

Hester hugs the baby to her chest, drapes the towel over the baby's small body, and then sits in the rocking chair by the fireplace. She wishes she had a fire going, but summers in July are hot even in the woods. Although the nights can be cool like tonight, especially when they're soaked in rain. She looks at the child in her arms. It's been so long since she's held a real infant to her bosom, she's afraid she's forgotten how. But her motherly instincts come rushing back, along with the memories of how she'd once held her own daughter by a campfire, cradling her, never wanting to let her go.

"Now, now. What's all this fuss about? It's just a thunderstorm. A little rain is nothing to cry about." She pulls the baby away from her for a brief moment, checks for marks on her skin as best she can in the dark, searching for cuts, bruises, signs of abuse. Other than being cold and wet and dirty, the child seems unscathed by whatever she has gone through tonight. Hester holds the baby close to her again, breathing in her scent.

The young woman returns to the living room carrying the lantern. She's wearing Hester's gray sweatshirt and sweatpants. They hang on her too skinny body. The afghan is draped around her shoulders.

"There's a clean rag in the drawer by the sink. You'll want to take care of that cut on your forehead." Hester thinks about asking the woman what's happened to her. Perhaps she's been in a car accident. Or maybe she's running from someone: a boyfriend or husband. She doesn't ask though. She'll wait for the right moment to bring it up, and she trusts she'll know when that moment is. Hester knows a thing or two about running away in the night.

The young woman goes into the kitchen, turns on the faucet. When she comes back into the living room, she's holding a rag to her forehead. Although the light from the lantern is dim and her features are shaded, most of the blood on the young woman's pale face has been washed away.

"Sit." Hester wants to get a better look at her, see who she's dealing with, and how far this young woman has come undone.

The woman approaches, tentatively sits on the floor at Hester's feet. The rifle is only inches away. For a second, Hester wonders if she'll reach for it. The rain continues pummeling the roof. A crack of thunder rattles the windows again.

"If you haven't noticed, the electricity is out. If you need to call someone, you'll have to wait until it comes back on."

"There's no one I need to call."

Hester nods. "Do you have a name?"

"Eve."

Hester suspects Eve isn't the woman's real name, but she doesn't push her for the truth even though she knows she should. She has no idea what kind of trouble Eve is in, and if she's brought that trouble to Hester's home. Now that she can see her a little more clearly, she's guessing Eve is no older than a teenager. She's not a young woman at all. She's a girl. There isn't a wedding ring on the girl's finger.

"And the baby's name?"

Eve hesitates. "Ivy."

The baby stops crying at the mention of the name, as if she knows they're talking about her. Her skin no longer feels cold to the touch, but Hester's not ready to hand her over to Eve just yet, so instead, she keeps the baby close to her chest. Besides, Eve hasn't asked her to give the baby back.

"How old is she?"

"A couple weeks."

Hester raises an eyebrow, tries hard not to be judgmental. A newborn has no business being out in this weather. She should be home, swaddled and safe in her crib, but what should be and what is are often two different things.

A loud bang comes from somewhere outside. Both women jump. It sounds close by. Hester gets up. She has no choice but to hand the baby to Eve, before reaching for the rifle.

"Who's with you? I can't protect you unless I know who I'm dealing with."

"No one's with me. I swear."

Hester puts her shoulder against the wall, rifle at her side, and peeks out the living room window. It's too dark and the rain is coming down too hard to make out anything other than the trees and the broken branch on the ground. "I'm going to check. You stay here and don't move."

"No! Wait!"

Hester stops from opening the door.

"Please. He didn't follow me."

So, not a car accident. Hester didn't really believe it was. It's what she suspected in her gut all along. Eve is fleeing from some rotten, no-good *He*. Hester knows all about what can happen when a young girl gets mixed up with the wrong man—the broken bones, the cuts, the bruised heart.

"How do you know he didn't follow you?"

"He didn't. Trust me."

CHAPTER
THREE

Noah opens his eyes and finds himself lying on his stomach on the cold, wet ground. Thunder rumbles and a flash of lightning splits the night sky. For a second, the woods are illuminated, as if the storm is saying to him: *Look where you are, dumbass.* To further its point, or maybe to just be a jerk about it, the rain not only hits the back of his head but also strikes the ground hard enough that it bounces up into his face.

Noah rests his chin on the back of his hand and licks the muddy water from his lips. There are several ways in which he can look at his current situation. If he tries really hard, he's certain he can figure out a way to get out of this particular predicament. Even in the worst-case scenario—such as this one—he has a knack for staying optimistic. If that doesn't work, well, he can always rely on luck. Ever since he was a boy, his adoptive mother, Madeline, told him he was lucky, and he's always been more than happy to agree with her.

So going with luck and in honor of Madeline's memory, he slowly pulls himself up to all fours. His head feels funny, and the ground seems to sway. Not to point fingers here, but if he had an inkling where the girl might be, he'd be pointing his finger at her for being the culprit, for making a mess of things, for surprising him.

And that's not an easy thing to do.

Nonetheless, the ninety-pound pissant hit him on the side of the head with a rock, knocking him out. *Man*, did she ever wallop him.

The rain continues to strike his head and back, where an endless stream drips from his hair and chin. He checks if the .44 Magnum is still tucked in his waistband. It is. His fingers sink in the soggy earth. Aside from the obvious, he's struggling to make sense of what went wrong.

Ah. On second thought, he knows exactly what went wrong.

He was rushed. The turnaround time his client demanded was nearly impossible, and he didn't have the luxury of overseeing any of the details.

"You pick it," he'd said to Shot. "Someplace remote, without cameras."

You pick it? Yup, that's what he'd said all right. How stupid can he be?

But he's here now, isn't he? He can still pull off the tight deadline even if he didn't choose the time and place, and the exchange wasn't exactly what he would call smooth.

Then he remembers: *the money.*

He sits back on his heels, checks he's not dizzy. He's not. The rain continues to hammer his head and shoulders with so much force it actually hurts. His clothes are soaked. The whole scenario is starting to piss him off.

Slowly, carefully, he stands and looks around, tries to see where he is and get his bearings. When he feels steady on his feet and somewhat certain of the direction he needs to go in, he takes a couple steps forward and stumbles, tripping over something, landing back on his hands and knees. *Shit.*

Sitting, he kicks a log. *Shit. Shit. Shit.* He kicks it over and over again. Somewhere in the back of his mind, it registers that this log is too soft. It's pliable where it should be hard. He taps it with his toe. It's squishy. Remembering his phone in his back pocket, he pulls it out, fumbles with it until he finds the little flashlight symbol so he can see what the hell he's tripped over.

The rain keeps coming, coating his face and lashes, and he wipes his eyes with the back of his hand as he shines the small beam of light on the ground near his feet. The log is wearing basketball shorts. Its shins are hairy. Noah scrambles backward when the beam of light bounces onto Shot's face. Shot's eyes are open, unblinking as the rain strikes his pupils.

His throat is collapsed.

Noah finds his legs, forces himself to stand again. Shot's windpipe must've been crushed when Noah throat-punched him. He must've suffocated. Noah really needs to work on his temper. He's too aggressive, forceful, and he makes a mental note to add it to his list of self-improvements.

Shining the light around, he looks for the bag full of money and avoids shining the beam on Shot's face, because who wants to see *that* again.

What about the girl? Where is she?

Based on the information he's dug up on Shot, the guy keeps his girls on a tight leash. He checks on them repeatedly when they meet with clients, keeping in constant contact as a way to control them. Eventually, he breaks them down into submissiveness, until they can't think or function without him. Most of the girls are runaways, drug addicts, or impoverished loners all but forgotten by society. Easy pickings for slimeballs like Shot. Noah understands how sex trafficking works, even though he's not a part of it.

He continues searching the ground. It's becoming clear he's not going to find anything in the dark.

Not the money.

Or the girl.

Or the baby.

Not tonight anyway.

Having no other alternative but to postpone his search, he uses the flashlight to guide him through the maze of trees, seeing only as far as the small beam of light allows. Hopeful that he's heading in the direction of the lake, he pushes the higher branches away from his face. With each step, his temple throbs where the girl struck him with the rock. In spite of what she's done to him, the trouble she's given him, he smiles. He can't help but feel a little bit of respect for her.

But that doesn't mean he's going to let her get away with it.

CHAPTER
FOUR

Eve refuses to talk, making it clear she's not going to elaborate about the kind of trouble she's in or who she's running from. Hester doesn't press her, not wanting to frighten away the only houseguest she's ever had. And the loud noise that made them jump was nothing more than a garbage can blowing over, striking the side of the cottage.

But Hester knows better than to trust her.

Eve is no longer sitting on the floor with Ivy. Instead, they're curled up on the couch, exhausted from their tumultuous night. Hester does the only thing she can and sits in the rocking chair in front of them with the rifle in her lap. Slowly, she rocks while she watches them and ponders her options. There's more than one way to get answers to the questions she has about the girl. All she needs is an opportunity to do a little reconnaissance work. If she waits long enough, she's certain an opening will present itself. The best way to keep them safe—herself included—is to know who she's dealing with.

The baby falls asleep, but Eve isn't nodding off so easily. The girl is fighting to stay awake, and she continues to fight for quite some time.

All the while, Hester patiently rocks and waits.

It takes the girl hours to give in to those heavy eyelids, but eventually she does. And still, Hester rocks and waits, listening for the sound of Eve's breathing, the kind that will let her know the girl has fallen into a deep slumber.

When it comes—the measured rhythm of someone whose heart rate is no more than a crawl—Hester makes her move. Neither the girl nor the baby stirs when she stands or when the floorboards creak underneath her feet.

Rifle in hand, she quietly leaves the cottage. She thinks about which direction Eve might've come from, before she'd pounded on Hester's door late last night. There's a path off the dirt road that veers toward the lake and Hester's canoe. It seems like the obvious choice.

She makes her way over to it, her sneakers sinking into the muddy puddles left by the storm. A warm breeze blows her hair across her back. The first slivers of sunlight poke through the tree branches as she picks her way through the woods, searching the ground for footprints or other signs that someone has been here recently.

It's not an easy trek. The rain has made the ground slick and moist. The vegetation has grown thick from all the summer storms and the path is rendered almost nonexistent. More than once she's thought about clearing the way, but now she's glad for the cover, for Eve's sake and Ivy's. It will help keep them hidden at her cottage, and, if she's honest, it's for her sake, too, because she doesn't want them found.

The image of Eve standing on the porch with blood on her face, the baby in her arms, its wails piercing the night, lingers in the back of her mind. It occurs to Hester that if Eve wakes and finds the cottage empty, she might flee with the baby. It's what Hester would do if the situation were reversed. If you're going to run and you don't want to be caught, then you need to keep moving.

The key in Hester's front pocket jabs her leg. It belongs to the El Camino parked alongside her cottage. She doesn't have a spare, and she's certain the truck will be there when she returns. Still, she finds herself hurrying, wanting to get home before her guests wake up. She can't believe she has actual guests—and a baby no less. She pinches herself just to check it's real and she's not dreaming.

She continues with her search, trying to find clues about where the girl came from.

Then she notices something white caught in a bush, and she pushes her way through the brush to get to it, but it's only an empty plastic bag. There's nothing written on it. It's just trash, and she sticks it in her pocket to toss out later.

Back to the path, she takes a couple steps and stops. Her skin prickles, sending goose bumps up and down her arms. She has that feeling you get when you suddenly realize you're not alone. Someone else is in the woods with her. Their presence furls through the air, crawling up her spine and nesting in the hairs on the back of her neck.

Soundlessly, she scurries toward a birch tree and places her back against the trunk. Raising the rifle, she peeks around the peeling bark.

Silence buzzes in her ears.

Crouching, she skitters through the thicket as quietly as she can, sniffing the air like a doe in search of predators, catching a sharp, tangy scent. The smell is stronger the closer she gets to the source, like meat left on the counter for too long. It can only mean one thing: Something big is dead.

Moving more slowly, she comes to an area between two small saplings and stops next to a pair of sneakers, which just happen to be attached to the feet of a man's body.

Well, what do you know?

23

She's seen plenty of corpses at the hospital, and she's not shocked by seeing one now. Apparently, Eve hadn't been kidding when she'd insisted the no-good He hadn't followed her.

Okay, she thinks. There must be something she can do to sort this out for the girl, but first, she has to do something about that smell.

She takes a moment and blocks the scent of decaying flesh from her mind, then replaces it with the more pleasant aroma of Baby Ivy's skin.

Hester can trick herself into seeing, hearing, smelling, feeling, believing anything and everything. The brain is a powerful tool if you know how to use it, and she knows how to use hers. All those nights putting puzzles together has kept her mind sharp. She's good at problem-solving, and this is one problem she wants to fix for Eve and the baby. And yes, sure, also for herself. No matter what her intentions, whether they are pure or not, in the end, it all comes back to the self. Why do people help others? Because it makes *them* feel good, that's why.

Every action, even if it's good, is selfish in nature.

Something to remember.

She circles the body, not finding any blood. He hasn't been shot or stabbed that she can see. Next to his thigh is something shiny. She kicks it to get a better look at it. It's a knife, but not just any knife. It's a switchblade. She picks it up and turns it over. It's probably what made the cut on Eve's forehead. She retracts the blade. Curious how it works, she presses the button on the handle, and it springs open again. Lunging at the air, she pretends to stab someone, dueling with an imaginary opponent. *En garde!*

"Huh." She considers how she feels about a knife as a weapon. It's pretty nice actually, and she retracts the blade again and sticks it in her pocket.

She turns her attention back to the body.

"So, what happened to you?"

Then she notices the bruise on his neck. *Well.*

She can't picture the girl having enough strength to choke him to death, but what does it matter really? No matter how he died, she still has to figure out what she's going to do with him. Someone will eventually be looking for him, and by the smell of him, he won't be too hard to find.

She contemplates burying him, but it will take up too much of her time, and besides, the trees and saplings and ground vegetation are too thick. There's not enough open space to dig a grave.

What to do? What to do?

Peering again at the dark mark on his neck, a smile forms at the corners of her lips as a plan takes shape in the back of her mind. Maybe she can fix this for the girl by making it look like the guy did this to himself. Or at least it could buy the girl some time before the cops start looking for her. It's worth a shot, and she searches for a tall tree, one with sturdy branches. All she needs is a rope. It's almost too easy.

Hester collects the rope from her toolshed, but only after she peeks into the cottage window to see the girl and baby still asleep on the couch. Then she hurries back to the woods and the man's body.

Standing over him, she weighs her options. He's young and rather thin looking. There's maybe a hundred and fifty pounds of heft to him, give or take a couple pounds. The tree she selects is close by, easy enough to drag him over to it. She grabs his ankles and pulls him close to the trunk and the branch with his name on it. She loops the rope around his neck, ties a secure knot. Living near the lake most of her life, she's been on enough boats to have learned basic seamanship.

After tossing the rope around the branch, she begins to hoist his body up. He's a lot heavier than she anticipated, but she's getting him off the ground: shoulders, hips, knees. He's a bit stiff *like a board*. It's probably from rigor mortis setting in. He must've died at least six or seven hours ago. It seems about right when she thinks back to when the girl came banging on her door last night and how the sun is now peeking over the mountaintop. Its rays are burning through the low-lying clouds, breaking through the tangle of branches and leaves, and making the humid morning feel that much hotter.

Sweat drips down the side of her face. With each tug and pull, she's lifting him up, up, up, and off the ground. The rope digs into her palms (new work gloves would come in handy right about now), and she leans back hard, putting all her weight into it. He's almost there, close to crossing the finish line, but the vegetation has something to say about it. Wet and slick from all the rain the night before, her feet slide out from under her, and she falls backward, landing hard on her ass. *Oomph*.

As she fights to hang onto the rope, it cuts deeper into her palms, but she holds on.

A play for the record books!

But from this position, she's struggling to keep him raised. She's losing him. The rope slips from her hands, and the next thing she knows, he's falling, falling, falling. When his feet strike the ground, something cracks. His knees lock, and he bends at the waist, his body folding like a lawn chair.

Well, that record was short-lived.

She pulls herself up, wiping the dirt off the back of her jeans. The birds are complaining, chirping, creating a fuss at all the commotion she's causing. "Oh, shut up."

She picks up the rope a second time. She's determined to string him up, throw off the cops, and save the girl and baby.

Yeah, keep telling yourself that.

Cops aren't stupid. Her cousin, the sheriff, isn't stupid. Hester just wants more time with the girl and baby, and nothing can change how motivated she is to see this through.

She pulls on the rope, yanking as hard as she can until he's off the ground again. His body swings and jerks with each tug, like a pendulum keeping time. A little more pulling and she does it; she gets him in the tree. Her tired limbs hum with exertion, and she's huffing and puffing, but holy shit, she's done it. If there was a crowd, they'd be cheering.

Taking a step back, she scrutinizes the scene. He's not as high off the ground as she would like, but it's going to have to do. Yet, something doesn't look quite right. *Oh!* It's his left leg. It's facing in the wrong direction, twisted at an odd angle with his foot pointing somewhere behind him.

"Let me fix that for you."

She grabs his lower leg, turning it at the knee, snapping and popping his hip not exactly back into place but closer to a more natural-looking position. Then she takes a step back again, looks up at the tree, hands on her hips, and admires her work.

"That's better."

She grabs the rifle and the extra rope she snagged from the toolshed that she didn't need. She makes her way home through the woods as though it's just another day, satisfied with a job well done.

All is quiet when she approaches the cottage. Hester tosses the extra rope onto the floor of the toolshed, and she throws the plastic bag she'd plucked from the bush into the garbage can. It's the same can that blew over the night before during the storm.

Scurrying to her truck, she hunches so the girl can't see her, and she feels around inside the passenger-side rear wheel well for the magnetic case. She finds it, pulls it out, and sticks the key she keeps in her pocket into the case. Then she puts the case back under the wheel well. It's a perfect hiding spot. Even if someone did think to check the wheel well for a spare key, they'd check the driver's side front wheel because that's what makes the most sense—but not to her. Her brand of common sense has always been skewed compared to most people.

Finally, she heads inside, stepping through the front door, rifle in her grip.

Eve is slouched on the couch. Her eyes are closed, and the baby's in her lap. In the light of day, she can see Eve's face more clearly. Her lips are full, her nose is crooked. Her skin is the color of ash. The gash on her forehead is at least an inch long and who knows how deep. It looks worse than it did last night.

Hester sets the rifle down, relieved to be home. Eve jerks awake suddenly and jumps when she sees Hester.

"Ivy's hungry," Eve says. "There's still no power, and I'm not sure how to heat up her bottle."

Hester glances at the diaper bag that's been lying on the floor since last night. She picks it up, heads to the kitchen.

Eve gets up and follows her, swaying on her feet, Baby Ivy pressed against her chest.

Hester pulls out a chair. "Sit." She considers whether Eve has stuck around not because she wants to, but because she's not strong enough to leave. *Yet.*

Eve eases herself into the chair. Her fingers touch her brow near the wound, and her eyelids droop. She appears to be struggling to stay awake. Baby Ivy, on the other hand, is alert, taking in her new surroundings.

Hester lights the gas stove, puts a pot of water on the burner. After pulling a can of formula from the bag, she pours it into the bottle, puts the bottle in the pot. While she waits for it to warm, she digs around the diaper bag, finding little in terms of supplies. The diapers are already gone. The formula won't last the day. Maybe Eve will consider breastfeeding.

When the bottle is heated, she holds it out for Eve. As the girl reaches for it, Hester eyes the mud caked underneath Eve's ragged fingernails. She's pushed the sleeves of Hester's sweatshirt up to her elbows, revealing scratches on her lower arms and some kind of writing on the inside of her left forearm, possibly a tattoo. Last night Hester had tossed Eve's wet, blood-soaked clothes into the washing machine, but only after she searched them for a wallet, ID, or weapon. Eve showed up with nothing on her, not so much as a penny. Her clothes sit in the machine unwashed, waiting for the electricity to be turned back on.

Eve hesitates, dropping her arm before grasping the bottle. "Maybe you should feed her."

Oh, yes, Hester wants to so badly, but she doesn't want to spook the girl by appearing too eager. Moving slowly, she reaches for the baby, cradles her in her arm. Ivy kicks her feet, eager to be fed. Hester can't help but smile at the pleasure this simple act is giving her.

Eve plucks a banana from the bowl on the table. "Do you mind?"

She doesn't wait for Hester to reply before she peels it and shoves it in her mouth.

Eve is too thin. Her body doesn't look like a woman's body should after giving birth. She doesn't have the pillow belly, the fat around the hips, the swollen breasts. She's possibly malnourished. The banana seems to perk her up, though, and she looks around the kitchen much like Ivy did moments ago. Hester wonders what Eve is thinking, if it's whether she can stay here, if it's safe.

"Do you live alone?" Eve asks.

"Yes," Hester says.

"Not married?"

"No."

"Is there a boyfriend? Or—maybe a girlfriend?"

"No."

"Any family?"

This girl is bold. Or maybe she's just being cautious. Still, Hester doesn't take kindly to her questions. "It's just me."

Eve seems to be satisfied it's the truth, because she doesn't ask her anything else. When Hester finishes feeding Ivy, she puts the baby on her shoulder, pats her gently on the back to burp her.

"I need to look at the cut on your forehead."

Eve's hand immediately goes to the open gash on her brow.

"Does it hurt?"

"A little."

"Are you dizzy?"

"Sometimes if I move too quickly."

"You're not going to pass out on me, are you?"

"No."

Once Ivy is sufficiently burped, Hester reluctantly passes the baby to Eve. After running a rag under the faucet, she gently cleans Eve's wound.

"It's deep. You may need stitches." Although she already knows the answer, she asks, "Do you want to tell me how you got it?"

Eve grabs Hester's wrist, taking her by surprise. The girl is stronger than she looks.

"No, I don't want to tell you how I got it."

They stare at each other. Hester sees now that she's underestimated her. Eve is a fighter. She's been through some things, maybe much harder than this. This is a good sign. Eve needs to be strong. She's going to have to be if she wants to keep her baby.

Hester pulls her arm away. "What should we do for diapers?"

CHAPTER
FIVE

Sheriff Laura Pennington hops out of her SUV and drags the horse barricade to the center of the road, blocking the entrance to the flooded cul-de-sac. She can't say how many times she's been called to this street after a thunderstorm. Too many to count.

Maneuvering around the rushing water, she makes her way to the nearest sidewalk, doing her best not to get swept away. The narrow storm drain at the corner of the block can't handle the amount of runoff that travels through the neighborhood. Whoever designed this section of town forgot to consider its proximity to the creek flowing from the lake.

She puts her hands on her hips and surveys the quiet street. It's too early for most of the residents to be up and bustling about before work. Their homes are dark, and they'll soon discover most of Bordertown is without electricity. The only fire department is currently busy putting out a small electrical fire caused by a downed wire, which means Laura's on her own here.

Cautiously, she inches her way closer to the water's edge where it careens over the curb. Through the tumbling white foam, she sees the bright red hat of Mrs. Pitchel's garden gnome. It seems to be wedged in tightly, doing a bang-up job of blocking as much of the drain's opening as it can.

Laura squats and reaches into the torrent. The water soaks her arm up to her shoulder and drenches the side of her uniform. She gives the lawn ornament a good yank, but it doesn't budge. After another strong tug and a little finagling, the gnome dressed as Santa Claus for the woman's Christmas in July display is freed.

Tucking the statue under her arm, she navigates her way back to the SUV and slides in on the driver's side. She drops the garden gnome onto the passenger seat. Then she shakes her wet arm and rubs the side of her uniform where it's soaked through.

For a panicked second, she grabs the front of her shirt, fearful the fading photo she keeps of a fourteen-year-old girl in her breast pocket is ruined. Thankfully, it's dry, and she covers her relieved heart. Underneath her palm, on the back of the picture, written in Pop's handwriting is *Kayleigh McBride, missing 2017*. It was his last case, unsolved, and the one Laura had promised him that wouldn't be forgotten. She wouldn't be able to forgive herself if she damaged the photo today of all days, on the four-year anniversary of his death.

I'll find her, Pop. I haven't given up.

Denise from dispatch comes on the radio.

"Go ahead," Laura says.

"Did you find the gnome?" Denise asks.

"I got it right here."

"Was it stuck in the drain again?"

"Yeah. I'll drop it off on my way in."

"Oh, the coffeemaker is on the fritz. You might want to grab a cup before you get here."

"Anyone else need some?"

"Bring as many as you can carry."

"Copy that."

Laura starts the engine and pulls from the curb, driving to the next block where Mrs. Pitchel lives. When she gets to the house—a small split-level surrounded by lush shrubbery—the first thing she notices is a large downed tree limb on top of the woman's car.

Laura picks up the radio. "Hey, Denise, we're going to need a tree service out here."

"I'll put it on the list," Denise says.

Laura grabs the gnome. It's going to be one of those days, she thinks, as she exits the vehicle.

CHAPTER
SIX

Five miles away from the sheriff and the garden gnome, Noah stumbles upon some kind of backwoods convenience store. The paint on the store's sign is chipped and some of the letters are missing, but he can still make out what it says: Fisher's Market, or rather Fi her's Ma ket. The screen on the front door is ripped. The place is run-down, neglected by its owners, but since it's the only sign of life Noah has found since stepping out of the woods early this morning and onto a winding, deserted road, it will have to do. He spent the night wandering around the maze of trees aimlessly, a little dazed and confused, perhaps from the blow the girl delivered to the side of his head. But now the haze has lifted. His head feels clearer.

The thunderstorm last night has left a mosaic of glass puddles in the gravel parking lot, and he jumps over them as though he's playing a game of hopscotch. His T-shirt is wet and dirty and clings to his skin. His jeans are waterlogged and feel as though they weigh ten pounds. The rainwater mixes with the sourness of his sweat.

The bell jingles when he steps inside. He shakes off the stares of two men dressed in camouflage shorts and muscle shirts. The cashier looks up from the paper. He's an older gentleman, conditioned to read the news in print.

Noah feels as though he's stepped back through time and the year is 1970 based on the wood-paneled walls. This is the kind of place where the locals will remember a stranger in detail, and it's a little unnerving. He's glad he dyed his hair blond after much internal debate before leaving the city and making the drive upstate.

The old man folds the paper, puts it aside. "What can I do for you?"

"Do you have a bathroom I can use?"

"There are plenty of trees to piss on outside, pretty boy," one of the camo guys says.

"Right. Thanks for the tip."

Noah picks up some beef jerky for protein and a jug of water, and he sets them on the counter. He would prefer a protein bar, but he's doubtful he'll find anything like that here. From a quick glance down the aisles, the shelves are mostly stocked with candy and chips, bread and cereal, laundry detergent and toilet paper. All the essential items and nothing more. There's an entire section dedicated to chewing tobacco.

"Where're you from?" the same camo guy asks, the one who not so politely told him to piss on a tree.

"Not from here." Noah winks at the guy. It's probably not the best way to handle him.

"Who the fuck you think you're winking at?"

The old man comes out from behind the counter. "All right, boys. That's enough."

"He started it," camo guy says.

35

"I know, but I'm ending it." The man ushers the guys out the door and returns to the cash register. "That'll be twelve forty-seven."

Noah tosses a twenty onto the counter.

The man gets change from the cash register and hands it to Noah. "Watch yourself around here. I wouldn't go picking a fight with the wrong people."

"I'll keep that in mind."

Noah shoves the change in his pocket before he picks up the jerky and the water and strolls out the door. He looks left and right, searching for the two camo guys, but they seem to have gone. All through prep school he had to put up with bullies like them, but back then he'd been teased about being adopted, not having the right pedigree or the right genes. It still gets to him sometimes, the ribbing and the insecurities about where he came from, chipping away at his self-worth.

He heads behind the store, walks fifty yards into the woods, and puts his purchases down. He hasn't gone to the bathroom outside since he was a boy, peeing behind the stables when he was too lazy to walk up to the main house where he lived with Madeline in Greenwich, Connecticut.

Oh, what the hell.

He unzips his fly and pees.

Somewhere to his right, twigs snap. His stream is flowing, and he decides not to interrupt it. He knows it's the two idiots from the store. They just couldn't help themselves. They just couldn't leave well enough alone.

They stand on either side of him.

"Boys."

"You a queer or something?" the same camo guy asks, the one who appears to do all the talking.

"No." Noah zips up his fly.

"Well, we don't like your attitude. Ain't that right?" the guy says to his buddy.

"Yeah, that's right."

"What's your problem, anyway?" Noah would really like to know before this goes any further.

"You're our problem." The chatty camo guy pokes him in the arm.

"Don't touch me."

"Yeah, what're you going to do about it, *pretty boy*?" Chatty camo guy pokes him harder this time, pushing Noah into the other camo guy.

Noah thinks quickly about his next move. It's two against one. Best-case scenario, they rough him up, steal whatever money he has in his wallet. Worst-case scenario—he can't even go there, not after their offensive, homophobic words. He doesn't see any other way out of this, and before either camo guy knows what happens, Noah's Magnum is pressed between the eyebrows on the chattier camo guy's forehead.

Camo guy puts his hands up. "Easy. We don't want any trouble."

"Like hell you don't."

Maybe it's because he's tired from walking around in the woods all night or the fact that his clothes are wet and he stinks. Or maybe it's because he has yet to find the girl and the money. He supposes it's a combination of all those things that makes him pull the trigger, catching the surprise in camo guy's eyes right before his knees buckle and he falls to the ground.

The other camo guy is running by the time Noah can line up a shot, disappearing behind a wall of trees. Noah is in no mood to chase the guy down. *Fuck it.*

He looks at his shirt that's covered in blood splatter. Several drops have landed on his sneakers. *Dammit.* He really likes these sneakers, and he wipes his foot in the tall grass trying to get it off, instead smearing it and making it worse.

Nothing about this job is working in his favor.

There's blowback on the end of the barrel, a little blood and bits of skin, and he wipes it on his shirt since it's already dirty. He tucks the Magnum back in his waistband and takes out a piece of beef jerky, chews on it while he mulls over what he's going to do with this asshole's body. Can he just leave him here? Or should he try to hide him from his dipshit friend? When he finishes chewing, he wipes the corner of his mouth.

It's probably best to hide the body.

He shoves several pieces of jerky into his front pockets, and then he takes several long swallows of water. He's feeling a little better now that he's hydrated, and since he's feeling better, he regrets losing his temper. Why does he let idiots like the camo guys get to him? He supposes it all started with those boys in prep school. They're the root of his rage, a reminder of his meager beginnings, the taunts of not being good enough, of being nothing more than an errand boy.

He looks down at camo guy and sighs.

What's done is done.

Noah grabs camo guy by the ankles and starts dragging his body deeper into the woods. It's not easy. The guy's got some serious mass to him, and he's not exactly helping with his arms flailing out and catching every tree and shrub. He considers dragging him by the arms, but that would put him near the head and the blood. He decides that pulling him by the ankles is best.

For the next thirty minutes, he schleps through the underbrush. Maybe he did provoke the guy by winking at him in the store. Noah is not gay. He likes women. It's just that he tires of them quickly, always finding some terminal flaw in their personality or appearance. His last girlfriend was a compulsive gum chewer and if that wasn't disgusting enough, she took it a step further, blowing little bubbles and popping them between her teeth. *Man,* was that ever annoying. No matter how good she was in bed, he couldn't get past the gum cracking. He hasn't lost hope, though. He believes there's a woman out there who won't piss him off regularly. Madeline had promised he'd find someone suitable. He just hasn't found her, yet.

The warm air collects in his throat and lungs, weighing him down. He needs to catch his breath, and until he does, he doesn't think he can take another step. He drops the guy's ankles. Wiping his sweaty hands on his thighs, he looks around. No matter how far he's walked, the trees all look the same, blending together like a room spinning after he's had too much to drink. Logically, he knows no two trees are the same, but they appear that way to him, every trunk and branch a replica of the one before.

He sits on the damp ground to rest and chews the last pieces of beef jerky he'd stuffed into his pocket. Not far from where he's sitting, something large is trampling through the brush. It's probably this asshole's friend coming back to even the score.

Noah reaches for his Magnum. He watches the dark mass move in his direction. It deftly navigates the maze of trees, ducking in and out of sight.

On second thought, he's pretty sure it's not the other camo guy, but whatever it is, it's big. Like really big.

Is it? Could it be?

Bigfoot?

No, Bigfoot is bipedal, so they say, if you believe in that sort of thing. This creature is on all fours.

It's getting closer. It's getting closer still.

It's a fucking black bear, and it's ambling toward him.

It's picking up speed.

Noah's heart seems to have stopped. He can't think of what to do. Shooting it doesn't seem right. The only other thing he can think of is to throw what's left of the beef jerky at the bear. Isn't that what you're supposed to do? Give the bear your food?

As the jerky leaves his fingers and before he can react, the bear is up in his face. The animal's hot breath presses against his skin. Its claws swipe his left shoulder. The pain is swift and searing.

He scrambles backward, and by some miracle (or because he's lucky?), the bear doesn't chase him. Instead, it stands between Noah and camo guy's corpse. It slams its front feet on the ground, grunting, blowing out air in what sounds like a giant exhale.

The bear is thinner than Noah first thought and kind of scrawny compared to videos he's seen on YouTube. It stares at him. They're in some kind of weird standoff. It seems to want something from him. Is it challenging him? Sizing him up?

Then it turns to sniff camo guy's body.

Holy shit. The bear is more interested in camo guy.

Noah starts moving backward, crab walking, cautiously, steadily, putting more and more distance between them.

The bear lifts its head, glances at him.

He freezes.

Then it turns its attention back to camo guy, and Noah starts moving again.

When he feels he's a safe enough distance away (he's only guessing here, having no idea how far a safe distance is from such a creature), he pulls himself up, despite the burning in his shoulder. He wills himself not to run, afraid the bear will only chase him if he does, and he walks away as casually as possible. His T-shirt is ripped where the claws have swiped him. His skin is sliced open. Blood drips down his arm.

A bear? An actual motherfucking bear. *Really?* He is *not* having a good day.

With each step, he sheds the shock, and yes, he admits the fear of coming into contact with such a beast. He's unsure where he's going, if he's heading deeper into the woods or making his way out, but he needs to keep moving, while his mind and body rids itself of adrenaline.

In his wake, he hears the sound of camo guy's flesh ripping, his bones breaking. It's a distinctive sound. It makes him sick. He throws up, spewing the last of the stress from his body. When he's finished, he feels better and stands straighter, taller. His left shoulder stings where the skin is torn open, but it could be worse. The animal could've ripped his arm clean off.

He laughs.

At first, it's an awkward chuckle, but then it gathers momentum, bubbling up from his stomach, until he's laughing uncontrollably.

He raises his arms to the sky, the pain in his shoulder protesting, as Madeline's words rain down on him like a rainbow.

Her angel.

It's only after the laughter wanes that he lowers his arms and takes out his phone. He pulls up the compass and turns in the direction of the original meeting place. It's time he starts at the beginning, retraces his steps, and finds the girl. He no longer has any regrets about killing camo guy, for he has fed a hungry bear.

He is Noah after all, and the world is his ark.

Tattooed on his back are angel's wings.

CHAPTER
SEVEN

After tying a tea towel around Baby Ivy's bottom, Hester watches her sleep on the couch. The towel was the best solution she could come up with, at least for now.

Eve is in the bathroom, showering. Her dirty clothes are still sitting in the washer. Hester knows they're still there because she's rummaged through them a second time, searching the pockets, looking for clues about her guest. She's found nothing about where Eve and the baby have come from. The pockets were empty. The shirt was torn and stained with blood. The amount of dirt on the knees of Eve's jeans makes her suspect the girl has spent some time kneeling. Was she on her knees begging for her life? Or crawling away from the man with the switchblade? The mud underneath her fingernails looked as though she'd been clawing dirt.

Hester glances at her wristwatch, relying on her battery-powered watch or the sun. She doesn't have a smartphone like everybody else. She has no one to call or text. At one time she had friends and coworkers at the hospital, but she hasn't spoken to anyone in three long years, not since she was forced to leave. It was one of the nurses—a big, fat know-it-all—who had complained to management about her. They'd warned her three, maybe four times (she lost count) to stay away from the maternity ward. They'd threatened to fire her if she didn't take the retirement package they'd only offered so they could get rid of her. She'd taken the money, of course, although she'd maintained she'd done nothing wrong.

The power is still out, and she can't log onto the internet on her iPad or check the local news on the television for reports about missing persons or babies. She can't even order diapers online and have them delivered. Baby Ivy's lips move as though she's sucking something, perhaps a binky. She must've lost it during the night. She's such a sweet child. Barely fusses.

"What are you doing?" Eve's helped herself to one of Hester's T-shirts and gym shorts. The shorts are big on her, and she's rolled the waistband to keep them from falling down.

Hester hadn't realized she was standing over the baby like some kind of watchman. She moves away, smooths the hair frizzing around her face.

"I was making sure she didn't roll off the couch."

Ivy is too young to roll over, but Eve doesn't seem to know this.

"Good thinking." Eve sits on the floor in front of the cushion where Ivy sleeps.

The baby doesn't wake from the sound of their voices. She's used to noises, people. It's possible wherever Eve has come from, it was a busy place.

"Was the water cold? No telling when the electricity will be turned back on."

She doesn't tell Eve how the power company sometimes forgets there's a cottage this deep in the woods, one with running water and electricity, putting Hester last on the list to get service back. From what she gathers, most of the town has gone dark. They hadn't seen a storm this fierce in some time.

"It got cold at the end. I guess I used what was left of the hot water."

Hester notices the writing on the underside of Eve's forearm again. "Is that a tattoo?"

Eve nods.

"What does it say?"

Eve holds up her arm for Hester to see. On the inside of her forearm, written in black ink, is the word *love*.

Hester never entertained the idea of getting permanent ink on her body. It's not that she's opposed to it. She just couldn't justify the expense, not when she's lived on a fixed income all her life.

"Did it hurt?"

"The tattoo? No."

"I knew a girl once when I was around your age." In juvie, she thinks but doesn't say. "She used to write *fuck love* all over her arms in pen."

Eve smiles, seemingly impressed, but what has impressed her Hester can only imagine. Is it the swearing or that she's known some interesting people in her past?

"Seems righter than this." Eve traces the letters on her arm with her finger. "The people who are supposed to love you, don't always, do they?"

"No, they don't."

Hester thinks of Mandy, although she has to remind herself how her daughter doesn't go by that name anymore. A perfectly good name in Hester's opinion.

Eve hunches over, touches her forehead. It's possible she's suffered a concussion. It will take time to heal. Hester will do everything in her power to offer both of them as much time as she can.

"Are you going to be okay in here for a while?"

Eve sits up straighter. "Why? Where are you going?"

"I have to check that maple out there that got hit by lightning last night. I want to make sure it's not going to come down on us."

She doesn't want to leave the cottage again, but in order to survive in the backwoods, there are certain jobs that can't wait until you feel like doing them.

Eve goes back to slouching, and then she pulls herself up a second time. "You'll lock the door?"

Hester stares at the girl. Maybe Eve isn't aware the man in the woods is dead. She thinks about asking her, but then dismisses the idea. The girl has made it clear that she doesn't want to talk about him or what happened. Eventually, though, they're going to have to sort out their little arrangement here.

"Sure," Hester says.

After grabbing the rifle, she heads outside and crosses the yard to inspect the damaged tree. She walks around its base. The tree is deeply scarred on one side where lightning has scorched a valley down its trunk. Large pieces of bark have been blown off, exposing its creamy insides and the parts no one is supposed to see.

Standing on tiptoes, she finds the exact spot where the assault took place, where the branch has been sliced and splintered. She's not sure the tree can survive the wound, and she debates whether the whole thing needs to be taken down. If the trunk is compromised, it could potentially fall on its own, landing on top of the toolshed or cottage. That would be disastrous. On further inspection, it appears to be sturdy. She'll have to keep her eye on it.

The branch on the ground, however, can be used as firewood, and she makes her way to the small toolshed. She pulls out the cordless chain saw and checks that the battery is charged. It has the power of a gas saw but with much less noise. If she had neighbors—which she doesn't—they'd appreciate the quietness of it. Now that she has a sleeping houseguest, her choice of quieter, pricier tools makes sense. She knew there had to be a reason why she chose this particular chain saw last summer when she'd first bought it even if she didn't know it at the time. It's what she calls having foresight.

Content with this knowledge, she gets to work.

The branch is thick. It takes an hour to cut it into manageable pieces for firewood. She's covered in sweat. It drips down her back, soaking the band of her jeans. It's too hot for pants, but when you work with tools, sharp ones that can sever a limb, you keep your body protected as best you can.

Her breathing becomes labored with the humidity. The sun is now hiding behind heavy gray clouds. Another storm is taking its time coming, gathering its strength. She rubs her knuckles, which seem to always be aching and sore.

Not far from where she stands, where the yard ends and the woods begin, the vegetation has been stomped on and flattened. Some of it has been cleared and dirt has been moved. It could be nothing more than a black bear searching for roots, but something in the back of her mind tells her it's not a bear. She grabs the .22 leaning against the tool-shed, carries it with her for a closer look.

She stops at the edge of the yard. The ground at her feet has definitely been disturbed. A lot of dirt has been displaced, and then someone has attempted to put it back where it was originally. She remembers the mud on the knees of Eve's jeans and how it was caked underneath her fingernails.

This is the girl's doing, and by the looks of it, she's been busy digging, burying something here in Hester's woods.

CHAPTER
EIGHT

Noah needs to check in with his clients. He's been avoiding the call all day. They'll just have to be patient for a little while longer and trust he'll deliver the goods.

He pulls his phone out. The battery is almost dead. Everything that could possibly go wrong with this job has.

He's been walking the shoreline of the lake for the last hour, listening to the sound of lapping waves. The air is heavy, rich with moisture. The sky is bruised, matching Noah's mood. He stops near the canoe that he'd used to cross the lake just yesterday. The plan was for him to enter the woods alone by way of the lake, make the exchange at a planned destination, and exit on the other side of the woods with the girl and baby where an SUV sits in a parking lot at the entrance of a local walking trail. It was supposed to be as easy as that. Enter one way, exit another. Keep it simple. Uncomplicated. Don't draw any attention to yourself.

Right. Keep it simple, my ass.

Noah looks inside the canoe and finds nothing but muddy water. He's hidden the paddle behind a bush as a precaution, because what if he needed the canoe again later? If he did need it, he didn't want to return to the shore only to discover it was gone.

He's closer to the original meeting place, and he checks the compass on his phone again. It's then he notices something in the near distance, some kind of structure. He heads in that direction and finds another canoe, but this one is upside down on a rack marked private. Someone has spray-painted the word *witch* on its side. There's an empty space on the rack for a second canoe. He looks out at the rough and tumbling water churning from the recent storm and wonders where the second canoe might be.

He considers whether the girl was here, found his canoe without a paddle, and used one of these canoes instead. Would she have attempted to cross the lake in the middle of the night during a thunderstorm? She's proven herself to be a fighter, and he has to assume she's not stupid. No one wants to be on the water in the middle of a storm as fierce as the one they experienced.

He continues walking along the edge of the woods, looking for a path in and finds one, although it's overgrown. It's similar to the path he followed late last night before everything went to shit. Some kind of vine ensnares his ankle, and he stomps his foot, kicking up whatever insects are hiding in the ground cover. He bats the flying pests away from his face. *Fuck.* He's really starting to hate these woods. His knowledge and skills are limited when it comes to outdoor survival, and now he can't help but think it's coming back to bite him. Literally.

Noah prefers his urban life: the concrete, the tall buildings and city views, the comfort of heaters and air conditioners, and the absence of whatever these biting insects are. Oh, and he can't forget about the bear. Now there's something you won't find on the streets of Manhattan. Madeline, however, loved the outdoors: riding horses, gardening, and hunting. Perhaps his love of the city comes from his birth mother, but he quickly dismisses that idea, ashamed of betraying Madeline even in thought.

He continues moving. The pain in his shoulder where the bear clawed him has subsided to a dull ache, and he pulls his T-shirt away from his skin where it's stuck with dried blood. At least it stopped bleeding: a small gift in an otherwise miserable day.

He pushes through the chaos of twigs and leaves, paying attention to where he's walking. The closer he gets to the meeting place, the fouler the air becomes. It gets so bad, he pulls his shirt up to cover his mouth and nose.

Not far from where he's standing, something hangs from one of the trees. In his subconscious, he knows that whatever it is, it's not natural, but it doesn't make sense in the rational part of his brain, so he ignores it. He moves cautiously forward, searching the ground for Shot's body, and, more importantly, for the bag of money. It's not until he reaches the spot where Shot's body should be—but clearly isn't—that he looks up and sees that the unnatural thing hanging from a branch is Shot himself.

What the—?

Noah's heart rate accelerates, pounds loudly in his ears. His shirt falls from his face when he reaches around his back and pulls out the Magnum. Someone else has been here—the girl perhaps—and it's possible he's walked into a trap.

Spinning in a full 360, he searches the brush and trees, ready to fire at anything that moves. Moisture from the humidity collects on the leaves. Even the trees are sweating. His shirt is soaked for the second time today. Not seeing anything other than trunks and branches, leaves and needles, he lowers his weapon and slowly makes his way over to Shot.

Shot's basketball shorts are sagging, exposing the top of his white underwear. Calvin Klein is written on the waistband. *That's interesting.* Noah wouldn't have pegged Shot as a designer underwear kind of guy.

Shot's head hangs to the side, and he looks much younger than he did last night. His cheeks are puffy like a child's. In the dark, his face appeared sharper, edgier, but maybe that was because he'd just slashed the girl's forehead with a knife. The little prick was trying to prove he was a tough guy, but what he didn't seem to understand was that Noah needed (and still needs) the girl unharmed. That is, of course, until he no longer has a use for her. He supposes it's the reason he throat-punched the guy in the first place, for pulling a knife on Noah and fucking with the girl's face.

Water drips from the prick's wet clothes, striking the ground like a leaky faucet. There are flies, a couple dozen maybe, swarming the areas of exposed skin.

Noah pulls his shirt up around his mouth and nose again, breathes into the cotton, while he tries to make sense of what's happened here. He circles around the tree to get a better look at the branch that Shot's hanging from. It's thick, and there aren't any signs of stress on the limb. He walks around the tree a second time, makes note of the rub marks on the branch. It's taken someone a lot of effort to string up the body this way.

Could the girl have done it? Could she be signaling someone? Or is this a message for him specifically? Maybe it's some kind of gang symbol he's not aware of? This was his first transaction with Shot. He came highly recommended through the elaborate networking system Noah has established through hidden sites on the dark web.

Noah doesn't know a lot about Shot, only that he operated an efficient business of moving girls across state lines and borders. It's the reason why Noah took a chance on working with him. What was it that

Shot had said when he was trying to convince him they should work together? *How hard could it be to move one little baby?*

Fucking hard, apparently.

Noah's had transactions go awry in the past where he's had to tie up a loose end (kill someone) and clean up messes (dispose of a body). But this is new and a little more perplexing, since it's the girl who has one-upped him, where it's usually Noah who comes out on top.

Sweeping the ground with his foot, he searches for the switchblade or possibly a phone. He doesn't find anything, and he realizes he's going to have to check Shot's pockets to make sure he's been wiped clean. It's something he should've done last night, but he wasn't thinking clearly, not after the hit he took to the head.

He tucks the Magnum back in his waistband. At the same time, his shirt, which he's been holding up to his face, falls and sticks to his neck and chest. Rubbing his hands together, he tries to work up his nerve. Most dead bodies he's handled in the past tended to be fresh, and he's not keen on having to touch one that's a day old.

When he's as ready as he's going to be, he says, "Sorry about this," and he stands on his tiptoes, reaching the very bottoms of Shot's basketball shorts, and he pulls them down. The flies scurry, buzzing around Noah's head as he turns the pockets out and finds them empty.

It wasn't his intention to kill Shot, and it doesn't feel right to leave the guy hanging with his pants down. So Noah attempts to push them back up, but he's not tall enough. He jumps, trying to pull the shorts up at the same time, but he can't seem to get them past Shot's knees before they fall back around his ankles.

Not deterred, he jumps again and again.

Another attempt and he nearly slips and falls.

The shorts are wet and heavy and refuse to cooperate.

Noah's out of breath.

Screw it, he thinks. He tried.

He turns away from Shot so he doesn't have to look at the guy or his underwear anymore. It suddenly occurs to Noah that the scene might've been staged to look like a suicide, as though Shot had done this to himself. It's not something Noah would've thought of doing, but it's certainly creative. If it's the girl's handiwork, he wonders again what her reasons might be. To buy herself some time, but time for what?

Either way, he decides he doesn't care.

He spends some time searching the brush, ripping through the vegetation, looking for the bag full of money, but it's becoming all too apparent it's not here. The girl must've taken it with her when she fled last night. It's what he would've done if he was in her shoes.

Noah sighs. He's thirsty and tired. Maybe it's because of dehydration or lack of sleep that he slips into one of his daydreams. He's prone to staring into nothingness for long periods of time—he can stay trapped inside his thoughts sometimes for days, happy in his solitude. It comes from being an only child: another gift Madeline has given him. He's never had to share anything.

What he envisions is the baby swaddled in a pink blanket. She's staring up at him. Under her gaze, his chest opens. Reaching in, she pulls out his heart, holds it up for him to see. His clients, Hillary and Emeril, appear like shadows floating on air. *Please*, they are saying. *Give her to us.* He places the baby in their arms, and his heart drifts back inside his chest, fuller than it was before.

The inked markings on his back begin to stretch and flex. The wings fan out from his shoulder blades, delicate and light. They carry him up high to a cerulean blue sky, and somewhere far behind this illusion where he portrays himself as an angel, in the darker recesses of his mind, he imagines a very different picture, one with seven figures padding his personal savings account. Seven figures, that is, if he counts Shot's half of the money.

And why shouldn't he count it?

The guy is dead.

Things change.

Noah's vision fades. He's not sure how long he's been staring into the trees, but he senses time sliding out from under him.

He has to move, finish what he's started, and there's only one way he knows how.

He has to find the girl.

Turning his back on the tree where Shot hangs, he steps onto the overgrown path that leads deeper into the woods.

CHAPTER
NINE

Hester doesn't mention the digging Eve has done in her woods, and she doesn't bring up what Eve has buried there. It's become their secret, whether the girl knows it or not.

Instead, she focuses on Ivy and the more pressing matter of baby supplies. She's made the decision to leave Eve and the child at the cottage, while she goes into town for formula and diapers. She isn't happy about leaving them behind, but it's not like they can go with her. Eve has made it clear under no circumstances can she be seen by anyone. Eve doesn't say why, but Hester assumes it has to do with the man she's strung up in the tree, and she supposes that is reason enough.

Hester lays the rifle in the bed of the El Camino, then she opens the driver-side door. In case Eve is watching her from the cottage window, she pretends to fiddle with something on the seat. When she feels certain she's not being watched, she lies on the ground and army crawls around the back of the truck to the passenger-side rear wheel well. Maybe it's a bit much, a tad overkill being this paranoid, but she doesn't want Eve to know where she's hidden the keys.

She backs up the same way she'd crawled around the bed, but this time in reverse. In a matter of seconds, she's behind the wheel, barreling down the long dirt driveway, the tires spinning and kicking up mud.

After fifteen minutes of winding backroads and constantly checking in the rearview mirror to see if she's being followed, she pulls the El Camino alongside the curb a block away from the small grocery store that serves the better part of the local community in Bordertown. The larger supermarket is located a few miles outside of town where the residents do their bulk shopping on weekends, but this is where she shops. You don't need bulk when you live alone.

Up the street from where she's parked, the power company's truck idles next to a utility pole. A guy in a hard hat gets out of the vehicle. He's talking on the phone. If some of the people in town are still without electricity, there's no telling how long it will be until she gets juice to her cottage.

Hester gets out of her truck and nervously looks around to see if anyone notices her. No one does. She hurries down the sidewalk and through the parking lot. It's full of cars, people stocking up on nonperishable supplies while they wait for their TVs and refrigerators to be turned back on. She grabs a small shopping cart from the stack located inside the automatic door, and she pushes it up and down the aisles. Nobody is paying attention to her. She's invisible in the crowd of people who are focused on the half-empty shelves. The possibility of being without power for more than a day has created a sense of panic. They're idiots, but it's working to her advantage.

Keeping her head down, avoiding eye contact with the other shoppers, she hurries toward the baby section. She's memorized where each baby item is on the shelves, and she can practically find what she needs with her eyes closed. She drops a binky into the basket along with a box of diapers, baby wipes, and a couple cans of formula. Then she heads to the fruit section and snatches more bananas for Eve. The girl seems to really like bananas since she's eaten four already. Hester picks up bags of pretzels and chips, hot dogs and rolls, and bagels. Glancing at the security camera, she places them just so on top of the diapers and formula, a sad attempt to hide the baby supplies from watchful eyes. She makes her way to the checkout counter. It's too bad they don't have self-checkout. If ever she could use it, it's now.

She's the fifth person in line.

She looks everywhere but at Barrett, the store's manager and only cashier at the moment. Maybe he'll be too busy to argue with her today.

Fourth person in line.

She should've tied her sneakers better. One of the laces is coming undone. The dried mud that's stuck to the rubber soles from when she was traipsing around in the woods falls off, onto the tile floor. She kicks the dirt nonchalantly, trying to push it away from her.

Third person in line.

The woman in front of her looks over her shoulder and notices the mud on the floor from Hester's dirty sneakers. The woman makes a face before turning back around. Hester sticks her tongue out at her.

Second person in line.

Hester doesn't move up, leaving more room than necessary between her and the judgmental woman in front of her. This way she can stay out of Barrett's sight for a little while longer.

First in line.

She places her purchases on the conveyer belt and tentatively pushes her cart up to the cash register.

"Hester."

"Barrett."

He plucks the pretzels and chips from the conveyer belt, scans them. He does the same with the hot dogs and rolls, bananas, and bagels, until only the baby items are left.

"You know I can't sell you these."

"I don't see why not. It's a free country."

"She wants you to leave her and the baby alone." He looks around, gauging if anyone else is listening. The person in line behind Hester pretends to be searching the magazine rack. "That's why your daughter has a restraining order against you."

Hester can't meet his gaze, and she stares at her feet, kicking more mud that has fallen off her sneakers.

"Here." He hands her the items he's already bagged. "That'll be eighteen seventy-one."

"You forgot these." She pushes the formula toward the scanner. There are more people in line behind her now. The crowd presses at her back.

He shakes his head. "Eighteen seventy-one."

She glares at him. This time it's Barrett who can't meet her eyes. He probably believes she's putting a curse on him right now. He thinks she's a witch just like everybody else in this town. She squints, hissing and wiggling her fingers at him.

He ignores her and pushes the box of diapers and bottles of formula to the side, out of her reach.

"Fine. Have it your way."

She tosses the money on the counter and grabs the plastic bag from his hand. She doesn't care what people think of her. They don't know her heart.

Outside the store, she lingers to the side of the glass doors and out of Barrett's line of sight. She considers driving to the bigger store on the other side of town, but that will take her at least twenty minutes one way. The thought of the long drive there and back creates a panicked fluttering inside her chest. Besides, they know her at the bigger store, too. Her picture is posted in the manager's office.

A woman and small child are crossing the parking lot, heading toward the automatic doors. When they walk past her, she reaches for the woman's arm.

"Can you do me a favor?"

The woman pulls her arm away and shakes her head, moving the child out of Hester's reach, never breaking her stride. At the same time, another woman exits the store. She's older, maybe pushing sixty and close to Hester's age.

Hester reaches for her. "Please, I just need you to buy some diapers for a baby. I'll pay you double what they cost."

"No," the woman says, and she keeps walking.

Barrett marches out of the store and grabs Hester's bicep, gripping it firmly.

"What? What did I do?"

"Come on, off you go." He escorts her into the parking lot.

"I didn't do anything!" She struggles to pull her arm away.

"You're scaring the customers! Look at you. You're all sweaty and covered in dirt. When was the last time you brushed your hair?"

Self-consciously, she touches her head where the wiry hairs stick up.

"Never mind. Just forget about it and go. Get out of here before I call the sheriff." He releases her. As he walks back toward the store, he calls over his shoulder, "And for god's sake, take a shower. You stink!"

"Yeah, well, you stink, too!"

When he disappears behind the automatic door, she sniffs her armpit. At the same time, a young woman exits the store, pushing a cart full of groceries. Strapped to the woman's chest is a front baby carrier with an infant inside. The woman stops next to a minivan to unload her purchases. On the bottom rack of her cart is a large box of diapers and a bag full of cans of baby formula.

Hester looks back at the store. There's no sign of Barrett. He's probably behind the cash register again. This is her chance and she rushes to where the woman is standing behind the minivan.

"I'll pay you twice what you paid for the diapers and formula." She holds up several twenty-dollar bills, waves them in front of the woman's face.

"Excuse me? What? No, please get away from me."

The woman's eyes are red-rimmed and puffy. She puts a protective hand on the baby carrier where the infant sleeps. Hester can just make out the precious soft spot on the infant's head.

"Please take the money." She tries to give the bills to the woman, but the woman pushes Hester's hand away.

"Look, lady. I don't know what your problem is, but I'm only going on a few hours of sleep here. I'm exhausted, and I really can't deal with this right now. Please just leave me alone." The woman turns back to her grocery cart.

It's a privilege to be tired, Hester longs to say to her. It's an absolute *privilege* not to have time to wash your hair for days, as she can see is the case with this new mother. This young woman has been given the gift of a child, one she can love and care for without ever having to worry about her baby being ripped from her arms. She has no idea how lucky she is, and Hester's heart tears in a place where she didn't think it could rip anymore.

"Please." She tries to give the woman the money again. "It's an emergency. I need these diapers and the formula."

"If you don't leave me alone, I'm going to call the sheriff." The woman reaches around her back and pulls a phone from her pocket.

Without thinking, Hester knocks the phone out of the woman's hand. It falls to the pavement and skids underneath the minivan. She's instantly sorry, and she's not sorry. She's desperate. While the woman gapes at her, Hester grabs the box of diapers and the bag with the cans of formula. It takes the woman a moment to realize what's happening. She seems shocked by Hester's actions. Hester is pretty surprised herself.

The woman comes around. "Stop! What are you doing?"

Hester throws the twenty-dollar bills in the woman's face, and then she takes off across the parking lot. The box is bulky under her arm. The bag with the heavy cans of formula bounces off her leg, hard, as she races toward the street, down the sidewalk, barreling toward her truck. Somewhere along the way, she's lost the bag full of snacks. Too late to go back for them now, and she tosses the diapers and formula in the bed, before jumping in on the driver's side.

The sultry air seems to have eaten all the oxygen, and she can barely catch her breath. The sticker in her side forces her to hunch over. The joints in her fingers scream as she shifts into drive. The wheel is sweaty in her grip. Her knobby knuckles are white and angry. She feels exhilarated and at the same time she's horrified by what she's done.

Fighting the impulse to drive faster, she takes her time, sticking to the speed limit, going along as though she's done nothing wrong and the sheriff has no reason to pull her over.

Hester parks the El Camino alongside the cottage. She's made it home without being followed, and she's giddy with her success. She can't wait to put Ivy in a nice clean diaper. The small tea towels they've been wrapping around her bottom have worked in the short term, but they can't be very comfortable.

She hides the truck's keys in the magnetic case on the underside of the passenger-side rear wheel well like she did earlier by army crawling around the back of the vehicle. Then she pulls herself up before grabbing the box and bag from the bed, leaving the rifle. She'll come back for it later.

"I'm home," she calls as she steps through the door, carrying the box of diapers under her arm and the bag full of formula in her hand.

Baby Ivy is sleeping, lying on the couch peacefully.

Hester is about to say, *look what I've got*, but she stops short at the sight of Eve standing in the middle of the living room. There's mud caked on her bare knees. Her hands and forearms are covered in dirt up to her elbows. There's a feral look in her eyes.

The box of diapers drops from underneath Hester's arm. It hits the floor with a thud.

"What did you do!" Eve's hands are balled in fists.

"Nothing. I paid for it. More than it costs, too, by the way." She wonders how Eve knows she's lifted the stuff off another young mother.

"I'm talking about the money! Where did you put the money!"

Oh. Right. Hester understands now. The dirt on Eve's hands. The mud on her knees. She was in the yard, digging up the money Hester has already dug up and reburied under the pile of firewood. It wasn't easy having to restack all that wood, and then she had to add the fresh cut pieces from the limb that had been struck by lightning to the top of the pile.

By hiding the money, she's taken away Eve's last chance of leaving with the baby.

Hester considers it her insurance policy.

Eve continues digging those dirty nails into her palms. "Do you know what you've done?"

Hester hasn't moved since dropping the box of diapers. She grips the plastic grocery bag in her hand. Her other hand flits around the pocket of her jeans like a fly who's trying to make up its mind where to land.

"Give. Me. The. Money," Eve says.

Hester can tell that Eve is trying hard to stay calm, to not wake up the baby who is sleeping on the couch. "I can't do that."

"Why not?"

Hester doesn't answer. Instead, she moves into the small kitchen and she puts the bag she's carrying on the counter. She starts to unpack it.

Eve steps toward her, but she stumbles, touches her head where it's been cut open. She has to support herself on the arm of the couch to stand upright.

"Still dizzy?" Hester asks, and she goes back to taking the formula out of the bag.

"Are you fucking crazy? Just tell me what you've done with the money!"

"I'm not crazy." Hester gives her a dirty look.

They both turn to the sound of a car approaching, its tires sloshing through the puddles on the dirt road.

CHAPTER

TEN

n here. Quick." Hester motions frantically for Eve to follow her.

Eve hesitates. The girl seems uncertain as to what she should do, then she scoops the sleeping baby from the couch.

Hester hurries Eve and the baby down the hall to one of the small bedrooms. She opens a doll-size door on the far wall next to the single bed with the wrought iron frame. Peering into the dark cubbyhole, she makes a quick assessment about the size of the space. Eve is tiny, nothing but a bag of bones. She'll fit easily enough inside, but she and the baby won't be able to stay in there long. It's going to be as hot as a closed-up car on a summer day.

"It's tight, but you'll be okay. It won't be for more than a few minutes."

Eve hesitates, hugging the baby close to her chest and out of Hester's reach, as though she doesn't trust her. And why should the girl trust her after what Hester has done? She's hidden the girl's money and trapped her and the baby here. Literally—she thinks when she looks into the black hole she's asking the girl to crawl into. But now is not the time to worry about such things.

"Haven't you ever seen a cubbyhole before? It won't bite. Now get inside."

Eve gets on her knees and crawls into the space inside the wall. The baby starts to fuss in Eve's arms.

"That's it, tuck your legs in. Hurry."

Eve is barely situated inside when Hester closes the door, knowing they'll be sitting in a sweatbox in utter darkness. She wishes there was another way but there isn't, and she's sorry she has to do this to them, as she slides the bolt and locks them in.

By the time she returns to the living room, someone is knocking on the door.

Hester smooths her hair down and pulls her shoulders back. Then she takes a deep breath and opens the door to find her cousin, Sheriff Laura Pennington, on the other side. Laura is short and stout—way shorter than Hester—but Hester isn't fooled by her cousin's small stature. Underneath that dark uniform is fifty-five-plus years of solid muscle built by spending an hour every morning at the local gym. Hester has felt Laura's strength up close and personal when she was tossed into the backseat of the sheriff's SUV.

"I was wondering if I could have a word." Laura peeks over Hester's shoulder.

Hester doesn't have to turn around to know that Laura has spotted the box of diapers lying in the middle of the floor where Hester had dropped them earlier. She didn't think to hide them. *Stupid, stupid, stupid.* From what Hester knows about the law from her cousin, any contraband in plain view gives her the authority to come into Hester's home. She feels as though she has no other choice but to step aside and let her cousin in.

"I gather you know why I'm paying you a visit." Laura points to the box on the floor.

Hester thinks of a quick lie. "I can show you a receipt for the diapers, but it's online and my power hasn't been restored yet. I don't suppose you know when it'll be turned back on."

"I'm sure your power will be restored soon. Wait. Are you telling me you're buying diapers online, too? Never mind. Forget it. We both know that's not where this box of diapers came from."

"They were delivered yesterday." Hester lies again, because there's no way she can get arrested. They may be cousins, but being family has never made a difference where Laura's job is concerned. It makes a person feel all warm and fuzzy on the inside, doesn't it? But whatever. Right now, she has to think of a way to get rid of Laura, and she has to do it quickly. Eve and the baby will not survive hours in the hole if Hester is sitting in a jail cell.

Laura is shaking her head. Her cousin then proceeds to look around the living room and kitchen. Eventually she notices the bag on the counter and the cans of formula Hester was in the process of putting away.

"All of it was delivered yesterday. I bought it all online. I swear."

"You were caught on their security cameras not a half hour ago. I know all about what happened inside the store and outside in the parking lot. There's no use lying to me about it."

"I paid the woman. I paid her twice the amount of what the stuff costs. I didn't steal nothing."

"I know. She told me."

"So what's the problem then? No harm done if you ask me."

"You can't keep doing this, Hester. Priscilla has a restraining order against you for a reason." Laura shakes her head again, but this time Hester suspects it's out of pity. "Look, Priscilla and the baby are doing just fine. Okay? You don't need to buy all this stuff for them. They're fine. Trust me. That's all you need to know."

But there's so much more Hester wants to know. You don't stop being a mother just because your daughter doesn't want anything to do with you.

"What did she name the baby?"

"You don't know?"

Hester shakes her head.

Laura must feel sorry for her because she says, "She named her Sophie."

Sophie. It's an alright name, but Hester still thinks Mandy is a better one. If Priscilla isn't going to use Mandy, the birthname Hester gave her, then she'd hoped her granddaughter would. It's such a little thing Priscilla could've given her, but she hasn't, adding another tear to her already shredded heart.

"I stopped to let you know the woman at the store isn't going to press charges. You're lucky you didn't break her phone or the situation could be very different." Laura turns toward the door and pauses, points to the diapers and cans of formula. "You need to get rid of this stuff. Maybe donate it or give it to someone else who you think might need it, but you're not to go anywhere near your daughter or her baby. Are we clear?"

"Perfectly clear."

"I'm trusting you to do the right thing here and donate it. This has to stop."

"Yes, I know. You're right." She'll say anything to get her cousin out the door.

Just as her cousin is about to leave, Ivy cries. The sound carries down the short hallway and floods the room.

The cry is immediately stifled somehow. Maybe Eve is finally giving Ivy a nipple to suckle.

Laura turns back around. "What was that?"

"I didn't hear anything."

Her cousin tilts her head, as though she's listening for it again.

The baby cries. A small chirp this time. It stops as quickly as it starts.

Laura stares at Hester. "What's going on here?"

Hester desperately searches for some kind of explanation, but she doesn't come up with anything. Maybe she should just hit her cousin over the head, knock her out, tie her up, but then what?

Oh! She thinks of something better. But no. She can't. It's too embarrassing, and yet, she knows it's what she has to do, if only she can bring herself to do it.

"Please, don't make me."

"Don't make you—what?" Laura stands with her feet slightly apart, her shoulders square, as though she's ready for battle.

"Please, I'm begging you." Hester can't bear the thought of showing her, but she can't think of anything else she can do. She has no other choice. How else is she going to get them out of this?

"Either you start talking or I'm going to search every inch of this house. I know what I heard."

"Fine."

Hester goes into the back bedroom, opens the closet. Inside is a toy crib, a small changing table, stacks of baby clothes, and a *look alive* baby doll that cries and pees. She picks up the doll and cradles it in her arms, caresses the doll's plastic cheek with her fingers.

Laura has followed her into the bedroom. She's standing in the doorway, looking back and forth between Hester and the open closet.

Hester forces herself to keep her eyes on her cousin and away from the wall where Eve and the baby hide inside the cubbyhole.

"This is what you heard." She squeezes the doll's tummy to make it cry.

Nothing happens.

She swears she can hear Eve breathing and Ivy making sucking noises.
She presses the doll's tummy again.

Nothing happens a second time.

"It's the batteries. They're going dead." She tries to explain why the doll isn't crying.

"Hester."

Hester is panicking. Is Ivy's sucking getting louder?

"Come on, Ivy. Work with me." She pretends to talk to the doll, when really, she's talking to the baby in the hole. She squeezes the doll's stomach harder.

Still nothing.

She begins to shake the doll. *Cry, damnit. Cry.*

"*Hester.*"

Hester ignores her and continues to shake the doll violently, madly, until finally, *finally*, it cries.

"There!" She holds the doll up triumphantly. "Did you hear it? Did you?"

"Wow. That is some seriously disturbing behavior, Hester."

Hester lowers her arms. "I wouldn't shake a *real* baby."

She's not crazy, although Laura's looking at her like she is. She's not pathetic either. Okay, maybe she is a little pathetic.

Laura touches Hester's arm, giving it a gentle squeeze. Then she fishes in her pockets, searching for something. She pulls out a card and hands it to her.

"It's for a social worker. She'll be able to hook you up with someone who can help. Because you do need help, Hester. You need help. You know that, right?"

She nods. *Sure. Yeah. Right. Whatever.* She can't stand the concern in her cousin's eyes. Her cousin needs to leave, and Eve and the baby need to get out of that hole.

"You'll call?" Laura's referring to the social worker's phone number. She nods again.

Finally, her cousin leaves the room. Hester follows her down the short hallway and into the living room. She's carrying the baby doll with her, cradling it.

"If your power doesn't come back on soon, you should probably toss any food in your refrigerator," Laura says.

"Yeah, sure, right. I know."

Laura looks at her and the doll, shakes her head yet again. "Seriously disturbing." She turns for the door.

"I embarrass you."

Laura pauses, her hand on the doorknob. "Call the number on the card," she says right before she leaves.

Hester waits for the rumble of the SUV's engine, listens for the sound of the motor to fade as the vehicle makes its way down the dirt road. Then she flings the doll onto the couch and races down the hallway to the bedroom.

CHAPTER
ELEVEN

Laura drives down the long dirt road, away from Hester's cottage. She swerves, trying to miss the larger potholes as the SUV bumps along, splashing through puddles left by the rain the night before.

She adjusts the vent in the SUV. The cold air pumping from the air conditioner hits her arms and neck, drying the sweat on her skin. The side of her uniform is still damp from when she reached into the storm drain to free the garden gnome earlier that morning. Since then, it's been one call after another.

She wipes the perspiration from her brow. Hester's cottage was a sticky hot sauna. Laura doesn't know how her cousin can stand that kind of heat, and then she thinks maybe she can't. Maybe the heat has finally gotten to her. Hester was acting strangely—even for her. Laura makes a mental note to check with the power company and make sure they haven't forgotten about the cottage in the woods. Her cousin doesn't have central air conditioning or a window unit, but at least she'd be able to turn on a couple of fans.

At the end of the road, Laura stops. Before she turns onto the paved road that will take her back into town, she picks up her phone.

"Hey, Priscilla, it's Lau—"

"What's she done now? Do I need to be worried?"

Priscilla has made it clear that the woman who raised her, her adoptive mom, is her mother, not the crazy woman who lives in the woods. *The witch.* That's what Priscilla had said when she came into the office six months ago and filed a restraining order. "You keep that *witch* away from me and my children."

Priscilla had spotted Hester in a tree outside her house, lying on a branch, binoculars to her face, looking into Priscilla's windows.

Laura doesn't blame Priscilla. A person has a right to choose who they want in their life and who they don't. Those around them either accept it or they reject it. Either way, there's not anything they can do about it. You can't make someone love you. You can't make them forgive you. The only thing you can do is offer yourself up and hope for the best.

"Hester was caught today buying some baby supplies. She got her hands on some diapers and formula. I told her that she's not allowed to go anywhere near you or the baby with the stuff, but I thought you should know in case she doesn't listen to me and she shows up at your house anyway."

"Why can't she just leave me and my family alone?"

Laura doesn't have a good answer for her and defending Hester isn't going to make Priscilla change her mind about her. "Do me a favor and call me directly if she turns up."

They spend the next few minutes catching up, talking about Priscilla's new baby girl. She thanks Laura for the basket of onesies, sleepers, and socks.

"Tell Charlotte I said hi," Priscilla says.

When they hang up, Laura finds herself calling Charlotte. Talking with Priscilla about babies has made Laura miss her own daughter.

Charlotte is currently in Brooklyn attending college. She's studying to be an architect. Charlotte's an only child and Laura's pride and joy. Laura's a single mom. She raised her daughter on her own since Charlotte was three years old. Laura's ex-husband, Bradley, was a decent guy, but he couldn't handle the demands Laura's job as Pop's deputy, at the time, had placed on her and the long hours it had required. They tried to make it work, though, for Charlotte's sake. They really did.

Laura is sent directly to her daughter's voicemail. "Hey, it's Mom. I just wanted to call to check in, see how you were doing. Call me when you get a chance."

She hangs up, disappointed. She really thought she would've heard from her daughter today. Charlotte must've forgotten it's the anniversary of Pop's death. Seems like a big thing to forget, but she supposes her daughter is just busy, caught up in her classes, her internship, and her big, new city life.

Laura covers her heart and the ache that seems to have permanently lodged there, missing her daughter and father, the two people she loves most in this world. She leans into the pain, if only for a moment. In her breast pocket, she feels the edges of the photo.

Another call comes in on the radio. Denise is saying they received a report about a bear attack. Did Laura hear that right?

"Say again?"

Denise says, "Bear attack."

CHAPTER
TWELVE

Eve crawls out of the cubbyhole. Her clothes are wet and sticking to her. It must've been a hundred degrees in there. Ivy hasn't made a sound ever since Eve put her breast in the baby's mouth. It was the only way to keep her quiet.

She looks at Ivy's face. Her eyes are closed and her skin is pink. Eve puts her ear to the baby's mouth, checks she's still breathing, and hears her soft baby's breath. Little red dots have broken out on the insides of Ivy's arms and behind her knees where the skin rubs. It could be heat rash, but what does Eve know about such things? Nothing. She knows nothing at all.

Hester is talking to her, but Eve is having trouble focusing. She almost passed out in that damn hole. She stares at Hester. The woman's face is blurry, as though someone has erased the lines where her nose and chin should be. It takes everything Eve has not to punch her.

"What the fuck were you thinking putting us in that sweatbox?"

"I couldn't think of anywhere else." Hester is looking around the room, as though she's searching for something.

Then Eve sees what Hester is taking stock of. There's a toy crib and changing table inside the closet. Doll clothes are neatly stacked on the shelves.

"What the hell is going on?"

When she was locked inside the hole, she heard a baby crying, and it didn't come from the baby in her arms. There's something strange here. Something close to dread circles her chest, tightening her rib cage.

"It was just my cousin, but I got rid of her. She's the sheriff, but she's gone now. We're safe. I mean, you're safe."

"Safe?"

She's starting to wonder if maybe the sheriff was a better option than Hester. It's not like Eve didn't think about pounding on the door, screaming to be let out, for whoever was on the other side to save her and the baby. She even went as far as placing her palm on the wood, poised to bang on it, but she couldn't get her arm to move, as though the bag full of money was weighing it down, reminding her of what she'd be giving up.

"Where's the baby?"

She's not talking about Ivy, but about the one she heard crying outside of the hole. Pushing past Hester, Eve rushes out of the room. There on the living room couch is a baby doll. Eve thought she'd seen it all but apparently not. Carefully, she puts Ivy on the cushion at the opposite end of the couch, then she picks up the plastic doll.

Hester enters the room. "I can explain."

Hester looks sad and pathetic, but Eve doesn't feel sorry for her. All she feels is rage. It's been building inside of her ever since this crazy old woman stole her money, trapping her here. Of all the cottages, she chose the one with a lunatic.

"You're batshit crazy!"

She chucks the doll across the room at Hester.

Hester has to duck to avoid getting hit.

"I can explain. Please, just let me explain."

Eve doesn't know if it's the heat or the missing money or having been shoved into a hole in the wall with an infant, but she leaps across the couch where Ivy has started crying, and she tackles Hester, knocking her to the floor. She lands on top of her. Hester cries out in surprise or pain or maybe both.

"Where is my money!"

She has never hated someone as much as she hates this woman right now, and that's saying something, considering where she's been and what she's had to endure.

"Please, Eve, let me explain."

Hester puts her arms up to block Eve from hitting her.

Eve isn't even her real name. It was the first name that came to her mind last night. It's the name on the fake passport Shot told her about, the one made for her by the asshole from the woods. She has no idea how he came up with it, and she wasn't about to ask. Questions only got her chained to a wall and several days without food.

Her head throbs, either from the gash made by the switchblade or from the bump when she'd hit her forehead after falling, running through the woods. The pain blends into a pot of hot stew, boiling her thoughts until they're murky and unclear. She can't even remember the name her mother gave her at birth. It's as lost as she is.

"I'm no one! I come from nowhere!"

Eve swings her arms wildly, smacking the side of Hester's head, her cheeks, and shoulders. She was so close to escaping. So close to freedom.

"You crazy old bitch!"

She pulls Hester's wild hair.

Hester struggles to get away, to get out from under her, but Eve is relentless, and she refuses to let her up. She's about to deliver another blow to Hester's face when the front door bangs open. From their position on the floor, both women look toward the sound and find a man standing in the doorway.

Eve recognizes him.

He's the asshole from the woods whom she punched with a rock.

He aims a gun at them.

CHAPTER
THIRTEEN

Laura gets out of the SUV and joins Deputy Joe Ives by his vehicle. Together, they carry a large branch off the roadway and heave it to the side. The entire area surrounding the lake is littered with downed limbs and in some places whole trees have been uprooted. In the near distance, the buzz of heavy machinery echoes through the tall trees.

"I know that look on your face," Joe says.

"You heard the call?" Laura is referring to the earlier report about Hester and the incident at the grocery store.

"I heard it."

"It's fine now. I took care of it." She doesn't want to talk about her cousin, and she changes the subject. "Last I heard, black bears don't attack people."

"Normally, I'd agree with you, but I'm not so sure now."

He's towering over her: a tall, lean, dark-haired man. Sweat stains his uniform under his arms and around the collar. A bead of sweat drips from his forehead, and she resists the urge to wipe it away.

"Do we know who he is?"

"Who? The bear?"

"Yes, Joe, the bear. Tell me, is it Yogi? Or Boo-Boo? Maybe it's Smokey?"

"Haha. Very funny. It's Derrick Fisher."

"Oh. Oh, shit. Who found him?"

"Karl Fisher reported it."

"Did he? Geez. I hope you were easy on him. You didn't talk too fast or anything like that, did you?"

"No, I was easy on him. He didn't say much anyway. We met here, and he showed me where I could find Derrick. He stayed far back from the body though. I guess he didn't want to get too close."

"Well, I can't say I blame him there."

Joe nods.

"Anyone else know about it?"

If it's a bear attack and the media get a hold of it, they could have a panic on their hands. Summer is a busy time in these parts with families camping, fishing, and hiking the trails.

"As far as I know, Karl hasn't said anything to anybody other than his dad."

"Sounds about right." The Fishers are a private family, known to keep to themselves. "Okay, well, you better show me."

They head into the woods and push through the dense trees, picking their way up the side of a steep hill. The terrain turns rocky, and Joe reaches back for her hand to help her over a particularly large boulder. If they weren't completely alone, she would never allow this type of physical contact between them, even a simple gesture of help. He holds onto her hand a little longer than he should.

They continue on and eventually find a narrow path made by the animals, and they take the animal trail the rest of the way. The ground is soft from the rainstorm, and the mud sticks to their shoes. The air is thick and hums with the sound of insects. Laura's sweating more than normal. It could be a hot flash, her way of flirting with the humidity. Or it could be from adrenaline and the anxiety she's feeling about what she's about to see.

"Here he is," Joe says.

They stop next to the remains of Derrick's body. There's barely any flesh left on his bones. He's been picked clean. The underbrush around him is flattened and bloody. Deep depressions of bear tracks are scattered in the surrounding soil.

"Better let Mason know."

Mason is the fish and game warden in the area. He's worked closely with the sheriff's department for the better part of eight years. He'll be able to tell them a lot more about how something like this could've happened.

"Joe already contacted me."

Laura jumps. She didn't hear him coming up behind them. "You're like a damn cat."

Mason smiles at her, and he nods at Joe.

"Thanks for getting here so quickly," Joe says. "Pretty sure it's a bear. We're hoping you can make some sense of it."

Mason moves closer to Derrick's body, watchful of where he's stepping. Then he moves some debris away from a print. "There's no question these are bear tracks."

"So, it's an attack?" Laura asks. "I didn't think this was normal behavior for black bear."

"It's not," Mason says. "They're typically shy animals. They'll avoid human contact if they can."

"This one certainly didn't avoid anything." Joe lifts his hat and scratches his head. "This is an all-out mauling."

Mason squats near the body, looking over the wounds on the torso. Laura rests on her haunches next to him. Derrick's arm has been nearly severed. It hangs by a thread of sinewy muscle and bloody ligament. The shredded parts of his body are hard to look at, but it's the expression on his face that she can't seem to turn away from. It's as though he's been captured in an eternal state of shock. Whatever happened here took him by surprise.

Mason moves to the other side of the body. Laura continues staring at Derrick's face. On his forehead, between his eyebrows, is a small hole. There appears to be black powder close to where the skin is puckered inward. There's so much blood smeared across his forehead and in his hair, it's hard to be sure, but from her position, it looks as though he's been shot at close range.

"We're going to need a medical examiner to confirm this." She points to the area between Derrick's eyebrows. "But this looks like a gunshot wound to me."

Joe leans over her. Mason does the same. They both agree.

"If that's the case, then the bear could've just been taking advantage of an opportunity," Mason says. "A hungry bear finds a fresh carcass. It's going to eat."

"You're suggesting he was already dead when the bear found him?"

"It's a more likely scenario."

Mason stands and takes a step back. Laura and Joe join him. Until they understand what's happened here, they have to treat the area like a crime scene and that means being careful not to destroy any evidence.

"Okay, this is something the state police should be involved in," she says.

The sheriff's department doesn't have the manpower to handle a homicide investigation on their own. They'll need the state police's forensic unit, as well as a detective to oversee the case. Laura and her deputies aren't equipped with either of those. The sheriff's department handles mostly traffic violations and domestic disturbances for the county. Bordertown's local police department (a two-man unit) was dissolved not two years ago. There was much debate between the local residents about whether it should be dissolved, but in the end, they just didn't have the tax dollars to fund it.

Laura gets Denise on the radio. "Hey Denise, looks like we're going to need the state police on this one."

"Oh yeah? Not a bear then?"

"Yes and no. It looks like the victim was shot. And listen, let them know we're dealing with a backwoods family here."

"Oh, right, okay," Denise says. The radio goes silent.

Mason has since stepped away from her and Joe, and he's pointing to another area on the ground farther down the hill. "Seems to me the body was dragged up here."

Laura and Joe come to stand next to him again. The ground vegetation looks as if someone has taken a comb to it, brushing it with heavy strokes uphill.

"Could the bear have done it?" she asks.

"Sure, it's strong enough," Mason says.

"Are you thinking this isn't the original crime scene?" Joe asks.

She nods. "That's what I'm thinking."

Joe says, "Maybe we should talk with Karl again."

"While you do that, I'm going to take a look around and see if I can find the bear. These prints look fresh. I should be able to track it and figure out if it's acting strangely. See how it behaves around me." Mason heads deeper into the woods.

Laura turns to Joe. "Head back to our vehicles. Shouldn't take long for someone from the state police to get here. I'm going to see if I can find where his body was moved from."

Laura follows the blood trail through the woods, leading down the steep hill. She slips in the slick vegetation, grabbing onto the trunk of a nearby tree, catching herself. It's not an easy climb—up or down—and Derrick is a big guy with a lot of weight on him. It must've taken a good deal of effort for the bear or someone else to drag him up here. It couldn't have been easy. Whoever has done this must've been highly motivated.

At the bottom of the hill, the trees start to thin, and the sky pokes through, gray and saturated with dark, soggy clouds. She'll need to get the flags from the back of her SUV and mark the trail before the rain comes and washes the evidence away.

Not far from where she's standing, she sees a jug of water about a third full and an empty bag of beef jerky. There's blood on the ground, probably from when Derrick was shot.

Okay, so this is the original crime scene. She looks around, tries to get an idea of where she is in relation to the road. About fifty yards away, between the snarled branches, she spies the back of Fisher's Market.

Laura pushes the market's torn screen door open. A bell jingles as she steps inside. Clyde is standing behind the counter. His eyes are bloodshot and teary. Karl is sitting on a chair next to him, hunched over. He stands when she approaches.

"Clyde. Karl. I'm so sorry."

Clyde looks like a man who's seen one too many tragedies, and it's finally broken him. He's whittled down to nothing but muscle and bone. He wears a permanent frown on his leathery face.

While she gives Clyde a moment to collect himself, she glances around the store. The tiles on the floor are peeling in places. Dust covers the shelves and coats the bagged and boxed food in the nearby aisles. In the corner above Clyde's head, there are water spots from a recent roof leak. It's probably from the thunderstorm they had last night. Near the water stain is a security camera.

"Can you tell me what happened?" Laura directs her question at Karl, making note of his large size and also his clothing. He's wearing camouflage shorts and a muscle T-shirt that looks as if it's been dragged through the dirt, but there are no noticeable blood stains. His skin is tan from spending time outdoors.

He talks into his chest. "A bear got him. Ripped him to shreds."

"Were you with him? Did you see it happen?"

Karl shakes his head.

"You weren't with him?"

"No. I wasn't with him."

There's anger in his voice, and Laura isn't sure where it's coming from. Is he angry at the bear? At the person who shot his cousin? Or is he angry at himself?

"Then how did you know where to find him?"

Karl shrugs.

Clyde clears his throat and says to Karl, "Go on, answer her," and then he adds, "the two are inseparable."

"But they weren't together when the bear attacked Derrick?" she asks.

"We got separated," Karl says.

"How did you get separated? What were you doing in the woods in the first place?"

Karl looks up, but he avoids looking directly at her when he says, "We were just walking around and got separated. That's all."

Perhaps Karl accidentally shot his cousin. Hunting accidents happen all the time, especially in small communities like Bordertown. But a shot at close range between the eyebrows isn't an accident. Still, she asks the question to see how he reacts. "By any chance, were the two of you hunting?"

"No."

"Either one of you have a gun on you?"

"No. I'm not allowed to carry unless it's hunting season."

"That's right," Clyde adds.

Karl wipes his eyes with his fists.

"I understand. But did Derrick have a gun? Maybe he was the one doing the hunting and you were just tagging along? In light of what's happened, I can't fine him for hunting out of season, but I need you to be honest with me."

"No guns. We weren't hunting."

"Okay. Was there anyone else in the woods with the two of you?"

"No." Karl glances at his dad.

Clyde stares down an aisle, not acknowledging anyone. Once he digests his nephew is really gone, Laura imagines grief will overtake him if it hasn't already. Derrick was like a son to Clyde ever since Derrick's father was killed in a boating accident.

She gazes at the security camera. Something about it makes her ask one last question. "Anyone come into the store lately looking for Derrick?"

"No," Clyde says. "No one's come in all day."

That can't be good for business, she thinks, and she points to the camera. "Mind if I take a look at the video?"

Karl whips his head around to where the camera is secured in the corner of the ceiling.

Clyde says, "It doesn't work anymore. I leave it up as a deterrent so customers think they're being videotaped. They stay out of trouble that way."

"Do you mind if I take a look anyway?"

"I said it's not working." Clyde plucks a rifle from behind the counter and lays it down in front of her. "This is what I use if I need it."

Is he trying to intimidate her? She's known Clyde her whole life.

He's not a man who is easily rattled or one who is prone to impulsive or violent behavior without some kind of provocation, but right now, he's emanating the same anger she feels coming off Karl like a smoking ember, waiting for a reason to catch fire.

She doesn't ask if he has a license for this particular firearm. You don't need a license to possess a shotgun or rifle in the state (with the exception of New York City), and just about everyone owns one or the other in this small town. Everyone but the occasional tourist, that is, who comes to vacation in the mountains and lake.

"Okay, good enough. I'll need you to stay out of the woods. The state police are on the way. Someone will be in touch with you shortly."

She walks out of the store, although she suspects the father and son duo aren't being completely honest with her. The way Karl's head snapped to look at the camera tells her it's working just fine, but she knows better than to back a Fisher into a corner. If she does, they'll just dig in, push back, and their paranoia will take a firm hold. It's best that she waits for the medical examiner's report, and then if she needs to, she'll have the state police get a search warrant to take a look at that video.

Right now, she has to get those flags from the back of her SUV so she can mark the blood trail before the rain washes it away.

CHAPTER
FOURTEEN

Noah aims the .44 Magnum at the two women on the floor. In his other hand, he grips the rifle he found in the bed of the truck outside. Or is it a car? What the hell is an El Camino, anyway? It looks like a car from the front, but it's got a bed in the back like a truck. All business in the front and party in the back. Like a mullet. Like someone else he knows, thinking of camo guy.

He makes a quick assessment of the cottage: stone walls, wooden floors, box of diapers, 1930s appliances, shabby '70s furniture. There's a short hallway that probably leads to a bathroom and bedroom. He scans the cottage for another door and second exit, but he doesn't see any. There's only one way in and one way out. That's good. The baby is on the plaid couch, crying, seemingly unharmed. That's also good. In the back of his mind, it registers that the bag full of money isn't anywhere to be seen and that's bad.

The women spot him and freeze in mid-battle, either in fear or surprise. The girl is clutching a fistful of the older woman's hair. The older woman's face is red, possibly bruised. There are large sweat stains under her arms.

The girl is just as sweaty, but she's covered in dirt up to her elbows. The cut on her forehead where Shot has slashed her with his switch-blade has started bleeding. The blood drips down the side of her face. By the look in her eyes, he's certain she recognizes him. She pulls her hand out of the older woman's hair and scrambles off her, lifting herself up to stand.

"No, no, no. Take a seat right where you are."

She sits next to the older woman. They are side by side on the floor. They watch him intently.

"Who the hell are you?" the older woman asks.

"It doesn't matter who I am, but I'm guessing you're the owner of the canoe out there by the lake. The one with *witch* spray-painted on it?"

"Maybe," the older woman says.

"I'm going to take that as a yes, so, you'll go by Witch."

"That's not my name. It's—"

"Stop. I don't want to know. Until I figure out our little situation here, you're Witch, you're Girl, and that's Baby."

"And what the hell do we call you?" Witch asks.

"Asshole," Girl says, and the witch smiles.

"Very cute." Noah considers the witch's question. He certainly can't share his real name or the name his clients know him by. "You can call me Sir." He likes that. It's respectable.

"Why should we listen to you, *Sir*?" the witch asks.

"Because Magnum here says so."

The witch crosses her arms. All the while, the baby continues to cry.

He holds up the rifle he's been carrying in his other hand. "I found this in the back of the El Camino outside. Do you have any other firearms in the car-truck? Or in the house? Or maybe in the toolshed out there?"

The witch shakes her head.

"Don't lie to me."

"That .22 there is it."

"Okay." He'll have to take her word for it. Hopefully, he won't be here long enough for it to matter.

The baby's crying gets louder.

"Girl. Tend to Baby."

The girl gets up and crosses the room without complaining. She picks up the baby and tries to soothe her, but all the while she's glowering at Noah. There's so much anger in her eyes and perhaps resentment, too. Noah has thwarted whatever plans she's made since fleeing last night, and he's not sorry for it. Not at all. Who does she think she is, anyway? What was it that Shot had said? *She'll do exactly as she's told. She won't give you any trouble.*

The motherfucker was wrong. Shot underestimated her, whereas Noah overestimated him. But Noah's clients needed an infant—a newborn of exactly three weeks old—and they needed her today. Shot just happened to have a girl who'd just had a baby and exactly what Noah needed.

Thinking of his clients (or rather their money), he's well aware of the amount of time that has gone by and how frantic they must be waiting for his call. His phone battery died right about the time he stumbled onto the small cottage.

"I don't suppose you have a phone charger?" he asks the witch.

"No, I don't have a phone. Only an iPad, but it doesn't matter anyway. The power's been out since last night."

"Does the iPad have cellular service?"

"No, it doesn't have cellular service. What would I need cellular service for?"

"Um, I don't know, maybe to call someone or to get on the internet when the power's out?"

She makes a face, as if his suggestion is ludicrous.

"Right." Another setback. What else could possibly go wrong? Not that he could use the iPad, anyway, since it's not secure. He kicks the door closed behind him, never taking his eyes off the two women. At least he won't have to worry about the girl attacking him, not while she's occupied with the baby. The girl doesn't seem to know how to soothe her. The child hasn't stopped crying since he walked in.

"I think she's hungry," Girl says. "Or maybe—" She holds the baby away from her and appears to inspect the baby's arms and legs. "I think she has a heat rash." She peeks under the rag the baby wears as a diaper. "Oh shit."

The witch is on her feet.

"Whoa." Noah points the gun at the witch. "Where do you think you're going?"

"I'm going to help her."

It probably couldn't hurt. It's important the baby is cared for. Noah needs the baby healthy for his purposes, and since he knows nothing about how to care for an infant, he motions with the gun, allowing the witch to help.

The witch pulls the rag away from the baby. "She has a diaper rash." Then she turns to Noah. "I've got cornstarch in the cabinet to the left of the sink."

"What? You want me to get it?"

"Yes." The witch and the girl lay the baby on the floor next to the box of diapers. The girl opens the box and pulls out a clean diaper.

"O—kay," Noah says, somewhat baffled. It's not exactly how he thought things would play out, but nothing about this job has gone according to plan. He sets the rifle on the counter. It's not loaded. The bullets are in his pocket. In the old wooden cabinet next to the sink, he finds the cornstarch, where the witch told him it would be. He hands it to her, then he picks up the rifle and steps back, making sure to always aim the Magnum at them. He's a good shot, and he's not worried about missing and injuring the child.

The baby's crying seems to lessen with her bottom sufficiently corn-starched and covered in a clean diaper, but she's still agitated.

"I think she's hungry." Witch gets up without asking Noah first. He watches her walk into the kitchen and open a can of formula. It's as though she's not bothered by the fact that he has a gun aimed at her. She acts as if he's just another houseguest. That's all fine and good for now, because he knows she'll be changing her mind about him soon enough.

The witch prepares a bottle and heats it on a gas stove. After it's been sitting in a pot of water getting warm for a few minutes, she tests it on her wrist before handing the bottle to the girl.

"Sit on the couch." Noah waits until the witch, the girl, and the baby are settled. The baby stops crying as soon as the bottle is in her mouth. The only other chair in the small living room is a rocking chair. It won't do. Noah doesn't want to get too comfortable in a rocker. He's been up for over twenty-four hours straight. His shoulder aches, and his stomach is empty. He can't get too relaxed or, worse, fall asleep. More importantly, he needs to be steady when he has to shoot the witch. But first things first, he wants to know where the money is.

Noah drags a chair from the kitchen table. It's wooden and sturdy and has a straight back. It will keep him upright and balanced. He places it a few feet in front of the couch, and he sits. The rifle rests across his lap. The Magnum, he points at the women.

Where does he begin?

He's so damn tired. His jeans are filthy. His shirt is torn and stick-ing to him. The scratches on his shoulder where the bear clawed him pulses with the pumping of his blood and the pounding of his head. It's like a damn drum playing inside of him, one painful beat after another.

Outside, thunder rumbles in the near distance. At least he's indoors and out of the coming storm.

"Now that we're all settled." He looks at the girl. "Where's the fucking money?"

CHAPTER
FIFTEEN

The state police have officially taken over Derrick Fisher's case, and Laura's off the clock. She's filed the last of the day's reports, and currently, she's headed to a section of the Burgh where drug dealers hang out in alleys and young girls walk the streets. The Burgh is the largest city in the county under Laura's jurisdiction and about twenty minutes south of Bordertown.

She drives past a laundromat and a corner store. The sidewalks are permanently cracked and the buildings are graffitied. Most of what's written on the walls are words Laura has never heard of before or ones whose definitions have been changed by a younger generation. Take, for instance, the declaration about somebody named Nathan, who apparently has a fupa. What does that even mean? Fupa? Maybe it's an acronym for something. Whatever it is, it doesn't sound good.

Laura passes an empty lot and a stretch of chain-link fence on her way to Clemons Street. At the end of the block, she takes a right turn, slowly cruising toward a cluster of women wearing tight clothes. One of them runs when they see her SUV. The woman probably has an outstanding warrant. Laura doesn't care. It's not who she's here for.

The other women turn to stare at her. The woman with the biggest attitude steps up, sticks her hip out, and puts her hand on it. Her nails are long, the tips filed to sharp points. Her skirt barely covers her bottom. She's the one who knows what goes down in the neighborhood, and Laura pulls the SUV alongside her, rolls down the passenger-side window.

"Look who's back," the woman says. "You miss us or something?"

"I wouldn't be here if I didn't."

"Sheeit." The woman laughs.

Laura holds up the photo of Kayleigh McBride. She was fourteen when she disappeared, and in her school picture she still has the chubby cheeks of a kid. There's always a chance one of the women might've seen her around since the last time Laura was here. You just never know. Sometimes all it takes is someone to say they might've seen someone who sort of looks like the girl and you have a potential new lead.

The woman barely glances at the photo. "I told you before, she doesn't look familiar."

"Come on, look again. I'm not here for anything else but to find this girl. She would be nineteen now."

Laura's not worried about the five years that have lapsed since the photo was taken. She'd compared Charlotte's pictures at fourteen and nineteen and there wasn't a big difference between the ages. It was easy to see she was the same girl.

The woman walks up to the SUV, leans in the window. Her roots are black and deep lines frame her mouth. Her teeth are stained and crooked. She takes the picture.

"Sorry, Sheriff. Haven't seen her. What'd you say her name was again?"

"Kayleigh McBride."

"Hey, Glitz, you ever hear of a Kayleigh McBride?"

"Not me, but no one goes by their real names 'round here. You should know that."

"She got another name?"

"Not that I know of."

"Can't help you then." The woman with the pointy nails hands the photo back to Laura.

Laura gives her a card. "In case you lost the last one."

The woman stuffs the card in her bra and blows Laura a kiss.

"You ladies be careful out here," Laura says as she pulls away from the curb.

After leaving the Burgh, Laura makes her way back to Bordertown, pulls the SUV into her driveway. She bought the small ranch-style house after her divorce from Charlotte's father nearly sixteen years ago. She got it for a good price, all 1,500 square feet of it, complete with three bedrooms, a decent-size kitchen and bathroom, and wall-to-wall carpeting.

It's nothing fancy, but it's home.

She cuts the engine at the same time Priscilla's Escalade pulls alongside her. Laura climbs out of her SUV.

"Hey," she says when Priscilla rolls down the window.

Priscilla leaves her big vehicle running, AC pumping. She's wearing the pink baseball cap, the one supporting breast cancer. Her adoptive mom died not two years ago from the disease. It was a rough time.

"Did something happen?" Laura assumes whatever it is, Hester's involved.

"No, I was driving around to get Sophie to sleep. She doesn't sleep. She cries all night." Priscilla wipes her eyes. "The boys can't sleep. Adam yells. It's a lot to deal with."

"Come inside. Let me get you something to drink. We can talk."

"No, I can't. Sophie will wake up if I turn the car off."

Laura peeks into the backseat at the sleeping baby. Sophie's cheeks are plump, and her lips are pink and full. Women would pay for lips like that. "She's so cute," she says.

"You'd never know she was a monster, would you?"

Laura laughs. "Is it that bad?"

"Yes. No. Sometimes."

"It'll get better. Remember the boys at this age? They grow so fast." Laura glances at her phone. Still nothing from her daughter. "Enjoy her while you can," she says. "Because one day you'll look around and she'll be gone."

For a moment they're quiet, watching Sophie sleep.

"Look, I stopped because you never told me how Hester got the baby stuff. Who sold it to her?"

"It doesn't matter, does it? I warned her not to bother you with it."

"I want to know, Laura. I want to talk to them, explain they're not supposed to encourage her. Because I just—I just can't deal with her right now. It took me weeks to get the boys to calm down after we caught her staring into our windows. They're afraid of the witch in the window. That's what they call her. They wake up crying, scared out of their minds."

"I didn't know." Although, Laura suspects the boys got the idea of a witch from Priscilla.

"Tell me who it was."

"No one sold her anything."

"She stole it?"

"Not really, no. She took it off some woman in the parking lot. She threw money at her, so I guess that's like paying."

"Jesus. She really is crazy. Why couldn't she just have another kid and leave me alone?"

"I told you before. They took her uterus."

"Yeah, right, complications—like it was my fault."

"No one said it was your fault." Hester had struggled delivering the afterbirth when she'd had Priscilla. The doctor had ended up scraping Hester's uterus, damaging it to the point of having to remove it altogether. Medical malpractice if Laura had ever heard of one.

"You sure you and the baby don't want to come inside?"

"No, I can't. I wish I could." Priscilla puts the Escalade in reverse. Sophie starts to cry. "I gotta go."

Priscilla waves as she drives down the road. Laura picks up the newspaper in the driveway. Most days she reads the news online, but she doesn't cancel her subscription because Tim Jr. is her paperboy. Laura may be the sheriff for the entire county, but she grew up here in Bordertown. She knows everyone, and everyone knows her. Tim Jr. is the son of Tim and Beth Culpepper. Beth's mother is a good friend of Laura's neighbor, Shari. Shari is a bank teller, who works with Bill Shaffer. Bill went to high school with Laura and married Laura's friend, Chrissy. Chrissy's maiden name is Fisher, and what Laura knows about the Fisher family is a lot.

The house is quiet when she enters. It's taken her a long time to get used to the silence. She tosses her keys and the paper onto the kitchen counter, then she rubs the back of her neck where it feels stiff, probably from stress. Most definitely from stress.

The clock on the stove flashes from when the electricity went out last night. The power has since been restored and the air conditioner kicks on, much to her relief. Her phone lights up with a text from the medical examiner, a professional courtesy since the state police are handling the investigation.

Derrick Fisher died of a single gunshot wound to the head.

Laura extends the courtesy and sends a text to Mason to let him know it was confirmed; it wasn't a bear attack. It will put the warden's mind at ease. Then she texts Joe, asks him to stop by.

She makes her way to the spare bedroom, which doubles as an office. Photos of Pop hang on the wall. In some of the shots he's wearing his sheriff's uniform, his expression businesslike and stern. Other shots are more candid, like the one of him holding Charlotte on her fourth birthday. Laura's favorite photo is of him sitting on the stoop next to Laura's mother, his arm slung around her mother's shoulders. They're both young and smiling. It was taken a few years before Laura was born.

On the opposite wall is a map of the county littered with pushpins. Laura picks up a chart from the top of the desk, marks the date and time, and pushes another pin on Clemons Street where she'd shown the woman with the pointy nails Kayleigh's picture for what seems like the hundredth time.

"Laura," Joe calls.

"In here."

He comes up behind her, looks at the map on the wall. He smells like the day's work mixed with the piney scent of the conifers from the woods.

"Anything new?" he asks.

She shakes her head. "I don't understand how she could've just disappeared. One fight with her mother sends her flying out the door and poof, she vanishes."

"Well, we know it wasn't one fight but several over a stretch of time." He rubs her neck, his thumb pressing into the knot that's been tightening all day.

She leans into his hand. "Did I ever tell you that Pop had an argument with Charlotte the same day Kayleigh went missing?"

"You might've mentioned it once or twice."

"You're right. I'm sorry. I don't mean to keep bringing it up."

"Hey, it's okay. I get it. She's the same age as your daughter. Some cases hit close to home. This one did for you and your dad."

"It really scared him, you know? And me. Like what if it *had* been Charlotte?"

"But it wasn't. You three were always close."

"Yeah, I know, but at the time it felt personal. It still feels personal. And Pop. It haunted him." She stares at the map, at the pins and strings, and the charts strewn on top of the desk. All of it started by Pop, then added onto by her. "I look like a person obsessed."

"No, you look like a person who cares."

"Well, someone has to. Kayleigh's own mother sure as hell didn't. She said Kayleigh went to live with her sister, Joe. It was a lie. We never found a sister even after the mother died. The poor girl has no one."

"Not no one. She had your dad and now she has you."

Laura nods. "I guess."

"Come on, we've been through this before, and it's been a long day." He takes her hand and leads her from the room. "What you need is a beer. I know I could use one."

In the kitchen, he pulls two bottles from the refrigerator and hands her one. "So, what did the ME say?"

"Derrick was shot. Single gunshot wound to the head like we thought."

He twists the cap off the bottle, takes a sip. "Who do you think shot him? Karl?"

"No, not Karl."

She considered that, of course, whether Karl had shot him, and whether Karl and his dad were trying to cover it up. But Derrick was shot at close range, execution style. It doesn't fit with what she knows of Karl and his affection for his cousin. Karl and Derrick were as close as cousins could be, unlike Laura and Hester. Some days she envies the Fishers for their acceptance of each other's—shall she say—idiosyncrasies. Although today is not one of those days.

"Who then?"

"I don't know, but you're right about one thing, it's been a long day."

She steps closer to him. He visibly leans back, and she takes another step closer, removing the bottle from his hand and setting both bottles on the counter.

"What're you doing?"

Laura touches his chest. He's already removed the bulletproof vest. So he was hopeful. She slips her fingers between the buttons on his uniform, feeling the heat of his skin, the patch of hair, the pounding of his heart.

"Are you sure this is a good idea?"

She unbuttons his shirt, slides her hand inside.

"You know, with it being your dad's—" He grabs her wrist, squeezes it. "I can't think when you're touching me."

"So don't think."

He pulls her against him, kissing her hard on the mouth, slipping into their act, playing his role obligingly.

"Is this what you want?" He grumbles into her lips.

"Yes." She rips his shirt open.

In one swift motion, he lifts her up, carries her to the bedroom. They shed their clothes. His eyes roam her body, her breasts, between her thighs. She is vulnerable, every inch of her exposed. It's what she wants, to relinquish control, to let herself go. She's tired of being the boss, of being in charge.

But most of all, tonight, she doesn't want to be alone.

CHAPTER
SIXTEEN

The blinds are drawn in the nursery. The last rays of daylight slip through a crack, cutting across the floorboards where Hillary stands. She stares into the empty crib. The mobile hanging overhead, the one with circus animals—giraffes and elephants and tigers—moves slightly when the air conditioning turns on.

If she squints and tilts her head just so, at just the right angle, she can still see her baby girl on the mattress sleeping blissfully. And if she tries really hard, if she concentrates, she can hear her baby girl's lips sucking the pacifier the doctor has told her not to use but she has used anyway. She understood the doctor's reasoning, not to use the dummy as a crutch to soothe a cranky child. It was a battle she wouldn't want to have with her daughter when it came time to take it away. But Hillary dismissed the doctor's concerns when she saw how comforted and happy Elsie was with the dummy in her mouth. And Hillary would always give her baby girl whatever she wanted.

The nursery door creaks open. She can feel Emeril's presence behind her. He carries his grief in the air around him, bringing it into every room in the house. It's suffocating, and she tries her hardest to bear it, but the truth is she can barely manage her own suffering.

"Hill, honey, why don't you come downstairs and have something to eat?"

"I'm not hungry," she says in a practiced British accent.

Her stomach rumbles. It's soft and cushiony like a pillow now that there's not a baby inside it. Just three weeks ago, it was large and round and so terribly hard. Nature is playing a cruel joke on her, she thinks. Her stomach rumbles again. She ignores it. How can she eat, when she can barely breathe? They're still waiting to hear from their contact. Whoever said waiting was the hardest part wasn't kidding.

Emeril checks the burner phone. She doesn't have to turn around to know he's doing it. He's been checking the burner phone every few minutes for hours now, the one that's untraceable according to some nameless guy who sold it to him.

"Something must've gone wrong." Emeril stands in the doorway, as though he's frightened to move, to come any closer. The threads that have been holding them together in the last seventy-two hours are fragile. One wrong word and they could unravel, shattering what's left of their hearts.

"Nothing has gone wrong. It's just taking longer than we expected, that's all."

"But every minute that passes makes it harder for us to get away with this. People will become suspicious. They'll start asking questions. They'll know something's not right."

Hillary rubs her brow. She doesn't want to have this conversation with him yet again. He's become so tiresome. It's because he's worried, she tells herself. When she married him, she assumed he was the stronger of the two. But with most everything that life tosses your way, you never really know which one of you will be better at handling the hard, bitter realities of this world until you're both tested.

Now she knows though, doesn't she? It's her. She's the stronger one.

"No one knows our baby is dead." Her words sound cruel even to her own ears, and still, she goes on. "Not the staff. Not the doctors. Not any of our family or friends." She pauses, waits for a break in the incessant pounding on the door from the room above.

When it stops, she continues. "We stick to the plan. We say I'm struggling with the baby blues. We'll explain to everyone how we needed some time to ourselves to adjust. They'll understand, and then when we do come out with our baby girl, no one will suspect a thing."

She hears how crazy she sounds. Maybe she really is suffering from some form of extreme baby blues. Or perhaps she's completely out of her mind with grief.

"And the nanny?" he asks.

They both look up at the ceiling. It's quiet. Almost too quiet.

"I don't know," she says.

"We have to do something about her."

"Yes."

"What should we do?"

"I said I don't know!"

He looks to the floor, hurt.

"I'm sorry," she says.

"Me too."

"Maybe we can tell her we had to quarantine her. Some illness she has or something. We'll convince her it's made her hallucinate. Or—or we'll pay her enough money to keep her mouth shut."

The more she talks, the crazier she sounds. She just can't accept her Elsie has died a crib death. How is such a thing possible in today's world? How could modern medicine not foresee something like this happening? How could they not have prevented it? It has to be a mistake. It *is* a mistake. Hillary refuses to believe her baby is dead and buried on the estate in the rose garden in an unmarked grave.

Was it three nights ago they buried her? Or four?

She's unclear of the time of the events as they unfolded. What she does remember is being woken in the middle of the night, the nanny shaking her shoulder, saying something is wrong over and over and over again. Hillary raced from the bed she shares with Emeril, and she rushed to the nursery. There in the crib, Elsie was sleeping peacefully, so peacefully, and yet, Hillary knew her daughter was gone without ever checking for her baby's breath. *She knew.* She picked Elsie up, her tiny body limp in her arms.

She's fine. She's hungry. I'll feed her, and she'll be fine, is what she told the nanny, but the girl wouldn't listen, saying repeatedly, *But ma'am. But ma'am. Ma'am!*

What happens next is a blur in Hillary's mind, a dark cloud that's impossible to see through clearly. Emeril grabbing the nanny, locking her in her room, telling her the baby is fine. Hillary is fine.

But why does he lock the door? From the outside?

Together she and Emeril rocked their little Elsie, Emeril promising he'd fix it. No matter what he had to do, he would make it right. Then he took the baby and put her in a box and placed it in the ground in the garden near a rose bush. The sound of his cries echoed in the night under a too bright moon.

No. She covers her ears. *No.*

She doesn't believe it. Her baby is out there somewhere. Her baby is on her way back to them. Hillary only has to wait for her baby girl to come home, so she can hold and love her once again.

Emeril comes up behind her and he puts his hand on her shoulder. She places a hand on top of his, pats it gently. They've shared so many whispers in the dark belly of the night. Discussing friends, friends of friends, powerful friends who could point them in the right direction, who had information on how they could go about setting things right. Of course, they'd heard there were ways to get certain things, seemingly impossible things—ancient artifacts, stolen paintings, banned products—but they've always heard of such occurrences from a distance and never up close and personal. And never about a baby.

Until they needed one, which couldn't be obtained in the usual way.

It was easier than they thought, getting the name of the one person who could help them get what they wanted, what they needed, and then it was as simple as setting their plan in motion. It would cost them though, a minimum of seven figures, but that's what having money can do for a person. It can buy them anything, and Hillary and Emeril are in a position to do just that thanks to Emeril's family wealth: old railroad money that's been passed from generation to generation for over a century.

"I would do anything for you," Emeril says. "Anything. You know I would."

Yes, she knows, but she reaffirms her position, because he needs to hear it. "Then you'll do this."

"Of course." He kisses her on the side of the head. Then he leaves the room, pausing in the doorway. "Please come down and eat something soon."

"I'll be down in a few minutes."

He's forgotten she has some staging to do, something which has to be done for their plan to fully work. There has to be proof of a baby living in the chateau these last few days in case there are any questions later. What better way than to have security camera footage of Hillary doing just that, doing something a new mother would do with her newborn child. Nothing too private or personal, but something that would reflect well on the family if the video ever needs to be viewed—dare she say it—by the authorities.

Hillary selects a simple white slip dress, light and airy, and a wide-rim hat with a silk sash. Breezy and elegant. Something a character in one of Jane Austen's novels might wear for a walk about the gardens. She considers a parasol, but since they locked the nanny in her room, someone has to push the pram. Hillary is American, but she speaks with a British accent, spending hours in front of a mirror practicing during the year she'd spent studying abroad. She fell head over heels for all things British, especially their words. Pram sounds much more glamorous than the American version—stroller. Compare dressing gown to bathrobe. She shudders. *Bloody hell*, there is no comparison. Even the curse words the British use sound highbrow to her ears.

The pram is the exact kind that William and Kate had used for their three children. Hillary knows because she and Emeril have a few similar acquaintances (and Hillary reads the tabloids, but only the articles about the royals' baby gear). Although Hillary has yet to meet the Duke and Duchess, she's hopeful.

Hillary pushes the empty pram around the English garden fountain that's circular in shape and three tiers high. It's really quite grand. Somehow, she makes it all feel normal: a stroll before dinner under the light of the setting sun. On occasion, she stops for effect, posturing and preening for the security cameras. The smile she presents is forced, but she does her best. Stiff upper lip and all that.

The fountain mist graces her arms, giving her skin a dewy glow. How divine she must look in this light under a heavenly sky. She raises her hand to shield her eyes from the glare as though she suddenly sees something of interest, a hummingbird perhaps, and she poses for the perfect shot. Then she slips the hat off, shakes out her hair, imagining the shot in slow motion. She reaches for the pram as if to say, *oh, darling, you must see this*, but the pram isn't there.

Whipping around, her hand flies to her mouth as she catches sight of it rolling down the garden path.

Bloody hell.

She should probably run after it since the cameras don't know the pram is empty. Yes, she should run after it, and she takes off at a speed a little faster than a jog, but the pavers are wet, and she slips in a puddle of water. Her body is propelled forward, uncontrollably, and she crashes into the pram. Her legs tangle and the next thing she knows, they're both careening, heading straight into a shrub.

Surprised and confused, she pulls herself out of the jumble of scratchy branches and turns around, faces the chateau. Tiny leaves stick to her skin and twigs poke out of her hair.

Stunned, she blinks.

Emeril appears in the doorway, a drink in his hand. "Oh, dear," he says.

CHAPTER
SEVENTEEN

H ester sits on the couch next to Eve and Baby Ivy. The baby is drinking from the bottle Hester prepared. Ivy is quiet, comforted for now, but oh, how Hester wishes she was the one feeding her.

Instead, she's looking down the barrel of a gun the man sitting across from her is holding. Her rifle is lying across the man's lap on top of his designer jeans. How does she know they're designer jeans? The doctors in the hospital where she'd worked had worn them when they were off duty. Sometimes she'd catch them when their shift was over, walking through the parking garage, heading to their cars. Sometimes she'd follow them home, trailing behind while they'd run their errands and carpooled their kids to soccer games and dance recitals.

Seeing this asshole in his ritzy threads, with the smug look on his face, brings back old feelings of loathing she's harbored for those same doctors not so long ago, especially the obstetricians, driving their shiny cars, flaunting their families. They'd oozed money and everything else Hester has never had. Just like fancy pants here sitting up straight in Hester's kitchen chair. Except fancy pants doesn't wield scalpels when he's playing God. No, this idiot holds a gun. He's like some goddam couture cowboy, and she hates him instantly.

"Where's the fucking money?" the couture cowboy asks Eve for a second time.

Hester waits patiently for Eve to answer him. Sure, she can be patient, because she doesn't have anything else to do. And these two aren't going anywhere, of that she's certain. At least not without their money. She glances at the baby, longs to reach out and touch her cheek, smooth the soft spot on her head.

It seems the cowboy is patient as well. He appears to be content to wait for Eve to answer him, for the time being anyway. Hester suspects if he has to ask Eve a third time, it will probably be her last opportunity to talk.

After an excruciatingly long silence, Eve says, "I don't have it."

"Yeah? Then who does?"

Hester picks this moment to speak up in an attempt to save her own ass. Eve isn't going to come to her defense, that's for sure. She can feel the anger coming off Eve like some kind of electromagnetic wave. The way she came at Hester, mouth open, shrieking, fists flying. She behaved like some kind of raging lunatic. Hester looks at the cowboy's stupid blond hair. Clearly a dye job and a bad one at that.

"Who do you think you are, anyway? Riding in here like you're some kind of cowboy in your fancy threads, asking all kinds of questions, making all kinds of demands?"

He stares at her as though she's suddenly piqued his interest. "Am I to assume you know where the money is?"

"If I did, I wouldn't tell *you*." She has never been so happy with herself for hiding that money the way she did.

He points the gun at Eve. "Where is it?"

"Do you think I know? If I knew, do you think I'd be sitting here right now? I'd be long gone, mister. I mean *Sir*. I'd be long *fucking* gone."

The cowboy leans back as best he can in the straight chair. He rubs his chin on his left shoulder, catching the sweat that's been running down the side of his face. As he does this, he winces. His shirt is in tatters where it looks as if he's been injured. It's a sore spot and it's a little bloody, although Hester can't get a good look at how bad he's hurt from where she sits. Maybe he's been cut by the switchblade, which feels as large as a sword in the pocket of her jeans.

They sit in silence, and it seems to Hester that the cowboy is weighing his options just as she is weighing hers. She looks out the window, watches as the gray sky darkens. It doesn't take long before rain hits the glass and strikes the stone walls and roof. Shadows start to creep across the wooden floor and soon it will be too dark to see.

"Turn on a light," the cowboy says.

Eve sets the empty bottle on the cushion between her and Hester, and then she leans forward as though she's about to stand up with the baby, but the cowboy stops her.

"Not you. You, Witch. Get up and turn on the light."

Eve lifts Baby Ivy to her shoulder and pats her back, attempting to burp her.

"I told you the power is out, but I got something that'll help." Hester puts her hands on her knees and pushes herself up. Her damn arthritis makes every joint stiff when she sits for too long and especially in this weather.

"Slowly now. Don't do anything stupid."

"Why? What're you going to do? Shoot me? Go ahead, asshole, then you'll never find your money."

She walks to the table where the puzzle she's started just last night sits untouched. So much has changed in the last twenty-four hours. Most of it good. Except for the cowboy. He's bad news, but just how bad, she's not really sure. She picks up the lantern and turns it on before returning to the couch.

"Set it on the cushion between you," he says.

The lantern lights up Eve and the baby, and its yellow beam flows onto Hester. The cowboy remains in the shadows, exactly how he wants it.

"You've got a smart mouth on you," he says to her.

"Fuck you, cowboy."

He chuckles. She has no idea what he thinks is so funny. Is he amused by her? Why does she care if he is? She decides she doesn't. Her mind is working on how she's going to get her and Eve and the baby out of this alive.

They sit in silence again, listening to the rain. The cowboy seems preoccupied with staring out the window at the streaks of water on the glass and the blackened view of the woods. What's he thinking? Whatever it is, Hester has to outmaneuver him somehow, and she comes up with a plan. It's not a very good one, but she has to do something to distract him until she can think of a better one.

"Well, I don't know about you, but I can't think properly when I'm hungry, and I'm starved." She smiles at Eve. *Agree with me, honey.*

"I'm starved, too," Eve says.

Good girl, Hester thinks. "I've got a fridge full of food that's going to spoil if I don't cook it up and fast. What do you say?" she asks the cowboy. "Are you hungry?"

He seems to mull it over. While he takes his time to make up his mind, she gets up from the couch in an attempt to make it up for him.

"Let the baby sleep," she says to Eve. "You can help me in the kitchen."

"I didn't say either one of you could move."

Hester picks up the lantern. "You'll be able to watch us the entire time."

He looks toward the dark window again and by a stroke of luck, thunder rumbles.

Hester assumes he's not planning on leaving in the middle of a storm and definitely not without his money. What she gathers about him in the short time he's been here is that he's too vain and most certainly too proud to walk away without it. What she's done is bought herself some time while he seems to be deciding his next move.

She heads to the kitchen and puts the lantern by the sink. It throws enough light to see the gas stovetop, the fridge, and the countertop. It's a fine lantern. Tonight, she wishes she would've bought a cheaper one. The cowboy will have no trouble keeping his eye on them. She's going to have to be very careful.

Eve sets Ivy on the couch. The baby seems content now that her belly is full.

Hester opens the freezer. Everything inside has thawed. The packages of meat and bags of vegetables are wet and dripping with water. She pulls out a pound of ground beef, peels back the plastic from the container, and she smells it. It's ripe, but she rearranges her face as though it doesn't stink at all, and she says to Eve, who has come up behind her, "We can fry this up."

Eve yanks the package out of Hester's hands, letting her know she's still angry with her. She holds the meat away from her face, probably because of the smell. Hester looks at her, imploring her to play along. If they can get the cowboy to eat the spoiled meat, he'll get sick, and if he gets sick, they'll have a chance at getting the gun away from him.

That's her plan. The whole of it.

If it doesn't work?

There's always plan B—the switchblade in her pocket.

Knives are messy work, though, and she'd rather avoid it if possible. She's never stabbed someone before, and she doesn't want to have to do it now, but she resolves to do whatever she has to do to get rid of him.

She pulls out a bag of mixed vegetables—corn and carrots and broccoli—which was supposed to be frozen but has also thawed. She doesn't have a lot of food stored in the freezer or the refrigerator. Why would she? She lives alone. Eats alone. And she's never been one to overeat. Gluttony is a sin. The parents and teenagers around town and the couture cowboy may believe she's a witch, but she's no sinner. At least not in her mind.

There's about eighty bucks worth of spoiled food. Maybe she can bill the power company for her loss for forgetting she's back here. She pays her electric bill just like everybody else. Shouldn't she expect the same kind of service as the rest of the town?

Hester pours the mixed vegetables in a pot to boil. It will make a nice side dish. Then she drops the beef in a frying pan and dumps the elbow macaroni in another pot. She finds cheese in the lunchmeat drawer. Add a little ketchup, salt and pepper, along with the cheese. A poor man's version of Hamburger Helper.

While she's busy at the stove, Eve finds a bag of baby carrots, and she nibbles on them.

"What do you need me to do?" She doesn't sound so angry anymore. Maybe she's caught on to Hester's plan.

"We'll need to set the table."

Hester slides open the silverware drawer. Next to the forks, spoons, and knives is a box of ammunition. She doesn't need a knife since she already has the switchblade, but it couldn't hurt to shove a couple of bullets in her pocket in case she needs them. Maybe she can steal her rifle back while he's shitting rotten meat.

She likes her rifle. She prefers it. If she tries to steal his handgun, she's not sure how good of a shot she'll be.

Eve reaches for a knife, but Hester shakes her head. Where would the girl hide it? The shorts she borrowed from Hester don't have pockets. Instead, Hester motions to the box of ammunition.

"What are you two doing over there?" the cowboy asks.

Hester nearly jumps, but she quickly recovers. "What does it look like we're doing?"

Abandoning the bullets, she lifts up the plates, and she sets them on the table. She'll have to try to get back to the drawer later, but then Eve makes a lot of noise with the silverware, clanking it together, before shutting the drawer and joining Hester with the forks and spoons. Hester has no doubt Eve has taken a couple of bullets, but where has she put them? In her underwear?

But what does it matter as long as she has them.

They're going to have to work together to get rid of the cowboy one way or another. Once they do, she'll try to strike some kind of bargain with Eve about the money and the baby. What kind of deal, she hasn't figured out yet. It's a problem she'll have to solve later.

Right now, she needs to think about what else she can cook, since she and Eve can't eat the meat. They'll have to distract the cowboy of this fact. There isn't anything left in the fridge that's salvageable. The only other thing she can think to make is soup. *Egads*, it's too hot for soup. She'll put out bread, but they'll have to eat it dry, since the butter has melted.

After adding the pasta and cheese to the meat, she mixes it around. She instructs Eve to stir the vegetables. For a moment, she pretends they're a family, preparing dinner, getting ready to sit down together to discuss the day's events. It's easy to play pretend. You don't have to be a child to do it. All you need is the right mindset and a lot of time on your hands.

The cowboy moves from the chair, and her little daydream dissipates. The floorboards creak when he walks over to the card table. He sets the rifle down, and he reaches for a puzzle piece.

"Don't touch that!"

He points the gun at her, not to shoot her, but more out of surprise. "What is your problem?"

"Just don't touch it. It's mine to solve."

Eve is staring at her.

"What're you looking at?"

Eve holds up her hands, as if to say *leave me out of it.*

The cowboy picks up the rifle and he steps away from the card table. It's as if he doesn't have the energy to fight with her. Good, she thinks. *Good.*

The cowboy remains standing, watching them closely.

After a couple of minutes, she says, "It's ready. Let's eat."

CHAPTER
EIGHTEEN

Noah is hungry and he really doesn't like to admit this, but he's also feeling weak and slightly confused. What was he thinking wandering over to the puzzle on the card table? He's never been interested in puzzles before. Clearly, he's not himself.

Thunder rattles the windows and rain powers down on the roof like an exclamation point, emphasizing how he's not going anywhere in this weather anytime soon. It seems he's stuck here, at least until the storm blows over. Wherever *here* is—he's lost all sense of direction in the maze of trees out there. It was sheer dumb luck that he'd stumbled onto the cottage the way he had and even luckier that he'd found the girl and baby inside. Lucky, that's him. But without his phone and its compass, it will be nearly impossible to find his way back in the middle of a stormy night, and now he has the girl and the baby to worry about, too.

Noah considers taking the car-truck outside, although he doubts the witch will just hand over the keys. He'd already searched the vehicle for them at the same time he discovered the rifle in the bed. Hot-wiring the car-truck isn't an option simply because he has no idea how to do it, and, quite frankly, it's an outdated street skill with newer models all using computer technology.

The witch is spooning food into bowls. He's made the decision not to kill her. Not yet, anyway. Since it appears he's trapped here, at least for the night, it gives him plenty of time to find the money and deal with her afterward. The girl carries the bowls to the table. When they finish putting the food out, he asks them to stand against the counter with their backs facing him.

"What the hell for?" Witch asks, but she does what she's told.

The girl joins her.

"Put your hands on the counter and spread your legs," he says.

"You arresting us?" Witch asks.

"I'm going to pat you down. I don't know what you're up to, but I know you're up to something."

Noah leans the rifle against the kitchen chair where he plans to sit. With the Magnum in one hand, he pats the girl down with the other. He chooses her first based on past experience and the hit he took to the side of his head. Starting with her waist, he works his way down her legs. No pockets in her baggy shorts. Her T-shirt hangs loosely, and he pats it to make sure she hasn't stuffed anything up it. She doesn't move, as though she's used to having unwanted hands touching her.

His shoulder aches and the wound reopens. For a second, he lets his arm hang at his side. Blood trickles down his forearm and onto his hand and eventually drips from his fingertips. So much effort to do a simple task.

"Stay put," he says to the girl, and he switches to pat down the witch.

"Watch where you put your hands, cowboy," Witch says.

As if, and he smiles to himself. He kind of likes this woman, or at least her feisty spirit. In the front pocket of her jeans, he feels something long and hard, and he pulls it out, surprised to discover Shot's switchblade.

Son of a bitch.

"Turn around. Both of you."

Noah holds the switchblade up for them to see. "Where did you get this?" he asks the witch. "Or did you get it from her?"

He points the knife at the girl. She flinches even though the blade is retracted. It's possible the memory of Shot cutting her forehead has flashed before her eyes.

"She didn't get it from me," Girl says.

By the way the girl is staring at the witch, he believes she's telling the truth. He's dealt with enough con men and women in his line of work to be able to spot when someone is lying. He turns his attention to the witch. "Where did you get this?"

"I found it in the woods."

"So it was you? You're the one who hung Shot in the tree?"

The witch shrugs.

"Why? What was the reason?" He's trying to figure out what her intentions are. Everyone has a motive. Everyone has a reason for doing the things they do. The witch is no exception. She wants something. Is it the money? According to her, she already has it.

The witch shrugs again. "I don't know. It just seemed like the right thing to do at the time."

"What does that even mean?" Shot was dead when Noah woke up after being knocked out by the girl. There's no question in his mind that he was dead.

"I don't like cops. I did it to mess with them a little, throw them off."

"So you made it look like he hung himself?"

"Yeah, if that's how you want to look at it."

"Why?"

"To help the girl and the baby."

"But why? You don't know them. Or do you?"

"No, not before she knocked on my door last night."

It seems too clean. Tidy. He's not buying this cop-disliking crap. The witch has an angle, and he needs to figure out what it is.

"Sit down. Both of you."

The girl and the witch sit on one side of the table. Noah shoves the switchblade in his front pocket, and he sits on the other side of the table, where he has a clear view of them. The lantern acts as a centerpiece. It throws off a good deal of light, enough for him to see the food in front of him. It looks like some kind of meat concoction with a side of vegetables. Far from the likes of anything he's seen before, let alone eaten. What he wouldn't give for a simple bowl of boeuf bourguignon. Even in this heat.

"What is this?" He dabs at the moisture on his forehead with the back of his free hand and the one he will eat with. Because whatever this shit is, he needs nourishment. And water. The Magnum is pointed at the cooks. The rifle leans against the table by his side where he last put it.

"It's my version of Hamburger Helper," Witch says.

"What the hell is Hamburger Helper? Forget it. I don't want to know." He grabs the girl's water and gulps it down just in case the witch has slipped something in his glass. Then he aims the barrel at the girl. "Eat it," he says to her.

"I'm a vegetarian." She stabs a piece of broccoli, puts it in her mouth.

"Bullshit." There's no way in hell Shot would've put up with a special menu for any of his girls. They ate whatever they were given, and he bet they never complained. He picks up his plate and leans across the table. "Eat it," he says to the girl, and without moving the gun, he says to the witch, "You, too."

For all he knows, the witch really is a witch, and she plans to poison him. He drops his plate between them with a clatter. Some of the mystery stew slops onto the table.

When neither of them takes a bite, he slams his fist down. "Eat it!"

Reluctantly, they pick up their forks and poke around in the meat. Eventually, they take several bites. Once he's satisfied they have both had a decent helping off his plate, he takes his plate back again and digs in. Between bites, he says, "Now eat yours."

He tries not to think about the disgusting smell and taste. It's food and water, and he needs his strength. Twice now, he's made the girl refill his water glass.

Once his belly is full, he's thinking more clearly. The witch was right about one thing, he does think better when he's not hungry. The baby has fallen asleep on the couch, and it's time he sorted out the other order of business.

"I'm going to make this really easy on everybody. I don't care where you put the money," he says to the witch. "You're going to get it and bring it to me. As soon as the storm blows over, me and the girl and the baby will vacate your little cottage in the woods, and you're going to forget we were ever here." The witch will forget once he puts a bullet in her brain.

"No way," Girl says. "I'm not going anywhere with you."

Noah ignores her. He can deal with her later. Right now, he's focused on the money. "Witch?"

"That's a no way from me, too. I'm not telling you where the money is, and I'm sure as hell not going to get it for you."

He sighs. Why is it that all the women in his life are nothing but one big pain in the ass? Except for Madeline, of course. She was a saint, but he mustn't think of her. Now isn't the time to get lost inside his thoughts. If he's learned anything in the last few hours in this stinking shithole of a woods, it's that he can't let his guard down.

Whatever these two were fighting about when he opened the door seems to have been settled. They're ganging up on him. If he can find out what the problem is between them, he can exploit it. Does he have time for that? He's lost so much time already. At least a whole twenty-four hours. An entire fucking day.

He supposes he could just kill the witch and forget about the money. He could leave with the girl and the baby at daybreak. The rain should stop by then. Sure, he could, and yet, he can't seem to pull the trigger. It's half a million dollars.

Relax, he tells himself. He still has time to find the money (and keep it, because his clients don't need to know Shot is dead). Once it stops raining and it's light enough to see, he'll figure out where the hell he is and how he's going to get out of here.

Besides, the thought of leaving all that money behind, well, Noah might as well put the Magnum to his head, pull the trigger, and be done with it. Giving the half a mil to Shot was the cost of doing business. He could've lived with it then, because he never thought of it as his. He was due to get his half when he delivered the baby. But like he said, things change, and the money belongs to him now. And once he gets something in his head, he can't get it out. And he can't stomach the fact that someone like this witch has taken it from him.

Speaking of his stomach—

His begins to churn.

CHAPTER
NINETEEN

Karl Fisher isn't dim-witted like everybody in town thinks. Sure, he was a poor student in school. It's hard to be a good student when you're hardly ever there. When he did manage to get out of bed and get to class, he did okay. He was pretty good at math if he could use his fingers. He was even better when he was given a calculator. Most of the time, though, he just couldn't see the point of it, and it's not as if his mom or dad was pushing him out the door or taking an interest in his grades.

Karl was already working part-time in his dad's store by the time he was twelve. He didn't aspire to be anything or anyone beyond working in the family's business, living in his family's house, being the cousin of Derrick Fisher. Maybe one day he'd branch out, get a place of his own if he ever found a wife, but that day seemed a long way off. After all, he's only twenty-four years old.

It's like Derrick always told him. "You're not slow, Karl. It just takes you longer than other people to understand stuff." Derrick would laugh, and then a few seconds later, Karl would laugh with him, because eventually Karl got the joke.

The sheriff, though, she believes he's slower than slow. The way she speaks to him, pronouncing each word clearly, carefully, as though she's talking to a child. It's the reason why he doesn't feel any guilt whatsoever for having lied to her. She represents the law, and like school, Karl doesn't have any use for it. It's not as though he's gotten into trouble in the past, nothing more than a parking ticket or two. It's just that he was raised by a family who takes pride in taking care of their own. They don't take kindly to outside interference in what they consider family matters and that includes the sheriff.

Karl sits on a metal chair next to his dad in the back office of the store. The chair is hard and cold. He doesn't mind. It's keeping him awake. He doesn't want to fall asleep. When he closes his eyes, all he can see is what's left of Derrick's body after the bear got him.

Karl doesn't blame the bear. The bear wasn't trying to be something he wasn't. He was just being a bear. An animal will do what an animal has to do and that particular bear was scrawny. He needed to eat. Karl knows, because he's the one who chased it away. If he hadn't, well, he doesn't want to think about what would be left of Derrick. Maybe nothing but a pile of bones.

"You paying attention to me, son?" his dad asks.

"Yes, sir." His hands ache from being clenched in tight fists for most of day. Hold it in, he tells himself. *Hold it in.* There will be a time and place to unleash the anger that has overtaken every cell and molecule in his body.

"I want you to study that face," his dad says. "That's the guy we're looking for. Do you understand? We have to be certain. We can't make any mistakes."

The video is paused on the stranger's face with the blond hair. The guy's hair has to be bleached. Karl has never known anybody to have hair that color yellow. It's obvious the guy didn't want to be recognized and dyed it as a disguise. How could anyone want their hair to be that color on purpose?

His dad rewinds the video, and they watch it again. They must've watched it fifty times or more. Each time, they're looking for clues, anything they might've missed about who this stranger is. They don't talk about why this particular stranger put a bullet between Derrick's eyebrows.

"It doesn't matter now, does it?" his dad asks. "Derrick's dead, and we can't bring him back. What's the point of discussing the *why* of such a thing."

But his dad keeps rewinding the video as though he's trying to go back in time, maybe stop it from happening. But you can't go back. Even Karl knows that. He doesn't mention to his dad how he'd warned Derrick not to screw with this guy. Karl won't admit this now, but at the time, the guy spooked him. There was something in the way the guy walked, like he had a certain swagger. And what was it that Karl saw in the guy's eyes? It was a look that screamed he wasn't someone to be messed with. Karl told Derrick all of this, but his cousin, being who he was, wouldn't listen. That was Derrick. A tough guy to the end. Big. Strong. Either you got out of his way when you saw him coming or you paid the price. Unless, of course, you were asking for his autograph.

In high school, Derrick played center on the ice hockey team. He was a natural athlete with the attitude of a star. Since hockey is the town's religion, everyone came out to watch him. There was talk about Derrick playing in the big leagues, capital B-I-G: the NHL.

After one too many concussions, though, the scouts stopped coming to see him, and then Derrick's dad died. Karl was sad, deeply pained by the loss of his uncle and the grief his cousin endured, but in the dark places he doesn't like to admit live inside him, he was glad his cousin would be sticking around.

And then there were the girls. Derrick had so many, a different one every few weeks. It seemed that way to Karl, anyway. His cousin wasn't stingy with them either. Derrick didn't mind sharing them with Karl. If it wasn't for Derrick's generosity, Karl would still be a virgin.

What a guy!

Most of all, what really mattered to Karl was how he felt important standing next to Derrick, like he was someone. They were more than just cousins. They were like brothers. Hell, they even looked alike to some extent. They had the same greasy brown hair, brown eyes, and large muscular frame. Although, Derrick stood two inches taller than Karl at six foot four. NHL material all the way. Karl played some hockey in school, but he'd get confused with the offensive and defensive tactics the coach laid out for the team. Because he couldn't quite catch on, he spent most of his time on the bench. It didn't matter to Karl, though, not when he had Derrick by his side.

Karl stands abruptly, the metal chair toppling over. The more he thinks about what the blond-haired guy did, what he took from him, the more incensed he gets. But there is something else, a sense of fear creeping in the shadows of his anger, lurking just out of reach. It's like an image he can only see out of the corner of his eye. He knows it's there, the panic, waiting to reveal itself in full view. *Who is he now without his cousin?*

Karl grabs a double-barrel shotgun from the gun cabinet. In his haste, the tip of the barrel catches the lip of the cabinet and pulls the whole thing over. The glass door shatters and shotguns and rifles clatter onto the floor. One of the guns goes off, the bullet lodging into the wall not far from where his dad sits.

Clyde springs from the chair. "You stupid idiot! Watch what you're doing! You could've gotten us killed!"

Karl scrambles to pick up the guns.

"Leave 'em. I'll get 'em. Just don't touch anything. Please. Just don't move."

"I'm sorry, Dad. It's just—I want to kill this son of a bitch."

"I know, but first we have to get rid of this video. You sure you'll recognize him?"

"I'm sure." Karl wipes his eyes. "How are we going to find him?"

"Do you remember where you last saw him in the woods?"

Karl nods.

"That's where we'll start."

Karl may be a little slow (and sometimes clumsy) when it comes to books and common sense, but there's one thing he's good at, and that's tracking animals. He follows the clues: snapped branches, fur caught in brush, prints. It's more than just following signs, though. It's a gut instinct, a primal thing, where he picks up the trail like a dog chasing a scent. And like a dog's nose that traps a scent in its glands, Karl's nose does much the same thing. If there's one thing Karl remembers most about the blond-haired guy—it's the way he smelled. The pretty boy must've bathed in some kind of expensive soap, one that Karl is certain he's never smelled in these parts before.

His dad starts picking up the guns from the floor. The rain that's been pattering against the roof is coming down harder. It's as though the drops are tapping Karl on the shoulder, reminding him how it's washing away the evidence the guy left behind, but Karl's not worried about the rain. He knows the exact location of the guy's footprints and the direction they were headed. He remembers the blood trail, and, most importantly, he memorized the guy's smell. It's all there, trapped in his nostrils, just waiting to sniff him out.

"Karl!"

"Yeah, Dad."

"Get your finger out of your nose."

126

CHAPTER
TWENTY

Eve is sweating, and not from the humidity in the cottage, which has reached suffocating levels. It's the kind of sweat that comes from sickness. She's both hot and cold, dying of heatstroke one second and chilled to the bone the next. She wipes her brow. Her body is working hard, attempting to rid itself of the bacteria that's been gnawing at her stomach ever since she was forced to eat the rotten meat. Picking through the hamburger concoction, she tried to avoid the bigger chunks of beef, nibbling on the elbow macaroni and cheese. Obviously, she must've swallowed some of it or possibly drank the meat juice that was mixed in with the entire slop.

It was a dumb idea, she longs to say to Hester, but she can't, not with the man sitting across from them at the kitchen table. What was it that Hester called him? The cowboy? It seems fitting. Eve glances in Hester's direction, giving her the side-eye. Hester's face is pale and her hair sticks to her wet cheeks. The woman looks as unhealthy as Eve feels.

The cowboy is talking. He's an idiot if he thinks he can negotiate an agreement with them. Eve is not going anywhere with him. She'd rather die than go back to being a Shot girl. Somewhere between fighting with Hester and the cowboy showing up at the door, she's made her decision—she won't accept anything less than the bag full of money and freedom.

The cowboy is eying her as though he's reading her thoughts. His face is also pale under the yellow light of the lantern, and he's sweating profusely just like they are. His gun is aimed in the space between her and Hester. Eve's stomach hisses and spits, and then a searing pain slices her abdomen, forcing her to lean forward, holding her belly.

The cowboy is the next one to clutch his stomach and bend over. Hester is the only one remaining upright, possibly because she's farted.

"I have to go to the bathroom." Eve bolts from the table, running down the hallway, gripping her side. She's careful when she rolls the shorts down to her knees. Tucked inside the waistband are three bullets that she's snagged from the box in the silverware drawer. The cowboy didn't find them when he patted her down. Too bad for him. Bending forward, she's still holding her stomach as she empties her colon. It feels so good to let it out. What a relief. But oh, the smell.

Someone is banging on the door.

"Let me in," the cowboy says.

"No!"

He kicks the door in, the gun in one hand, the other pressed against his stomach. Hester is behind him, bent over.

"Get the fuck out!"

"Get up. Now," the cowboy says.

"Hurry," Hester says. "I'm next."

"Like hell you're next." He pulls Eve off the toilet, and he struggles getting his tight jeans down. The cowboy sits just in time. By the look on his face, you would think he just had the best orgasm of his life. He aims the gun at them. "Sit where I can see you."

For the next few hours, they lie in the hallway with the bathroom door open, taking turns on the toilet. There is no shame exposing themselves this way. They're sick and in pain, and they have no sense of pride. They focus on making the cramps go away. No exception. Get it out of their systems. Make it stop. With each passing minute, Eve silently begs for it to end. When she thinks she's as empty as she's ever going to get, another round comes on.

"What the hell did we eat?" the cowboy asks. They ignore him.

Hester says to Eve, "Lie on your left side. It helps relieve the gas pain."

"Are you a nurse or something?" Eve flips to her left side.

"No, I wasn't a nurse, but I worked in the hospital in housekeeping. I paid attention."

They're lying in the hallway. The cowboy is in the bathroom, pointing the gun at them. Always with the damn gun. Eve's stomach hurts so bad, she has half a mind to tell him to shoot her now and get it over with.

Baby Ivy cries. She's been sleeping on the couch most of the night. At first, her crying is quiet, a test to see if someone will come running. When no one answers, the crying intensifies.

"I'm next." Hester is on all fours, ready to take her turn again after the cowboy.

One of the bullets in Eve's waistband pokes her side. An idea forms in the back of her mind: a better plan than the stupid spoiled meat one. During their haste to make it to the bathroom, they all forgot about the rifle. It should still be in the kitchen, propped against the chair at the table.

"I'll check on the baby." Eve crawls to the living room with the lantern. Behind her, the cowboy says, "Where do you think you're going? Get back here!"

Eve ignores him. When she reaches the baby, she touches the child's bare chest. For a second, Ivy stops crying, comforted by Eve's hand.

"Hang tight, little one." She talks to her as though Ivy can understand what she's saying. "I promise I'll take care of you right after I take care of that asshole."

Using the arm of the couch, Eve pulls herself up. Standing upright is excruciating, so she hunches and makes her way to the kitchen table. Searching the rolled waistband of the shorts, she finds the bullets. Her hands are shaking, and her ass is on fire from all the wiping. It feels as though she's sat in a pile of fire ants. She doesn't know how to load a rifle, but she's smart. She'll figure it out. Maybe it's already loaded.

She pulls the trigger.

Nothing happens.

Someone is coming up behind her.

She hears their footsteps, but she doesn't have time to react when her arm is struck, sending the bullets flying from her fingers. They scatter across the wooden floor. The cowboy's hand squeezes the back of her neck, forcing her chin into her chest. His fingers press into her skin like a vice. He could snap her cervical spine if he wanted to.

The baby continues to cry.

Somewhere, sometime, from that forgotten life before she ran away, a memory surfaces in her mind. She was ten or eleven years old when a police officer had visited her school and talked about stranger danger. What to do, how to react if she was ever grabbed from behind. Eve is surprised she remembers, but ever since being in the woods when this asshole presented her with an opportunity, she's let a slice of home in, along with a sliver of hope. It seems she'd been waiting for a chance to escape even if she hadn't been fully aware of it, at least not in a conscious way. And now that a bit of hope seems to have taken a firm hold of her, she can't let it go. Maybe she can't ever go home again. Or can she? At the very least, she can become someone else, someone new, reinvent herself a third time. What she wants most of all, what she dreams of is a simple life: a soft pillow for her head, a clean pair of socks, and shoes that fit.

Money.

Eve drops to her knees like the police officer told her ten-year-old self to do. The cowboy's grip on her neck loosens. Throwing her elbow up and back, she hits him hard between the legs.

He groans, gripping his junk.

She doesn't waste any time. She grabs the rifle, crawls across the floor, knees scraping the wood, the rifle hitting the floorboards every time she puts her hand down.

Swish thump, swish thump, swish thump.

There are shadows everywhere. It's hard to see between the darkened room and the blood from the gash on her forehead, which has reopened once again and is dripping in her eyes. Her hands sweep across the boards, searching for a bullet.

Just one.

That's all it will take.

Just one.

Somewhere behind Eve, Hester staggers into the family room, and she stops next to the couch.

"Shh," she says to Ivy. "It's okay. I'm here."

"Help me, you stupid bitch!" Eve says.

The cowboy grasps Eve's ankle. She kicks, trying to get him off. Hester jumps on his back, but apparently, she can't hold on, because she slides off.

"Oh." Hester doubles over. "I'm not going to make it." She's fiddling with her jeans.

The next time Eve catches sight of her, Hester is holding her side, running down the hall toward the bathroom.

Eve swings the rifle. It hits the cowboy's shoulder where he was bleeding earlier. If he feels it, he doesn't let it show. She continues kicking, swinging the rifle at him, but he's strong, and he drags her across the floor. She grabs onto a kitchen chair, anything to help anchor her, but all she ends up doing is pulling it along with her. He dumps her and the chair in the hallway and yanks the rifle from her hand.

"Stay." He talks to her as though she's a dog. He leans the rifle against the far wall all the way across the room.

Hester remains in the bathroom, cursing and moaning.

Eve curls into a ball, holding her belly again, while the cowboy searches for the bullets that Eve has dropped on the floor. From her fetal position, she counts how many times he bends over. Three. He's found all three bullets.

"Is that all of them?"

Eve doesn't answer.

The cowboy crosses the room and tosses the bullets out the front door. The rain has stopped and the air outside is quiet, except for the sound of crickets.

The baby continues to cry.

Hester emerges from the bathroom and stops in the hallway where Eve lies on the floor. "She needs to be changed. She's probably hungry again, too."

"Why didn't you help me?" Eve asks.

"Wait till you get old, then you'll see. The plumbing doesn't work as well as it used to."

If only Hester could've held her damn bowels. *Christ*, the woman can't do anything right.

"What?" Hester is saying to Eve.

The cowboy's in the kitchen now, opening cabinets. Some of the dishes fall out and crash to the floor.

"Hey!" Hester says.

"Take care of the baby." He yanks open drawers. He pauses suddenly as though he's found what he's looking for. The cowboy turns around with the box of ammunition in his hand.

Eve can't quite make out his face, but she would swear he's smiling. Yes, she's sure of it. It's a satisfied smile. He marches to the front door, which has been left open ever since he got rid of the other bullets. He's arrogant enough to believe they won't try to run. His arm cocks back as though he's a baseball player about to throw someone out at home plate. Then his arm pitches forward, and the box full of opportunity sails into the dark night.

A perfect toss.

Strike two. The rotten meat was strike one, which means she has one strike left.

One more weapon in her arsenal.

Eve has got to get back inside that silverware drawer.

For a knife.

CHAPTER
TWENTY-ONE

By the time Laura is showered and dressed, Joe is gone. He slipped out of bed at the crack of dawn, back to his place in the Burgh.

Laura grabs Kayleigh's photo from the desk in the spare bedroom and glances briefly at the map on the wall before putting the girl's picture in the breast pocket of her uniform. In the kitchen, she grabs her keys, picks up her phone, and notices a text from Charlotte.

Sorry. Forgot what yesterday was. I miss Pop, too. Talk later? Red heart, sad face emojis.

That's it, the extent of the message. No mention of how her summer internship is going, who she's hanging out with, or what she's doing that she's too busy to call her mother back.

Laura texts: *It's okay, Char. Talk later.* Red heart emoji. She touches her pocket with the photo, and then she adds: *Be safe.*

She leaves the house, climbing into the SUV, as her radio goes off.

"Hey, you're never going to believe this," Denise says. "But we've got another dead body in the woods. FBI's involved. They're asking for you."

"Really? Why me?" Her first thought is of Kayleigh. She's never gotten much help from the feds in the past. Laura's requests have always gotten buried in the thousands of other missing persons cases they deemed more pressing.

"I don't know," Denise says. "They didn't say."

"Is the victim male or female?" Laura's heart seems to have stopped, waiting for an answer.

"Male. I'll tell them you're on your way."

Within minutes of getting the call from dispatch, Laura is standing a few feet from where a man's body hangs from a tree. The man is dressed in a T-shirt and basketball shorts. The shorts are pulled down around his ankles. He wears designer underwear and high-end sneakers. His shoulders are rounded. His head hangs forward.

He's been dead for some time; lividity has set in. There appears to be blood on his arm and more blood on his shirt. The pockets of his shorts are turned out. Was he searching for something? Or was someone else? She files this away.

The FBI have cordoned off the entire area surrounding the body. No one is getting in or out without their knowing. Why the feds have asked for her specifically, she still doesn't know, but she's sure as hell going to find out.

The agent in charge, the one in a dark suit and tie, comes to stand next to her. He's a big guy, broad shoulders, biceps the size of boulders. For a moment they're quiet, watching the evidence response team unpack their gear. Then he turns to look at her and smiles. There's a large gap between his two front teeth, and his whole face lights up. It's disarming. He's one of those guys you can't help but instantly like.

He shakes her hand. "Special Agent Ring."

"Sheriff Pennington."

"I guess you're wondering what we're doing here and why I asked for you specifically."

"I am."

"What do you make of this?"

They turn to face the man in the tree.

"At first glance, I'd say suicide. The shorts around the ankles is interesting."

Agent Ring nods. "Do you recognize him?"

Laura takes a closer look. "No, I don't. I don't think he's from around here."

It's his clothes, she thinks. The shorts and sneakers aren't the typical brands a person would wear in this area. They're not from Walmart or Kohl's or any of the other stores in town. It's not just what he's wearing though. There's something else about him, something *city*. She can't say why she feels this way, but it's what her gut tells her. This young man is a long way from home.

"Is he wanted?" She's figuring he must be on their most wanted list. Why else would the feds be here?

Laura moves closer to the victim, careful where she steps. The ligature appears to be an ordinary rope. She wants to see the knot. The knot can tell a lot about the person who's tied it. Was he a boy scout at one time in his life? A fisherman? Or perhaps he was someone who engaged in autoerotic fantasies. It might explain his pants being down. Laura was called to a scene one time where a man dressed in female clothing and a blond wig had accidentally hung himself from his weight machine in his garage. The knots in the rope, the escape release, were sophisticated, suggesting it wasn't his first time partaking in this kind of activity.

From her angle on the ground, she can't see the knot clearly. The evidence response team will eventually cut the rope well above the knot and tie the ends with string or wire to prevent it from unraveling. The victim will be transported with the noose around his neck until the pathologist removes it. An expert in knot forensics can answer any questions after that.

The body rocks slightly, which is odd, because she doesn't feel a breeze. The branch he's hanging from creaks like an aging bone. Something about the scene doesn't feel right. The blood on his arm and shirt doesn't make sense, unless it's from self-inflicted wounds that she can't see from her position on the ground. Perhaps he cut himself somehow before jumping from the tree.

Laura watches where she steps again, making sure she's not walking on any footprints and destroying evidence. She circles around the tree to get a better look at the branch he's hanging from. It appears to be sturdy and she doesn't see any signs of stress on the limb. It will hold until they're ready to cut him down. She's about to turn around when she notices the rub marks on the branch where the rope has stripped away the bark. It could be from the wind blowing the body around during the storm, but it seems to her the stripping of the bark looks more forceful than something wind alone could do. It's as though he was hoisted up in the tree rather than jumping from it, and if he was hoisted up, it means he wasn't alone.

He had help.

Laura steps back to get out of the way of the team. She's strictly an observer here. It's Agent Ring's case. What was his reason for calling her to the scene? Was it just to see if she could ID the victim? Or maybe he just wanted to know if she's ever seen this guy's face around town before. She hasn't. Agent Ring is watching her.

"What're you thinking?" he asks.

"I'm thinking he looks young. Maybe twenty-two or twenty-three."

"Seems about right," he says.

"Did you see the way the bark is stripped from the branch?" She's almost certain he has, but she's playing along with him. The agent is clearly testing her, seeing if she's some kind of backwoods hick, a redneck sheriff who doesn't know shit.

"I did see it. What do you make of it?"

"It looks to me like someone raised him up there. Like someone staged the scene."

"That was my assessment, too."

"Did I pass your test?"

"Yes, you did." He laughs, and dammit, she can't help but chuckle along with him. It's that smile of his and that silly gap between his teeth. Witnesses and criminals don't stand a chance against that kind of grin.

Since she's passed his test, she hopes he'll give her some information if she offers some to him. "The other day, another man's body was found about five miles from here. Gunshot wound to the head."

"Derrick Fisher. We've taken over the case."

It's the first she's hearing that the state police aren't handling it anymore. They failed to notify her, and she's a little miffed about it.

"Do you think it's possible this guy in the tree might be connected to Derrick's shooter?"

"That's why I asked to speak to you."

"Okay." She wonders what the hell that means.

"What do you know about Derrick Fisher?" he asks.

"He's a local guy. Born and raised here in Bordertown. He was a big hockey star in high school. A couple of unfortunate hits to the head knocked him out of any chance of going pro. He lost his dad soon after in a boating accident. He works for his uncle at a small, family-owned market on the outskirts of town. Other than that, he mostly keeps to himself."

"Ever wonder why that is?"

"The fact that he keeps to himself? No, not until now."

Agent Ring smiles again. "Come with me." He leads her away from the scene. They pick their way through brush and trees, side by side, as best they can.

"I'm sure you've figured out by now that Derrick's involved in some things that we're very interested in."

"Like what things?" She stops walking, stunned that Derrick or any of the Fishers could be involved in something big enough to get the attention of the feds.

"Keep up," Agent Ring says.

Laura crosses her arms, refusing to move, feeling defensive. This is her town, after all, and these are her people he's talking about. "You didn't answer my question. What things do you think Derrick Fisher is involved in?"

Agent Ring stops and turns around. "You're on a need-to-know basis, and right now that's not something you need to know."

Laura doesn't move, keeping her arms tightly folded.

He grins and shakes his head. "The guy in the tree back there. His name is Logan Mense. There might be some retaliation for his death. Consider yourself warned. In the meantime, I'll need you to keep your eyes and ears open. Call me if you see or hear anything that's unusual for this place. You know the people in this town better than anyone."

It occurs to her that he knows much more about her, and she knows nothing of him. "You were digging up information on me."

"Just doing my job." He starts walking again.

This time Laura follows him. It seems Agent Ring knew the tree guy's name all along. At least he's given her something to look into, although he hasn't given her much else. They stop at the edge of the woods. He's led her directly to the lake parking lot where her SUV sits alongside a half dozen FBI vehicles. He hands Laura his card at the same time Joe pulls into the lot. They both watch as he parks his car.

"Let's keep this between us." He motions in the direction of her deputy.

The agent's about to turn around and head back into the woods, but she has one more question for him. Several questions actually.

"What kind of gun was used on Derrick?" Clyde had set a .22 rifle on the counter for her to see. At the time, she thought he did it to intimidate her, but perhaps he was trying to tell her something.

".44 Magnum revolver."

"Really? Like the Dirty Harry gun?" Laura had expected to learn it was a hunting rifle.

"Yeah, but shorter barrel. Know anything about it?"

Laura shakes her head. "What exactly is Derrick involved in? Why can't you tell me that?" But Agent Ring is already walking away, checking his phone, disappearing behind the trees.

Joe is headed in her direction. Seeing him for the first time since last night is awkward, but if she's going to continue like they have been for longer than she cares to admit, she has to learn how to deal with it. She walks up to him, meeting him halfway, trying hard to situate her face into the business one of sheriff and not the moony-eyed one of a lover.

"I don't know much. FBI is taking over."

"I can see that." Joe alludes to all of their vehicles in the lot. "Why? What the hell is going on?"

"I wish I knew. It's obvious they don't want us directly involved." Laura got that message loud and clear, but at least Agent Ring gave her the name of the guy in the tree, which means she has a place to start. But only after she talks with the Fishers, because she's going to talk to them whether the agent likes it or not. This is her turf. Whatever is going on has been happening under her nose and that doesn't sit right with her.

Not at all.

They fall in step and head in the direction of their SUVs. The sun is hot in the open parking lot. The heat comes off the macadam in waves. Neither one mentions the night before, but the intimacy between them lingers.

"What about the guy in the tree?" Joe asks. He was on the radio when she got the call from dispatch.

"It looks like a straight-up suicide at first glance, but I suspect the scene may have been staged. The ME will need to confirm it."

"Do we know the vic?"

"I've never seen him before. He's not someone from around here."

"Does this have something to do with Derrick Fisher?"

"I think it's a very good possibility." Laura wipes the sweat from her forehead, hoping it's not the start of a hot flash where her body becomes a blazing furnace.

"Shit," Joe says. "Did they give you any information at all about what's going on?"

They stop next to their vehicles.

Laura hesitates, but only for a second. "No, they didn't tell me anything."

"You know the guy in the tree is pretty close to your cousin's place."

"Yes."

"You don't think—"

"No, I don't, but she'll know they're in her woods."

Laura hopes Hester's dislike of law enforcement will keep her away. The last thing Laura wants is for her cousin to embarrass her in front of the damn FBI.

Laura goes to get into her SUV. She has work to do at the office. There's a ton of paperwork she has to catch up on, not to mention the additional reports she needs to file for the last two days, but first she's going back to the Fishers.

"Laura, wait. About last night."

Her heart seems to stutter, and she immediately looks around to see if anyone else heard the warmth in Joe's voice when he said her name. There's a family getting out of their minivan. The dad keeps glancing in their direction. Seeing the sheriff and her deputy in the public parking lot at the lake along with all of the other law enforcement vehicles on one of the hottest days of the summer can be alarming. The dad wants to know if there's a problem, if something has happened, and whether it's safe for his family to spend the day on the water.

"Not here." Joe cannot do this to her now, in public, not when she's in uniform. Not ever. That's not how this works. It's hard enough as it is to keep her distance from him.

She climbs into the SUV and starts the engine, then she puts the vehicle in reverse. Joe gets in his SUV and slams the door, letting her know how he feels about the way she's dismissed him.

Laura pulls alongside the family who have been eyeballing her. "It's nothing to worry about. Just stay away from the northern end of the lake."

"Sure, okay," the dad says, and he directs his kids toward the beach entrance.

Laura leaves the lake parking lot, punches the steering wheel with her palm. Joe cannot do this to her when she's on the clock. What the hell does he think he's doing? Whatever it is, he's just going to have to deal with it.

It's not long before she pulls into the lot for Fisher's Market. There's a closed sign hanging on the store's screen door. Not surprising giving the family's loss.

She swings the SUV around and enters the dirt driveway of the Fishers' home. It's set back in the woods a little way down the road from the store. Like the store, the house has seen better days. It's missing a couple of shutters. The once white siding is covered in grit. Faded green plastic lawn chairs clutter the front porch. The place looks deserted, the windows and front door buttoned up tightly. It's possible the family went into town to make funeral arrangements.

It couldn't hurt to take a look around, and she gets out of the SUV. The porch leans on one side, held up by a couple of cinder blocks. She steps onto it gingerly, hoping it will hold her, and knocks on the door. No one answers. Near the top of the door is a security camera. It seems odd somehow, out of place. She looks around, sees nothing but woods. How many visitors could they possibly get way out here?

She circles the house, finding cameras all around the property. It's quite an elaborate system for a backwoods home that's practically falling down. Then she notices the brand-new heating and air-conditioning unit.

She tries the back door, knocking and calling for Clyde or Karl. When she doesn't get an answer for a second time, she peeks in the window. The kitchen at the back of the house has been remodeled. The stainless-steel appliances look new, as do the countertops. There's even an island with barstools.

Laura looks in the other windows, stopping and staring into the living room at a flat-screen TV, leather furniture, and a ficus tree near what looks like a fancy massage chair.

What the hell is going on?

She takes a step back, not believing what she's seeing. Then she peers in the window again to make sure she's not imagining it. It doesn't make sense. The interior of the home doesn't fit with the exterior.

What are the Fishers involved in? Could it be drugs? But what kind of drugs? Heroin? Cocaine? Prescription pills? Whatever it is, it's the reason why the FBI are involved.

Poor Karl, she thinks. In ways, he's a lot like Hester. He needs a bumper between him and the rest of the world. He probably doesn't even realize the extent of trouble Derrick has gotten him into. Although Laura's not sure what that trouble is exactly, she's going to find out. Agent Ring might not be willing to give her all of the information he has on Derrick, but he never said anything about her checking things out on her own.

She circles back to the driveway where her SUV is parked, and she takes another long look at the outside of the house: the crumbling steps, the missing shutters, the filthy siding. If you're involved in illegal activity, you wouldn't necessarily bring that activity into your home. You would hide it somewhere else. The Fishers' store doesn't make sense, unless it's a front for money laundering. It's a possibility.

But there's something else she remembers about the Fisher family. Clyde's hunting cabin.

CHAPTER
TWENTY-TWO

Sometime in the small hours of the morning, Noah must've drifted off. The chair he's sitting on is tilted back on its two legs, propped up by the wall behind it. The two women are sleeping on the floor in front of the couch. The baby sleeps between them.

Slowly, he rocks the chair forward until it's setting on all four legs. He's feeling better. Not great, but better. His stomach has stopped tap dancing. His clawed shoulder aches. The sleeve of his T-shirt is once again sticking to his skin with dried blood.

The thunderstorm ended sometime late last night while he was shitting his goddamn brains out. Now, sunlight explodes through the open door. It's hot on his face, and for a moment, it blinds him. He gets up and kicks the door closed. The sound wakes the witch and the girl. They sit up, rubbing their eyes.

Noah takes a seat back in the chair and points the Magnum at them. "I'm guessing the meat we ate last night was spoiled."

"Ya think?" Witch asks.

Noah's not amused like he was before by her smart mouth. In fact, it's getting on his nerves. Even the look on her face chafes him. And what is that god awful smell? Is it him? Them? It's the whole stinking cottage.

"Open some windows," he says to the witch.

The witch pulls herself up and opens the two windows in the living room and one in the kitchen. When she passes the kitchen table that's covered with their dirty dishes from last night, flies scatter. They must've come in overnight through the open door. The thought of the meat, the smell of it cooking, causes warm saliva to pool on the back of his tongue.

Every minute he sits here is a minute too long. Time keeps slipping away.

He stands. The witch's and the girl's eyes are on him, watching his every move. They would be dumb not to. Now that it's daylight and he's no longer sick to his stomach, he makes the decision to search for the money and the car-truck keys himself. He'll have to tie up the witch and the girl first though. He doesn't trust them to sit patiently while he takes a look around. The witch strung up Shot in the tree, so she must have rope around here somewhere. Probably in the toolshed out there.

Noah picks up the rifle just in case there are bullets lying around the cottage that he hasn't tossed. He doesn't count the five bullets he shoved in his pocket when he first found the rifle in the car-truck and unloaded it. Between the bullets and the switchblade, his jeans are pulled tight, more than usual. He's fit and lean, so why the hell shouldn't he wear skinny jeans?

"Let's go, both of you. You're coming with me."

"Where are we going?" Girl asks.

"To the shed out there."

"Why?" Witch asks.

"None of your fucking business. Man, can't you just do what I ask? What is it with you two?" Perhaps the witch has hidden the money in the toolshed along with the keys. Couldn't hurt to check while he looks for some rope.

"What about the baby?" Girl asks.

"Bring her with us."

The girl scoops up the baby. For a moment the baby fusses, but then she quickly settles into the girl's arms.

"Come on, move it." He motions with the Magnum for the witch and the girl to go out the front door.

The witch glares at him.

"Get moving," he says to her, and he follows them outside.

Noah stays close behind them, poking them between the shoulder blades with the barrel of the gun to keep them moving, to remind them he's armed, and they shouldn't try to run. They cross the small yard, walking through some kind of ground covering. It's not exactly grass. It looks invasive. He has to squint from the bright sunlight. He could use his designer sunglasses right about now, which are stashed in the glove box of the SUV, along with three fake passports. They stop next to the shed. On one side of the shed is a stack of firewood. Some of the pieces on top look freshly cut.

Surrounded by woods, he tries to see through the trees, searching for something and finding nothing but more trees. It's quiet except for the birds and the chatter of squirrels. Even when he lived with Madeline in Greenwich, he doesn't remember it being this quiet. There was always someone around: the small staff, the horses, the visitors. But here there is nothing. No one.

The feeling of isolation creeps over him, spooks him. There's something about this place, these woods, that confuses the brain. Every time he's near these trees, standing in the thick of them, he becomes disoriented. They close in on a person. At first, it's discomforting, but Noah can see how after a while, a person could start to rely on them: the tall, wooden sentinels standing guard against outsiders and trespassers.

He glances at the witch. She's standing in front of the toolshed, facing him, eying him up, but it's not her eyes he feels on his skin. Whatever it is, it doesn't seem as though it's from this world. It's the best way he can describe it, although it sounds ridiculous. Maybe the girl hit him in the head harder than he thought.

"Open it," he orders the witch.

The girl cradles the baby. She doesn't move while the witch yanks on the door handle. It opens easily. Noah peeks inside. It's organized, and he has to give the witch credit for keeping it that way. He can't stand messes, and he's glad he doesn't have to search through one now.

He finds power tools and gardening supplies, a small ladder: everything one would expect to find in a shed. What he doesn't find is the bag full of money or the car-truck keys, but it's not a wasted trip. On the floor at his feet is a coil of rope. It's the only thing out of place and not on a shelf or hanging on a hook. The witch probably tossed it into the shed in a hurry after stringing up Shot in the tree. He grabs the rope and pokes the witch and then the girl in the arm with the barrel of the Magnum.

"Back to the house."

They make their way through the yard, back to the cottage. It's a relief to get out of the bright sun, into some shade, and away from the ghoulish woods. Noah closes the door. He flips the switch to see if the electricity has been turned on. It hasn't.

"Put the baby on the couch."

Girl gently lays the baby down.

He leans the rifle against the wall. Holding the Magnum in one hand, with the rope tossed over his good shoulder, he grabs the girl's arm with his other hand and marches her over to one of the kitchen chairs. He pushes her down on it. The girl doesn't make a sound when he ties her wrists behind her back.

"You're next," he says to the witch. "Sit."

The witch plops down on the other chair. Her hands are sweaty, and he ties her wrists extra tight because of it.

"What's this about?" Witch asks.

Noah leans over, puts his lips close to her ear. "I'm going to find my fucking money," he says, but what he feels like doing is shouting it at the top of his lungs. He's really trying hard to control his temper.

He starts searching the kitchen, rummaging through the cabinets now that it's daylight and he can finally see clearly. Finding the box of ammunition last night in the dark in the silverware drawer was lucky. Yes, indeedy, he's lucky.

He double-checks the drawers, even the impossibly small drawers that could never hold the amount of cash he's looking for, but they could hold a set of car keys. Or maybe the witch has divvied the money up, stashing small piles throughout the cottage. He finds a couple of butter and steak knives, which he tosses out the open window, hoping he's finally gotten rid of any possible weapons these two wenches could use against him.

Satisfied there's not a single one-hundred-dollar bill in the kitchen and the keys are nowhere in sight, he moves into the living room. He shoves his hand deep inside the pockets in the back of the couch, and he looks for holes in the cushions while trying not to disturb the sleeping baby.

The witch and the girl aren't talking, but he senses their eyes on him, watching his every move. Noah squats next to the stone fireplace, looks in and then up. Nothing. Next to the fireplace, tucked into the corner of the room on the floor is a toy doll. *Weird*.

In the master bedroom, he tears through the drawers and the closet, yanking out the witch's clothes and tossing them onto the floor. Of course, he checks underneath the mattress. Everyone knows it's a common place to hide things, but the witch isn't stupid, or maybe she is. Cooking the rotten meat was pretty fucking stupid. There's nothing under the mattress.

The bathroom is tiny. There's room for a toilet, pedestal sink, and a tub with a curtain around it. Noah looks behind the curtain and even checks the back of the toilet. No money. No keys. He takes a piss. Then he looks in the cracked mirror over the sink and rubs the stubble on his cheek. He has to admit, even dirty and scruffy, he's a good-looking guy.

There's one more room he hasn't searched, but he stops in the hallway to listen for any sounds coming from the kitchen. He doesn't hear anything, but he assumes they're trying to work their hands free. They can try until their wrists are bloody. They're not going to loosen the rope. He knows how to tie knots. It was all part of his training where he'd paid some rough characters to help groom him for his role as angel. If he was going to work with scumbags, it was best he knew not only how to defend himself, but also how to perform basic skills, some as simple as knot tying.

He enters the spare bedroom. At the far end of the room, on the other side of the bed, a small door in the wall has been left open. It's some kind of storage area. Getting down on his hands and knees, he pokes his head inside. He's too big to crawl into the hole, but it's not deep, and he can see where it ends. It's empty. He tosses the bed. Nothing. Then he checks the closet and finds more baby toys: a crib and a small table. Baby clothes are folded and stacked on the shelves. The whole thing feels strange and wrong. Maybe the witch really is a witch like the ones in fairy tales he read about when he was a boy. Maybe she boils children and eats them. After the dinner she served last night, anything is possible.

Noah returns to the kitchen. They were trying to untie the rope. It's written all over their guilty, dirty faces.

"Where's my fucking money!"

He startles the baby, and she begins to cry.

"Fuck you," Witch says.

Noah has kept his temper compartmentalized for as long as he can. It's an improvement over yesterday's throat-punch to Shot and trigger-happy finger with camo guy. He congratulates himself on his ability to stay calm for as long as he has ever since entering the witch's lair. While he's mentally patting himself on the back, he crosses the room, picks the witch up by her hair, and tosses her against the kitchen cabinets.

"Where's my fucking money!"

He can be tolerant for only so long. She can't expect him to play nice forever. She *poisoned* him for god's sake. He grabs a fistful of her hair again. Her wrists are tied, and she struggles to fight back, twisting and turning, trying to get out from under his grip. She kicks him in the shin. It hurts, but he barely registers the pain.

He swings her around and throws her against the card table, the one where she keeps her precious puzzle, and she falls to the floor. The puzzle pieces scatter around her. One quick foot to her stomach, and she's curling into a fetal position, moaning. He kicks her again, because he doesn't know where he is or which direction he needs to take to get out of here. He kicks her a third time, because he still doesn't have his money.

He's breathing heavily and sweat is dripping off him. The cut on his shoulder feels as wide as a valley. Blood soaks his T-shirt for the umpteenth time.

Fuck, it stings.

The baby continues crying. It's loud and he wants it to stop. On top of everything else, it's giving him a headache.

"Untie me," Witch says from her tucked position on the floor. Her lips are wet with saliva and stained with blood. "I need to take care of the baby."

"Girl takes care of Baby."

"But she'll need my help to prepare a bottle and change her diaper. And what about that rash?"

"Let her help me," Girl says. "She knows all about taking care of babies. She's been practicing on that one over there long before we ever got here." The girl motions to where the doll lies on the floor by the fireplace.

Noah looks at the doll and then at the witch. She's pulled herself up to a sitting position. Her frizzy white hair crowds her face. Her head is turned in the direction of where the *real* baby cries.

He scans the room. There aren't any pictures hanging on the walls in the cottage. No framed photos of grandchildren or family members on the end tables. The refrigerator door is free of magnets and kid's drawings, the kind with lemon yellow suns and stick figures.

And yet, the witch has a doll on the living room floor and a closet full of toy furniture and baby clothes.

It's an interesting observation.

Creepy, but interesting.

CHAPTER
TWENTY-THREE

Hester is sitting on the floor next to the card table that's been knocked over. Puzzle pieces are strewed all around her. If her wrists weren't tied, she'd pick them up, count them, make sure to find every last one of them. There's nothing worse than finishing a puzzle only to discover there's a piece missing. It's annoying as shit.

Well, actually, there are things which are worse and far more annoying. Being manhandled by the couture cowboy for instance. He almost pulled her hair out by the roots. Not to mention the kicks to her gut. She's had punches to her stomach before back in juvie. She's even had a metal nail file aimed at her throat. If the cowboy thinks roughing her up is going to get her to tell him where she's hidden his money, he can forget it.

The cowboy unties Eve. *Girl takes care of Baby,* Hester mocks to herself. Eve starts fumbling around in the kitchen. She doesn't seem to know how to use the gas stove or what to do with the bottle.

After about two minutes, Eve says to the cowboy, "I could use some help here."

"Fine." The cowboy reaches under Hester's arm and pulls her up. "Turn around."

He proceeds to untie her wrists. Then he sits in the chair. He slumps on the side where his shoulder has started bleeding again, and his face is looking a little peaked, possibly from all the blood he spewed while tossing her around.

He's weakening. This is good news.

Hester blocks out the pain in her abdomen (remember, her brain is a powerful tool), and she fills a pot with water, sets it on a burner, and lights the gas stove. She shows Eve how to prepare a bottle.

While Eve waits for the bottle to warm up, Hester changes Baby Ivy's diaper, sprinkling more cornstarch on the baby's bottom. Hester could use some cornstarch on her own bottom after all the shitting she's done overnight. Eating spoiled meat wasn't one of her better ideas. It was worth a shot, though, and she doesn't dwell on the fact that it has failed. She's the type of person who learns from her mistakes and moves on.

She picks up Ivy and cuddles her, cooing and breathing in the baby's scent. Ivy pulls her feet up, kicks. Hester rocks her gently. "Your bottle will be ready any second now."

"Shh," Eve says. "Do you hear something?"

Hester puts the baby on her shoulder and listens. It sounds like an engine and a loud one at that, possibly from a large truck, bumping along the dirt driveway.

The cowboy is up and out of the chair.

"Get the baby," he says to Eve.

The girl takes Ivy from Hester's arms.

The cowboy peeks out the window. "It's the power company." He looks at Hester. "Get rid of them or the baby gets the first bullet."

"No!" Hester says.

He knows. He knows. He knows. Somehow the cowboy has read her heart, and he has figured out how to manipulate her. You stupid, old woman, she thinks, but quickly dismisses the thought. He hasn't read anything, not without her showing it to him.

"I'll get rid of them. I promise. Don't do anything stupid in the meantime. Just go in the backroom. Wait. Here. Take the bottle."

She grabs the bottle from the pot on the stove and hands it to Eve. The formula isn't as warm as it should be, but it will keep the baby quiet. The last thing she wants is a repeat performance of what happened when her cousin dropped by unannounced and the baby cried.

Hester hurries out the front door, closing it tightly behind her. She waits on the top step of the porch. The air is fresher out here even if it's stifling hot, and yet, there's something different about the atmosphere. She first noticed it when she stepped outside with the cowboy earlier. It's the feeling you get when you walk into your home and you know someone else has been there. The energy of the space is altered somehow. It's as though the stranger has left a part of himself behind. It's the same feeling she had standing by the toolshed and now on her porch, but it's not the cottage that's been tampered with.

It's the woods.

She knows its beats, the sounds it makes, and right now, its pulse is off. It's no longer tranquil, but rather it's in a state of turbulence. Something or someone has disrupted its peacefulness, bringing a kind of commotion and fury into the very heart of it.

The utility man gets out of his truck, and she holds up her hand to stop him from coming any closer. He gets the message, and he stops and stands next to the front bumper. He's wearing a hard hat, yellow vest, and gloves.

"Hi, there." He waves.

"It's about time you got here." Hester's impressed with how cool she sounds, considering how hard her heart is thundering inside her chest.

"Yeah, I'm really sorry about that. In truth, we forgot you were back here."

"It wouldn't be the first time." She recognizes him. He's the dad of one of the teenagers who egged her house. She took pictures of the little bastards with the iPad and brought the photos to Laura's office. The utility man in front of her was one of the parents who made his son apologize, and because of that Hester didn't press charges.

He stands by his truck, nervously fiddling with his gloved fingers. It seems he remembers her, too. "I just want to say again how sorry I am about what my son did. I gave him a stern talking to, I can assure you."

"Yeah, whatever. Water under the bridge."

She has to get rid of him, or at the very least, get him working on turning her power back on, but he's not moving. He's standing there like he's expecting her to offer him a cold beverage. Well, he can forget it. Let him sweat his balls off. It's what she's been doing these last few days (if she had balls, that is) not being able to turn on a stinking fan.

"How long till my power's back on?"

"An hour. Maybe a little longer. We'll be working on the pole at the end of the driveway. I just came back here to let you know. If you need us for anything, that's where we'll be."

"I appreciate that."

He still doesn't move. *What's he waiting for?*

"Are you okay? It's just—your face looks so pale, and I think your lip is bleeding."

She dabs her lip with the back of her hand. "It's because I didn't have any goddamn electricity to keep my food cold. I had to eat something, didn't I? Damn near poisoned myself with spoiled meat."

"I'm sorry to hear it. You should probably throw out any food that's left."

"Just get my power back on."

He bumps into the truck when he turns around and he scrambles to climb into the cab. He's afraid of her. He probably believes the stories his kid tells him about her being a witch.

"Boo," she mutters, and she has to stop herself from wiggling her fingers at him.

He maneuvers the big truck into a K turn, before he heads down the driveway. He sticks his hand out the window and waves. She resists the urge to flip him off. Instead, she waves back, all nice-like. She wants her electricity turned on.

When she steps back into the living room, Eve is standing by the couch with the baby in her arms. The cowboy is next to her. They're both staring at her as though they're waiting for her to say something.

"What?"

"What did he want?" Eve asks.

"Oh, the utility guy? He said the power should be back on soon. I'll run some fans as soon as it is to cool the place off." The inside of the cottage feels like she's wading in a bowl of curdled soup.

"All right. Why don't you take a seat on the couch? Both of you." The cowboy directs Eve to sit with the baby. Hester sits on the cushion next to them.

Once they're settled, he says, "Until the power company is finished and gone, we'll all need to be on our best behavior." He picks up her iPad, sits in the kitchen chair that faces the couch, and then he puts the tablet on his lap.

What the hell does he want with her iPad?

CHAPTER
TWENTY-FOUR

I t's erased," Emeril says.

Hillary lifts her head from the nursery rocker. She must've dozed off after her little mishap with the pram in the garden. A tiny leaf sticks to her arm. Emeril is standing in the doorway. He looks horrid. His face is puffy and his eyelids are swollen. She nods to let him know she understands what he's said, that he's deleted the footage from the security cameras.

"You can give it another go today." His mouth twitches as though he's trying hard not to smile.

"Oh, shut up." But even she can see how there must've been something funny about seeing her dive headfirst into a shrub.

Pulling herself up, she looks out the window. When did it become daylight? She's surprised to see the sun's rays brightening the garden, shining light on the rich, red rose petals. The last time she remembers seeing the sun, it was setting, the moon was making its appearance in the darkening sky, and her head was stuck inside the shrubbery. It must've taken Emeril all night to figure out how to erase the security camera video. This is why they have staff, she thinks, to do the things they can't do themselves.

Like push a pram through a garden.

Ma'am! Ma'am! Bang. Bang. Bang.

They both look up at the ceiling.

"We should bring her something to eat," Emeril says.

"Yes."

"I'll get a tray ready." He leaves.

Hillary turns from the window. The bright sunny day suddenly feels like an insult. How dare the birds sing when her arms remain empty, and her lips tremble with the words of a lullaby. She hates the robins and blue jays and cardinals. She hates the bees pollinating the flowers that grow near her daughter's grave. How can nature continue? How can the world go on when hers has been completely and utterly shattered?

Hillary is unable to move forward or backward. This is what it means when time stands still. But it's not standing still, is it? No, it's not, and it's this realization that makes her suffering unbearable. Everything feels wrong: her thoughts, her skin, her tears, her smile. The angel is the only one who can make it right, who can help her become whole again.

Emeril's voice carries up the stairs and into the room. He's pacing in the foyer, talking on the phone. He can't think or talk unless he's moving. Her husband is in constant, perpetual motion, keeping his shape because of his inability to sit still. Thank goodness for this small quirk in his personality that some women might find irritating. Hillary will never complain about his need to keep moving. An inert man is a lazy man in her eyes. A fat man.

She couldn't be married to a man with a potbelly and love handles. Just the thought of the possibility of Emeril having a fat stomach one day, one that hovers over her in bed, while he thrusts himself between her thighs, is enough to make her gag. If they had a prenup, which they don't because she refused to sign one, she would've made it grounds for divorce if he ever weighed more than one hundred and eighty pounds (give or take five pounds because she is reasonable).

Hillary understands that in their world of privilege, image is everything. She and Emeril are the image of a perfect couple: young, attractive, thin. Hillary wears a size two, or at least she did before the pregnancy. The extra weight won't be a problem. She hasn't eaten in days and when she does nibble on a celery stick, she can't hold it down. Soon, when she rejoins the world with her baby, she'll once again take her private aerial silks classes with her personal instructor. Hillary will return to her old body before the pregnancy, although she'll miss the baby bump and the special attention she received because of it.

Hillary goes to the top of the split staircase. It's as grand as it sounds and one of the many features of the spacious chateau that she'd fallen in love with ever since she'd first set eyes on the estate. The chateau was a wedding gift from Emeril, a summer home for them to escape to, to get away from the city, and to enjoy the holidays in the countryside. It's one of many gifts he's given her in their six-plus years of marriage. Whatever her heart desires, he delivers.

The entire estate costs millions: fifty acres of beautiful Quebec land-scape. Although it's considered a chateau, the architect designed it after an English manor. A perfect fit for Hillary's love of all things British.

The dining room seats twenty-two people. The great room has a Rumford fireplace. The rest of the chateau has a library, a billiards room, and an indoor pool and spa. Emeril has a scotch room for his love of the drink. Hillary has what she fondly refers to as her Noah's ark kitchen that comes with two of everything: two stovetops, two ovens, two microwaves, two dishwashers, two islands with marble countertops.

Of course, she has staff who take care of the cooking and cleaning for her. (*Ma'am! Ma'am!*) And what chateau is complete without its very own chapel, where they renewed their vows in front of family and friends on their fifth wedding anniversary.

It's the rooms upstairs that are waiting to be filled, lived in, and loved by children. Hillary wants three kids, maybe four (she'll wait and see what William and Kate do). Her dreams are big like her multiple homes and her husband's bank account. But right now, for the love of God, she will settle for just one child, one baby. *Elsie.*

For a moment, she can't breathe, listening to Emeril on the phone as he paces on the black and white checkered floor below. Maybe it's the angel calling, telling them he's on his way with their bundle of joy. Emeril puts the phone back in his pocket and looks up at her.

It wasn't the angel.

Emeril's eyes are glassy and his grief rests on his shoulders. She looks away from him, and she stares at the crystal chandelier above his head, the one they bought in New York. For a second, she thinks about pulling it from the ceiling where it's bolted to a beam behind the drywall, watching as it falls on top of him, crushing him. Such a rich fantasy life she lives inside her mind.

Hillary doesn't really mean him any harm, and she curses herself for thinking such dark thoughts. She loves him. None of this is his fault. She just wants him to fix this pain inside her heart. He's given her everything else she could ever ask for, but waiting however many months possibly years to become pregnant again, and then another nine months for a baby, is just too damn long. Hillary's not accustomed to waiting, and she's already had to wait two long years before she was even able to conceive the first time. Emeril must understand this. Why doesn't he understand the anguish she's going through? Why isn't he fixing this? If anyone is to blame for her temper it's Emeril, for constantly spoiling her.

Hillary came from a family of doctors. Both her parents were surgeons and she thought her family was rich, because growing up, she doesn't ever remember not getting what she'd wanted. It wasn't until she went away to an Ivy League school in Rhode Island and then spent a year studying abroad that she'd learned there were different degrees of rich. Hillary might've come from an upper-class family, but when she'd stepped out with a classmate to attend a charity gala ball on a yacht, she was introduced to a completely different style of living. A class above the upper class. The superrich. Theirs is the kind of wealth most people can't even come close to imagining, and Emeril's family are members of this unique club.

In fact, it was at that very same gala where she'd first met Emeril. The ball was on his yacht. Her practiced British accent was what grabbed his attention. "What country are you from?" he'd asked, and she'd said, "Connecticut."

While her mum considers Hillary's accent eccentric, Emeril finds it entertaining.

All these years later, Hillary can't recall which charity Emeril was supporting at the time. They've attended enough of them through the years that they all start running together in her mind. Only their accountant knows what causes they are for, which ones they contribute to, and where their money is spent.

Now that she knows what Emeril's money can buy, she can't unknow it. She can't go back to living in the kind of world that most people would consider a good life, not after she's been exposed to the kind of wealth and the better life she has now.

Emeril is pacing again, talking on his phone. He's had to call the staff—all but one—and put them off for another day.

"Yes, we'll need you back. Yes, you'll be paid for the extra time off." He runs his hand over his head. "Thanks. I'll tell her. I'll give her your best." When he hangs up, he stares at her again, pleading with her to see how hard he's trying. "Something's happened."

"Do you know that for sure? Because unless you know for certain that something's gone wrong, I wish you would keep your negative thoughts to yourself. It's not doing either one of us any good to listen to your worries when they could simply be unfounded."

She knows she sounds cross. She *is* cross, but not at him. She's mad at the angel for not behaving like an angel at all. He's the devil, making them wait like this. Maybe this is what happens to you when you make the kind of deal they've made, burying their child and buying another.

Why is she doing this? What is it all for?

Deep down, far below her grief, is the voice of reason. Hillary knows she could never replace her daughter. She's trapped between the truth of this and the misguided belief that she can rid herself of this pain if she had another baby girl to hold.

This is her own special hell.

Emeril comes up the stairs, carrying a tray. "Ready?"

They take the steps to the third floor and stop outside the room where the nanny pounds on the door.

"We're coming in," he says.

There's shuffling on the other side and then silence.

Hillary unlocks the door and opens it.

Emeril steps inside with the tray. Hillary trails him.

"We thought you might be hungry," he says.

Rachel backs away from them, sits on the bed. Tears streak her full cheeks. She's in her dressing gown, the same one she was wearing when she came into their bedroom to tell them something was wrong with Elsie.

Emeril sets the tray on the bedside table. He's not able to look at Rachel. It seems he looks everywhere else but at the nanny.

Hillary tries to speak, to console the girl in some way, but before any words come out, Rachel flips the tray over. The croissant drops onto the bedspread and the juice spills onto the floor. Then she smacks Emeril. Strikes him hard enough to turn his face away.

"What in the world," Hillary says, as Rachel slaps Emeril a second time. "That's quite enough."

Rachel smacks Emeril a third time.

"Stop it!" Hillary says.

The nanny slaps him again. Why isn't he defending himself? Why is he just standing there, taking it?

"Rachel, stop it!"

The nanny smacks him again and again. The girl is hysterical. He puts his arms up to protect his face and block the blows.

"Emeril, *do* something." Now's not the time for him to be chivalrous, but no matter the circumstances, her husband would never hit a woman or child.

The nanny continues flailing her arms around, slapping his shoulders, his head. Shrieking.

Hillary can't stand by and watch the horror of this—this violence against her sweet, kind-hearted husband. She shoves Emeril out of the way, picks up the vase from the bedside table, lifts it high above her shoulders. The dying flowers fall out and water spills on her arm. She brings the vase down hard on Rachel's head.

Thunk.

The nanny falls to the floor.

Hillary looks at Emeril. His cheek is bright red.

"I was going to suggest valium, but a vase to the head is just as effective."

Oh, how Hillary loves him for his humor.

He squats next to Rachel, feels for a pulse.

"Is she dead?" Hillary asks.

"No, just knocked unconscious. Help me lift her onto the bed."

Emeril grabs her shoulders, and Hillary grabs her legs. They put her on the bed. Rachel's lips move, and Hillary swears she hears the girl say, *Ma'am*. They pick up the tray, find the croissant under Rachel's arm, and wipe up the spilled juice. They put a new tray of food on the bedside table and discard the broken vase.

"She'll be fine," Emeril says, and they exit the room, locking the door behind them. "I'll check on her again in a few minutes."

Hillary closes her eyes, takes a deep breath. *Rachel*. The eighteen-year-old girl they'd hired to stay with them for a few weeks over the summer. Someone to help with Elsie. A child taking care of a child. Hillary sees that now. She never wanted to hurt the girl.

What's happening to her? To them?

"Have we gone too far?"

Emeril picks the tiny leaf off her arm. "Let's give it a little more time."

He's right. She knows he's right. The angel will come through.

He has to.

CHAPTER
TWENTY-FIVE

aura's hand rests on the gun on her belt, ready to pull at a second's notice.

She should've told someone where she was going. Perhaps she should've mentioned it to Joe. It didn't occur to her until she was deep in the woods, where radio signals are sketchy at best, that she might need backup.

Clyde Fisher's hunting cabin isn't easy to get to, and the trek has taken up a good part of her day. The trees provide a nice canopy from the hot sun, but it doesn't keep her from sweating like it's nobody's business. It's a nervous sweat, reeking of adrenaline.

A few feet away from where she stands, resting in a blanket of pine needles, is the cabin. It's been close to thirty-five years since she's seen the place. It's a little more spacious and upscale than the typical shack. There's a narrow porch and a working chimney. Clyde's kept it nicer than she would've expected given the state of disrepair to his house and store. Laura spent time here when she was in high school. Clyde is a few years older, but occasionally they hung around the same crowd.

Growing up in a small town, there wasn't much choice. There weren't enough kids to pal around with if you stuck within your own age group. Around the same time she'd started hanging out at the cabin, Hester was serving a fourteen-month sentence in a juvenile detention center for girls.

Laura keeps her distance, checking the cabin from all angles, looking for signs of life. It doesn't appear there's anyone around. The small window over the kitchen sink is boarded up. The window in the only bedroom in the back of the cabin (where she let Chad, her first boyfriend, feel her up) is also boarded up. There's only one window, next to the front door, that's functional, which seems peculiar. Maybe Clyde— or rather, Derrick—doesn't want to look out into the dark night and see glowing eyes staring back at him. Or a more likely scenario, he doesn't want anyone to be able to see in.

She's a bit unnerved seeing the place after all these years, but she walks up to the front door anyway, making sure to announce her presence by stomping through the brush.

"Hello, is anyone here?"

The last thing she wants is to startle someone who might be inside. There are some hunters who shoot on sound alone, sight unseen. It might not be hunting season, but she has to assume most people walking in the woods are carrying.

Laura knocks on the door. "Hello."

She looks over her shoulder. She has the feeling she's being watched. There's something in the air that doesn't seem quite right. She scans the trees, but doesn't notice anything unusual. Then she peeks in the only window. It's dark inside, and she can just make out the shape of the furniture: a couch, table, and chairs.

Laura tries the door, but it's locked. Not unusual. The Fishers wouldn't want vandals or vagrants to be able to get inside. She takes a step back, ponders her next move. If she's ever going to figure out what the Fishers are up to that's serious enough for the FBI to be involved, she's going to have to take a look inside one way or another.

Then she remembers climbing through the window once when Clyde had forgotten the keys. It's worth a shot, and she slips her fingers under the lip and pushes up. She's able to raise it just enough to get her whole hand under.

Looking over her shoulder again, because she can't shake the feeling of someone's or something's eyes on her, she lifts the window up a little more. She gets it halfway open before it gets stuck. She bangs on the frame with her palm and then her fist to get it to move. Dirt falls onto the sill when she strikes the wood. After pounding on it several more times, she manages to get it unstuck, and she opens it all the way.

Poking her head into the room, she shines the small flashlight she carries on her belt and she looks around. She's not going to crawl through the window unless she sees something illegal. Laura doesn't want to be accused of breaking and entering. Never mind about the breaking part.

The air inside the cabin is hot and stale and smells like urine. She's not seeing any drug paraphernalia out in the open. Probably not a meth lab. She doesn't know if she's relieved or disappointed.

Backing out of the open window, she turns off the flashlight. She has a decision to make. Break the law and enter without a warrant or turn around and go back to the office not knowing for sure if the cabin is being used for what it's meant to be used for—hunting and partying teenagers—or if it's being used for something else.

She's come this far. What's the point of breaking in if you're not going to add entering to the charge? She takes a peek over her shoulder one more time, and then she climbs through the window.

Once she's inside she calls, "Hello," for a third time, triple checking she's alone. All is quiet, except for the squirrels chattering in the trees.

Laura slips on a pair of the latex gloves that she carries in the front pocket of her uniform and turns on the flashlight again. There has to be some kind of battery-powered lamp or spotlight around that she could use for more light. Shining the flashlight into the small kitchen, she's not watching where she's going, and she bumps into the edge of the couch.

On the countertop, she finds a lantern meant for camping. She turns it on. That's better, and she puts the flashlight away. She pulls open a small cabinet, not finding anything other than a few glasses and a couple plates. Then she looks inside the silverware drawer. Several girly magazines are thrown in with the forks and spoons. Not surprising to find porn in a man's cabin in the woods. They need some kind of entertainment, because God forbid they neglect their penises for a couple of hours.

She checks out the table and chairs, feeling a wave of nostalgia, having played drinking games with her friends in this very spot. But the table and chairs are different from the ones when she was a teenager. The couch doesn't look familiar either. This one is in tatters, and it smells moldy.

There's a set of antlers on the wall and a box of empty beer cans on the floor. Next to the box is a plastic cup full of some kind of brown liquid. She picks it up. It doesn't look like beer or urine—she guesses it's someone's spit from chewing tobacco. There's no telling how long it's been here. Behind the box of beer, she finds the empty can of snuff: cool spearmint flavor.

Turning away from the trash, she heads to the only bedroom.

The door is closed.

"Hello," she calls one more time in case someone's in there sleeping and didn't hear her the first few times.

When she doesn't hear any sound coming from the other side, she slowly turns the knob, pushes the door open, and holds the lantern up.

She jumps.

It's just her shadow.

It's not like her to be so jittery, but all this sneaking around has her on edge.

The bedroom is mostly bare minus a thin mattress sitting on top of a rusty frame. Two metal rings about two feet apart are bolted to the wall where a headboard should be. They look like something you would see in a barn to tie a horse to for tacking up. She tries not to think about what the metal rings are used for, and she doesn't want to jump to any conclusions, but her mind goes there nevertheless.

In her gut, she knows there's something very wrong here, something dark, and it has nothing to do with the boarded-up window and the lack of light. The room feels different, as if whoever was here has left a part of themselves behind. Laura can smell their fear in the walls, as though the logs have absorbed the emotion, making it a permanent part of its structure.

She holds the lantern over the bed. A graying blanket is bunched up at the bottom of the bare mattress. The mattress is yellow and stained. As she moves closer, she kicks something on the floor. Shining the light down at her feet, she finds a small trunk.

She sets the lantern down next to it and discovers the key is sticking out of the lock. There probably isn't anything valuable inside if the key was left in it, or maybe the last person to open it has been careless. Either way, she doesn't have a good feeling about it. Kneeling, she fiddles with the key until she hears the click. Tentatively, she lifts the lid.

Well, shit.

Inside, she finds handcuffs, duct tape, rope, some kind of harness, zip ties, and a whip. A creaking noise comes from somewhere behind her. Her hand flies to the gun on her hip. Peering over her shoulder, she stares at the open doorway. She has the same feeling again of being watched.

"Hel-lo?"

She strains to listen for any sounds.

All is quiet. Almost too quiet.

She waits another second, but after not hearing anything, she quickly closes the lid to the trunk. It's more than a box of kinky sex toys. It's a murder kit. For kidnapping? Rape? Karl's not equipped to handle something as dark as kidnapping and rape. This has to be Derrick's doing.

But still.

Still.

Her stomach churns, bringing up bile in the back of her throat. She fights the urge to run from the room, but she can't leave. Not yet. There are a couple more places she needs to check. She peeks under the bed. Nothing but dirt and dust bunnies. Then she gets up from her knees, pauses to listen again for any sounds.

Silence.

She puts her hand back on her gun and stands in front of the closet door.

She has to look.

She knows she has to. There's no way around it.

Slowly, slowly, slowly, she turns the knob, opening the door an inch at a time.

Please don't let there be someone inside.

The door swings open.

She pulls her weapon.

The closet is empty. There's not even a wire hanger on the clothes rod.

Satisfied there's nothing else in the room, she holsters her weapon and rushes out, closing the bedroom door behind her. Returning the lantern to the counter, she bumps into the couch again before scurrying through the open window by the locked front door, exiting the same way she came in, getting out of there as fast as she can.

Breathing in large gulps of fresh air, she tries to calm herself down. Then she asks herself, *when were you boys here?* She sweeps the small plants and debris with her foot, searching the ground, looking for shell casings, footprints, or anything else that might help her determine the last time Derrick and Karl were up to nothing good.

Not far from the front door she spies a wad of chewing tobacco. She squats, picks it up with her thumb and pointer finger. If it wasn't for the gloves, she wouldn't be touching something so disgusting. She's not a chew expert but it looks fresh to her, and she can still smell the flavor. It's surprisingly minty. It can't be more than a couple days old, and she tosses it back on the ground.

After combing the rest of the area around the cabin and not finding anything else, she takes the path through the woods, heading in the direction of where her SUV is parked on the dirt road only the locals know exists. While she ducks under low-lying branches and winds her way through the brush, her mind searches for an explanation as to why there's a box full of what anyone in law enforcement would consider suspicious contents in the Fisher's cabin. Nothing she comes up with is remotely logical other than the kidnapping and rape explanation, and by the time she reaches her vehicle, she feels unmoored.

One thing is for sure. The Fishers have some explaining to do.

Laura stops short at the sight of Agent Ring leaning against the front bumper of a black sedan. Immediately, she feels a sense of unease, although she has no reason to. Or does she? He wears a badge same as her, but she's alarmed as to why he's here, parked behind her SUV, blocking her in.

Reminded again of her mistake of not telling anyone where she was going, she glances around the woods. The feeling she had earlier of being watched may have been more than just a feeling. There could be another agent hiding among the trees right now, spying on her. She gazes back at Agent Ring.

"Did you have me followed?"

"Sorry about that." Agent Ring tosses his disarming smile her way, as though that could make up for his actions.

She doesn't smile back. "Did you know about the cabin?"

"Not until now."

"What exactly are they involved in?"

"Kidnapping. Rape. Trafficking. More or less."

Although he's confirmed what she's suspected ever since she entered the small bedroom and found the trunk, there's a part of her that can't quite grasp the Fishers could be involved in something so horrible.

"You're telling me they're involved in sex trafficking?"

He nods.

"Well that explains the box of toys."

She gauges his reaction, whether he knows about the trunk and its contents. His expression remains unchanged. It's somewhere between amused and serious. It's the amused part that bothers her. She doesn't appreciate being followed and ambushed.

"Thanks to you," he says, "we now know how they've been moving the girls through the area."

"They're trafficking girls through these woods?"

"They have several connections across the border. The hunting cabin—which one of my men just saw you break into illegally, I might add—we're assuming it's the last stop before they cross the girls over. It's the one place we haven't been able to locate until today."

It makes sense, Laura thinks. The Canadian border is anywhere from twelve to fifteen miles away depending on where you are on the winding back roads.

"Derrick has to be the one orchestrating it. Or maybe Clyde. There's no way Karl could pull off something like this, not on his own. He's not smart enough. You see, he struggles sometimes. I wouldn't say he has special needs or anything like that, but more along the lines of someone who has slightly below average intelligence."

"Well, we're pretty certain Derrick's our guy."

"If you've known all this time what's going on and that Derrick was involved, why didn't you stop it? Why didn't you arrest him? He might still be alive if you had."

"You bring up a good point and I have to tell you, I was surprised to learn he was dead. And this is between us, you understand? But nothing came through intelligence that would've suggested he was being targeted."

"Why are you telling me this now? Why didn't you say something to me earlier about all of this?"

Agent Ring pushes off the sedan, walks to the driver's side door and opens it. "You're on a need-to-know basis, remember?"

"And now you think I need to know this? Why?"

"That, I'm afraid, you don't need to know."

He gets into the car, looks over his shoulder as he backs up, and then pulls forward alongside her vehicle. At the same time, a line of black cars and two black vans are coming down the dirt road. More FBI agents and their evidence response team. Soon, Clyde's hunting cabin will be swarming with feds.

Agent Ring gets out of his sedan. "Thanks for all your help today."

Laura takes the hint: She's being dismissed. On shaky legs, she gets into her SUV. After rolling down the window, because she can't let the fact that he had the nerve to follow her go, she says, "Next time you want to know something about the people in this town, just ask me."

He's smiling at her again. "Will do."

As she's driving away, it occurs to her that he wants her to look into the case on her own. Otherwise, why bother telling her anything at all? He's under no obligation legally or professionally. It's almost as if he's playing games with her, baiting her, but why? For what purpose?

Laura's not a mile down the road when she has another thought. She touches the pocket holding Kayleigh's picture. Could Kayleigh have been kidnapped and trafficked? *By Derrick Fisher?* It seems incredible, and then there's Pop's voice in her head telling her how not every case is about Kayleigh.

And yet, she can't help but think it's possible this one could be.

The girl just up and vanished. What if she's been trapped inside a trafficking ring this entire time? It could explain why they haven't been able to find her.

It's possible, Pop.

This time it's entirely possible.

CHAPTER
TWENTY-SIX

Noah's sitting in the chair with his back against the wall, overlooking the small family room and kitchen. The unloaded rifle is on the floor underneath the chair by his feet. The electricity has finally been turned on. There are two fans blowing: one fan blows on him, the other one blows on the baby. The witch and the girl are sitting on the couch in front of him. Their faces are wet with perspiration and their cheeks are flushed.

Let 'em sweat, he thinks.

He's logged onto the internet on the witch's iPad, and he's searching Google Maps and Google Earth to figure out where he is and where his SUV is located in relation to the cottage. If he can't find the keys to the witch's El Camino (which seems to be the case) to drive to his SUV that he's stashed at the southern end of the lake, then at least he'll know which direction he has to take through the woods in order to locate the canoe.

Although, he's not keen on trekking through all those tall trees again.

His clients must be out of their minds with worry, but he's not able to contact them, because the stupid witch doesn't have a phone charger. Who doesn't have a smartphone these days? The iPad is old and its charger isn't compatible with his new phone. He can't use the iPad to contact his clients because it's not secure, and he won't do anything to expose their identity. If he's being honest, though, that's not what really concerns him. What's bothering him is how they must be thinking he's failed them. It's unacceptable to assume he isn't going to deliver what he's promised. His record is impeccable. Anything less is unimaginable in his mind. His business wouldn't survive otherwise.

If only he could call his clients, tell them he's on his way. They'll just have to be patient for a little while longer. He has a portable phone charger and a burner phone in his SUV. Once he gets to his car, he'll call them then.

The witch's cottage is starting to make him sick. Its rank smell, the dirt, and the foul women. The baby hasn't stopped crying for what feels like hours. The claw marks on his shoulder scream along with her. The wound broke open again when he was tossing the witch around. Fresh blood drips onto the encrusted dried blood that covers much of his arm.

"You're bleeding," Witch says.

Noah ignores her, and he rips what's left of his black T-shirt off his chest. The cotton tears at his back and splits. He wraps it around his shoulder and arm. It's not easy to do with the Magnum in his hand. All the while, he keeps his eyes not only on his shoulder, but also on the witch and girl.

"Do you need my help?" Witch asks. "I used to work in a hospital, you know."

"Yeah, as a cleaning lady," Girl says.

"No, I don't need your help. Just see why the baby's crying."

The witch and the girl kneel on the floor with the baby. The witch changes the baby's diaper, while the girl puts her face close to the fan.

"The diaper rash doesn't look so angry anymore," Witch says.

That's good to hear, although he doesn't think diaper rash is a deal breaker. His clients won't mind little red bumps on the baby's bottom, at least he doesn't think they will. His knowledge about babies is limited. Closer to nothing actually. He gets the T-shirt secure around his shoulder and ties it off. Then he stands and stretches, makes sure it's on tightly. The witch is eying him.

"What?" he asks.

"What's that on your back?" Witch scoops up the baby and cradles her in her arms.

The girl sits on the floor with her back against the couch, letting the cool air from the fan blow across her legs.

"It's a tattoo." He acts as if it's nothing when, in fact, it's everything. If she's trying to get him to turn around and put his back to them, she can forget it. He's not falling for it.

"I figured it was a tattoo. What's it a picture of?"

"Wings." He refuses to elaborate. The inked wings seem to know when they're being talked about, and they ripple across his skin. Instinctively, he flexes his muscles as though at any second, he could fly away.

"What kind of wings?"

"Angel's wings," Girl says.

He stares at the girl, and she stares right back. He wonders just how much Shot has told her about Noah's business. Whatever she thinks she knows, she's wrong. The little pissant doesn't know anything about him, and yet, he can't take any chances, can he? The girl has just hinted at having some knowledge about who he is, and knowledge can be a dangerous thing in his business. It looks like she won't be meeting with that caretaker across the border as originally planned. Instead, she just bought herself a date with one of his bullets.

"Both of you shut up." He sits in the chair again. Blood from his shoulder blossoms onto the shirt, which now doubles as a bandage. The wound will stop bleeding soon. He tries to ignore it. It's a minor inconvenience.

The baby is blissfully quiet. She's content in the witch's arms, and Noah can finally hear himself think. Noah, the girl, and the baby are either going to take the car-truck or they're going to walk to the lake and take the canoe, but either way, they're going to get to his SUV now that he knows which direction to take, and then they're going to cross the border.

The first thing they'll need to do, though, is take a shower. They need to be presentable, an ordinary, everyday family in the eyes of border patrol.

How does he accomplish cleaning them up? He can't trust the girl to do it herself. He's learned that the hard way. Subconsciously, he touches the side of his head by his temple where she hit him on that first night in the woods. The skin is tender. It's possible it's bruised, although he didn't see a mark when he looked at himself in the cracked bathroom mirror.

His hand drops to his lap. The girl has to be in his line of sight at all times. She'll shower first, while he waits in the bathroom until she's done. Then he'll tie her to the sink pipes, while he showers with the curtain open. He can't close the curtain, because he refuses to take his eyes off her.

Noah won't let her surprise him again.

The witch must have T-shirts they can wear, at least until he can get to the SUV where he's stashed a change of clothes. The doll clothes the witch has stored in the bedroom closet will come in handy. He figures some of them will fit a newborn. An infant carrier is already installed in the backseat of the SUV. Three passports are stored in the glovebox. He can't remember the names on the passports. Something simple like Smith or Johnson. He'll just have to look before they get to the border.

Okay, he knows what he has to do. It's going to kill him to leave the money behind, but Madeline would want him to finish what he'd started and give the baby a better home like she'd given him. It's the reason he took the job in the first place when he got the call initially. Well, the money was a big fat reason, too.

Since he's running out of options, he makes the hard choice to walk away from Shot's half of the money. He can always return later and search for it again after he delivers the baby and sees a doctor about his shoulder. But what if he comes back and can't find it? He's wasting time playing tug-of-war in his mind. Round and round he goes.

Enough.

"Girl, take the baby."

When she hesitates, he brings his arm back and makes as though he's going to hit her. She flinches, and then she wrestles the baby out of the witch's arms.

Noah points the Magnum at the witch. "I've come to a decision about our little predicament. I'm giving you one last chance to tell me where you put the money."

"And if I don't tell you?"

"If you don't tell me this very second, I'm going to put a bullet in that stupid fucking head of yours."

"Then do it."

"No! The money!" Girl says. "What about the money?"

"Why do you care so much about my money?"

Noah doesn't understand what the girl's problem is. When he walked into the cottage, the girl was ripping the witch's hair out of her scalp. She was swinging away at the witch as though she wanted her dead.

"You can't kill her. You don't understand." Girl turns to the witch. The baby is crying again. "Please, tell me where you hid it. I'm begging you. Tell *me*."

The girl not only ran with the baby, but also with the money. She wants the money. Of course, she does. It's always about the money. The thought of her taking half a mil from him is fucking ridiculous. He laughs.

"I don't see what the hell is so funny," Witch says.

"No, I guess you wouldn't." His finger is on the trigger, and he eyes up his favorite shot, the one right between the witch's eyebrows. "Last chance."

Before the witch can answer and before he pulls the trigger, the front door swings open.

CHAPTER
TWENTY-SEVEN

Laura is standing in an alleyway not three blocks from Clemons Street. She was going to turn around and talk with Agent Ring about Kayleigh's case, but she got a call from dispatch about a young woman's body found in the Burgh.

The news of another fatality in a matter of days has her rattled, and she's not sure what she's thinking or feeling. If anything, she seems to have gone numb.

It's late afternoon and the heat from the sun presses down on her shoulders. Behind her, the streets hum with a moody energy. Traffic is steady, nearing rush hour. Car windows are buttoned up tightly. Cool air pumps from air conditioners. The muffled sound of a bass drum thuds from someone's speakers.

The woman was found behind a coffee shop's dumpster. Her upper body slumps against a brick wall. Her legs are splayed out in front of her. Her skirt is short and pulled up around her thighs. She's young, relatively thin if not for the bloating. Her hair is tangled and dirty. Her lips are stained with a frothy substance. Not far from where she's sitting there appears to be vomit on the ground.

The city police are at the scene along with their forensic unit. The alleyway is being photographed and pictures of the woman are being taken from every angle. The officers are working quickly, efficiently, but to Laura, they seem to be moving in slow motion. Their chatter sounds as though they're talking underwater.

Joe's speaking to one of the cops, but she can't make out what he's saying. When he sees her, he makes his way over to where she's standing, stopping next to her, close to her side.

"Do we know who she is?" Laura asks, but even her words seem to drown in her ears.

"No."

"But could it be her? Could it be Kayleigh?" She can hear Pop's voice in her head again saying not every case is about Kayleigh.

"No, it's not her."

Laura breathes out slowly as her mind absorbs the news. *It's not her.* The activity around her suddenly reverts to regular speed. The officers are once again talking normally, moving routinely.

"Where've you been?" Joe asks. "I've been trying to reach you all day. You didn't answer your radio or phone."

"I was out of radio contact."

Laura avoids telling him where she's been and what she's been doing. She doesn't want him to know how she broke into Clyde Fisher's hunting cabin. He wouldn't like it, and she can hear him saying how it sounds reckless, like something her cousin would do.

"Out of radio contact? Where would you be for that to happen?"

She gives him a look and evades the question. "Who found the body?" she asks.

"One of the employees in the coffee shop came back in the alley to throw some trash in the dumpster. He can't say why he checked behind it. He just thought something smelled funny so he looked around. Anyway, he ran back into the shop and called 911. That was about ninety minutes ago."

He's making a point about the time and how long it's taken her to respond to the call. The sheriff's office is in the Burgh, about an eight-minute drive to this particular alleyway.

Laura ignores his comment. "But you're sure it's not her?"

"I'm sure. It looks like the body's been here for a couple days. From what the detective told me, probably a case of drug overdose, but so far, they haven't found any drug paraphernalia. There aren't any obvious signs of foul play from what they can tell."

"They'll need to do an autopsy."

Joe nods. "What are you thinking? Runaway? Homeless? Drug addict?"

"Yes," Laura says to all three possibilities. "I want to take a closer look." She has to make sure it isn't Kayleigh. It's the only way she can silence any doubt in her mind.

They make their way over to the victim. Someone has already placed a body bag next to her. They're getting ready to transport her to the medical examiner's office.

"Hang on," she says to one of the techs.

Laura bends over the body, pulls back slightly from the smell. The queasiness in her stomach when she was in the cabin kneeling in front of the trunk hasn't completely gone away. She notices a tattoo on the underside of the girl's forearm. Written in black ink is the word *love*.

She gets down on her hands and knees and looks up, directly into the girl's face. It's like Joe said, she's been here for a while, but it's clear she isn't Kayleigh. Even with the puffiness, the blanched skin, Laura can make out the oval face and dark brown eyes. Kayleigh has a heart-shaped face, light eyes, a splattering of freckles across her nose.

There's a commotion at the entrance of the alleyway. A large man in a dark suit and sunglasses is flashing his ID around, capturing the attention of the team.

"Thanks for all your hard work." Agent Ring shakes the hand of the police officer who's handling the crime scene log. He then goes on to shake the hand of the detective in charge, putting his other hand on the man's arm, flashing his gapped-tooth smile. "I'll be taking over from here."

"What the hell is going on?" Joe asks.

Laura gets up off the ground, wipes the dirt from her hands. Before she can answer Joe, Agent Ring walks up to them. He stands over the body, looks at the tattoo on the arm, and then he says to the techs, "Bag her." He turns to Laura. "Sheriff Pennington. Twice in one day."

"Lucky me." She introduces him to Joe.

They step back as the techs straighten out the body bag. No one talks as the techs roll the woman to one side and slip the bag underneath her. Then they roll her as best they can to the other side. When it's completely under her, they lift the sides and zip it up. Someone is filling out a tag as they load her into the back of the coroner's van. She'll be taken to the morgue, where they'll learn from the autopsy exactly what happened.

"Do you mind telling me what your interest is in this case?" Joe asks Agent Ring.

"Actually, I do mind. Will you excuse us?" Agent Ring attempts to guide Laura to the far end of the alleyway and away from Joe.

"Again. What the hell?" Joe asks.

"Just give me a minute," Laura says to him, and then she follows the agent.

They stand in the shadows of the setting sun, where it's a little cooler but not by much.

"I don't appreciate you being rude to my deputy," she says.

"I'm sure you can smooth it over with him later. Did you see the tattoo?"

"I saw the word *love* written on the underside of her forearm."

"Our guy brands all his girls. I suppose he convinces them that he really does love them. It's one of the ways a Romeo pimp manipulates them. He makes them think he's their boyfriend and that he'll always take care of them. Nice, huh?"

"More like disgusting."

"You won't hear an argument from me."

"This girl looks like she overdosed."

"I wouldn't be surprised. A couple of the girls have been lost in the last few months to fentanyl overdoses. It's a real problem. Whether he's giving them the drugs or not remains to be seen. My guess is that he is. It's another way he can control them. Get them addicted so they're dependent on him. They'll do whatever he asks just so they can get their next fix. Some of the girls were probably addicted before they were turned out."

"Is she from the Burgh?"

"Very few are local from my estimation."

Laura reaches in her pocket, holds Kayleigh's picture up to his face. "Does she look familiar to you? Is she one of the girls in your case?"

Agent Ring takes the photo, looks at it closely. Shrugs. "She doesn't look familiar, but I can't be one hundred percent sure. Who is she?"

"Kayleigh McBride. Local girl. She was fourteen when this was taken. She went missing about five years ago."

He glances at the picture. "You know there's software you can use to get an idea of what she looks like now."

"We don't have the budget for it, and when there isn't anyone in the family pushing for something to be done—" She pauses. "The free software online makes people look like caricatures of themselves." She doesn't tell him how she'd compared her daughter's pictures at the same ages, and there wasn't a big enough difference to matter.

"If you want, you can leave this with me, and I can have it done for you."

Laura takes the photo from his hand and puts it back in her pocket. "I'll send you a copy."

"Don't you trust me?

"No."

"Wow, that was honest." He smiles and turns to walk away, saying over his shoulder, "Oh, I left you a little present at your back door. You can thank me later."

After Agent Ring leaves, Joe walks up to her.

"Well?" he asks.

"I showed him Kayleigh's photo."

"And?"

She shakes her head. "Although, he did offer to have her image put through their age progression software."

"For no cost? That's nice of him."

"Yeah, he's a real peach."

"What's really going on here, Laura?"

Joe doesn't like to be left out of the loop. She doesn't blame him. If she were in his position, she wouldn't like it either.

"It's nothing I can't handle."

"That's not what I asked."

"I know, and I promise I'll explain everything to you when I can," she says, and she rushes to her SUV.

CHAPTER
TWENTY-EIGHT

Eve scrambles from the floor and onto the couch, pressing her spine against the back cushion. She recognizes the man standing in the cottage doorway, pointing his gun at them. He's known as Fen, short for Fenton. She knows what he's capable of.

She blinks, an attempt to clear her vision and remove the hallucination, if that's what this is. Eve's had dreams of moments like this, Fen showing up in her nightmares to punish her for something she may or may not have done. The infractions aren't important. It's how he's going to punish you that matters. It's what drives him. She's watched him shove an ice pick into a girl's ear for eyeballing another pimp, an out-of-pocket behavior that's against the rules of the stable.

An ice pick in the ear is not like stabbing someone with a knife, where the blade goes in and comes out in quick strikes. The opening of the ear canal is small and it's met with the resistance of cartilage and bone. It requires precision to shove a pick inside it and it takes a lot of force. Fen excels in both.

Eve sits on her hands to keep herself from covering her ears, fearing the act will not only amuse him but also entice him. The last Shot girl who had an ice pick in her ear didn't die right away. For days, the girl stumbled around unbalanced and unable to walk. She vomited and complained of dizziness, confusion, and then one night, Eve found her lying on the floor, her body twisting and contorting as though a demon possessed her. The girl was seizing. The blood had been slowly leaking into her brain. She was dead by morning.

It was a warning to all the girls not to partake in eyeballing behavior, and it was effective.

Eve doesn't want to die by the ice pick Fen keeps strapped to his calf, hidden by his black jeans. She prays for a bullet to her heart or head, whichever is the quickest way to go. It's funny to be praying for a swift death, especially for someone so young, but that's what she's doing in the seconds it takes for Hester and the cowboy to grasp what's happening.

Keep up, Eve wants to scream. *Our lives depend on it.*

The sound of the fans blowing is the only noise in the room. Eve can't breathe. She's waiting for someone to make a move. Fen aims the gun at the cowboy, but Fen's eyes are on her. His threatening glare has everything to do with her betraying his boss. Fen is small for a guy and not much bigger than her, but size doesn't matter when you're as mean and ruthless as he is.

"Hello, Trix," he says. "You look like hell. What happened to your forehead?"

Eve touches the area near the gash on her brow.

"Who the hell is Trix?" Hester is cradling the baby. She had taken Ivy out of Eve's arms at the exact moment Fen had appeared in the doorway.

Eve is amazed by how well Hester handles surprise guests and changes in circumstances. "It's my professional name," Eve says.

So far, the cowboy hasn't moved other than pointing his gun at Fen, rather than at her and Hester.

"Get a load of you," Fen says. "Professional name." He chuckles, and a chill runs up the length of Eve's spine.

"Shoot him," Eve says to the cowboy.

"Now, now, Trix. Let's not forget your place," Fen says. "I think our friend here is going to want to hear what I have to say."

"Professional name?" Hester asks. It seems to take her a second to catch on. "You're a prostitute?"

Eve glances at Hester, then says to the cowboy, "Shoot him."

"Hold on," Hester says. "If you're a prostitute, then who was that guy in the woods? Was he a john? Was he even the baby's father?"

"The guy in the woods was Shot's brother," Eve says.

"Who's Shot?" Hester asks.

"What did you just say?" the cowboy asks. He's leaning his elbow against the arm of the chair, the gun lazily aimed at Fen. It seems he's finally taking an interest in what's going on. "Are you telling me that's not Shot hanging in the tree out there but his *brother*?"

"Hanging in the tree?" Fen asks. "Who put him in a tree?"

"That would be the witch," the cowboy says.

Hester nods, apparently happy to take credit for her part in this whole mess.

"So, you're telling me it's not Shot in the tree?" The cowboy obviously needs this clarified.

"Yeah, that's what we're telling you," Fen says. "And someone's going to have to pay for that, too."

The cowboy sits back. "He didn't meet with me himself? He sent his *brother*?"

"Yeah," Fen says.

The cowboy's face is all scrunched up, and he seems insulted by the fact that it wasn't Shot who was handling the exchange.

"Shot thought it was just easier to send his brother," Eve says.

"Uh huh," the cowboy says, glaring at Fen. "And who are you again?"

"His name is Fenton, but the girls call him Fen," Eve says.

"I don't understand what's going on," Hester says. "Would someone like to explain it to me. It's my home you fucking barged into, you know."

Eve turns to Hester. "They're trading up babies, not just girls," she says, although she has no idea why she's explaining any of this to the old woman. Maybe if they keep talking there will be less shooting. Every second that passes is another second she's alive.

"You're selling babies?" Hester asks the cowboy.

He shakes his head. "Buying, not selling. And I bought this one right here."

"You sold your baby?" Hester asks Eve. The baby is fast sleep in Hester's arms, innocent and unaware they are talking about her.

"What? No," Eve says.

"You piece of shit." Hester turns on the cowboy, spit flying from her mouth. "You're *stealing* the baby from her?"

"Buying, not stealing. And just this one here."

"Who do you think you are? God?"

Eve isn't paying attention to what Hester or the cowboy are saying at this point, because Fen is aiming the gun at her, and she suddenly realizes her mistake. She's told Hester and the cowboy too much. It's an infraction for telling anyone outside the stable about what goes on inside it.

Eve has given them Fen's name.

She's talked about the business.

"You can't kill me." Eve pleads with him. "I make too much money for Shot. I'm a bottom girl, remember?" She's not proud of it. It's something she loathes about herself, and there's plenty on her list of detestable deeds. But she's moved up in the ranks, and it's not by choice. She either does what Shot asks or she pays the price with Fen's ice pick.

"Trix, Trix, Trix, you're so cute when you beg, but you should know better." Fen taps his ear and laughs.

She tries hard to keep her hands at her sides, to not cover her ears, but they go there anyway. It doesn't matter that she's a bottom girl. It never did. Somehow, she has to convince the cowboy to shoot Fen. If she doesn't, she's as good as dead. They all are.

Fen points the gun at the cowboy. "You and Shot had a deal. Now, I understand there's been a bit of trouble, but Shot is willing to be reasonable. If you give me the money and let me take care of the girl, he'll consider it square with him."

Eve turns to cowboy. "He's lying to you. It's not going to be square with Shot."

"Shut up," Fen says.

Hester is rocking the baby. She turns to Eve. "I'm not one to judge. We all have to earn a living. Your job has given you something precious and I won't let them take her from you."

"Who is this bitch?" Fen aims the gun at Hester.

Eve can't believe how obtuse this old woman is. Can't she see their lives are at stake?

"I'm the bitch who's the only one who knows where your stupid money is."

"Is that true?" Fen asks.

"Yeah, it's true. Unfortunately," the cowboy says.

Eve turns to the cowboy. "He'll kill you as soon as he gets the money.

192

You killed Shot's brother. Shot won't let you get away with that. I know him. He won't let you walk away from this."

"I agree with—Trix, is it?" Hester asks. "Shoot this guy," she says to the cowboy.

Finally. The nutty old woman is starting to understand how dangerous their situation is.

"Is that your plan?" the cowboy asks Fen. "You're going to kill me after I give you the money? You? You think *you* can kill *me*?"

Eve sees what's in Fen's eyes. It's a look she's seen before, the one that darkens his features right before he strikes.

"Shoot him or we're all dead," she says to the cowboy.

Fen aims, and Eve has to give it to the cowboy, he pulls the trigger before Fen can even get a shot off.

Fen drops to his knees and falls to his side. The bastard hasn't even taken his last breath, and already Eve is thinking about the ice pick strapped to his calf, and how she's going to get her hands on it.

CHAPTER
TWENTY-NINE

Laura has every intention of going home to see whatever Agent Ring has left at her back door, but instead, she finds herself turning right, heading in the direction of Fisher's Market. She's not sure what she's intending to do once she gets there.

Ever since leaving the alley, she's felt an angry knot forming in the pit of her stomach. Pop had said someone in the Burgh had to know something about what had happened to Kayleigh. How it was only a matter of finding that person and getting them to talk.

Is it possible now that this person doesn't live in the Burgh at all but has been living in Bordertown this entire time?

She pulls into the gravel lot. The closed sign hangs on the door, but there's a light on inside the store. She steps out of the SUV and glances up at the sky. The sun is setting behind the trees. Soon it will be too dark to see anything but stars.

Laura's never been nervous about entering Fisher's Market, or any store for that matter, and especially in Bordertown, but she's feeling anxious and sticky under her arms as she walks up to the door now.

The sign may say closed, but there are men's voices coming from inside. She tries the handle and the door opens.

"Clyde," she calls as she walks in.

Clyde appears behind the counter.

Laura lifts her hand, waves, a friendly gesture in hopes of neutralizing him. This can go one of two ways and by the look on his face, it's not going to go the way she wants.

"We're closed," Clyde says. He's dressed in head to toe camouflage. There are dark smudge marks on his neck and chin, remnants of some kind of face paint.

"I just have some follow-up questions." She's wondering where he's been and why he's dressed as though he's been hunting when everybody knows hunting season doesn't start until autumn.

Karl steps out from the backroom office. He stands slightly behind his father, towering over him. Laura has always known Karl to be big not only in height but also in width, but he seems gargantuan now. Standing next to Derrick all these years, Karl appeared much smaller than he actually was. He's also dressed in camo gear. The two of them look as though they've just returned from war.

"Hello, Karl." Laura smiles, hoping to put him at ease. "Am I catching the two of you on your way out, or did you just get back from somewhere?" She smells the sweat on them along with the woodsy scent of moss and wet leaves.

"What do you want, Sheriff?" Clyde asks.

"What were you two doing, anyway?" She motions to their getup. "I'm assuming whatever it was, you were in the woods."

Karl's shaking his head before she can get the last words out. She waits for one of them to answer her, but neither one says anything.

"Does it have something to do with the guy we found in the tree?"

"We don't know what you're talking about," Clyde says.

Laura can see in Karl's eyes that he knows exactly who she's talking about. "Do you know who the guy is, Karl?"

"I—"

Clyde slaps Karl in the chest with the back of his hand. "No, he doesn't."

"What's going on, Clyde? Why are the two of you dressed up like some kind of SWAT team or something?"

"This has nothing to do with you, Laura. I think it's best if you just leave."

"Come on, Clyde. You know me. I'm here because I want to help, but I can't help unless you tell me what's going on."

Laura realizes the reason she drove here instead of going straight home is that she not only wants the truth about what they're involved in and if they know anything about Kayleigh, but also her original intentions have somehow become twisted with her feelings about her own cousin. If she can help Karl in ways she isn't always able to help Hester, maybe she can keep him from making any more mistakes. She has no doubt Derrick has talked Karl into doing things he never would've done on his own, and now that Derrick's gone, Karl is going to be the one who goes down for Derrick's crimes. Karl won't survive in prison. He might get by on toughness and sheer size alone at least for a little while, but he's going to need wits, and that's where he's lacking.

"When was the last time you were at the hunting cabin, Karl?"

"I don't remember."

"Was it in the past couple days?"

"I guess that could be right."

"Do you bring girls there, Karl?"

"Don't answer that," Clyde says. He gives Laura a hard look. "I don't know what you're accusing him of, but unless you have something to charge him with, I think it's best if you just get the hell out of here."

"I'm trying to help him. If he comes forward now, if he tells them everything he knows, they might go easier on him."

"Who's they?" Clyde asks.

Laura can't tell him that, of course. She's not sure what she thought would happen by coming here tonight. Did she really expect Karl to just open up and tell her the truth about what he and Derrick were doing with the girls in the cabin? *With Kayleigh?*

She looks toward the corner of the ceiling, where the security camera should be, but isn't. Perhaps it's already in Agent Ring's hands. Clyde follows her gaze.

"I took it down. I thought it was time I got it fixed."

"Is that so?"

"Yeah, that's so."

For a second, they stare at each other. It seems he's challenging her to go ahead and accuse him of destroying evidence, but why say it when they both know that's what he did. It's not going to change anything one way or the other, so instead, she turns to Karl and holds up Kayleigh's photo.

"Do you know who this girl is, Karl? Ever see her before? Is she one of the girls you took to the cabin?"

"No." He turns his head away.

"Look again, Karl."

He glances at it. "Never seen her."

"You sure? You don't seem sure."

"No."

"No, you're sure? Or no, you're not sure?"

"No. I—I don't know. You're confusing me."

"It's a yes or no question, Karl."

"That's enough. Stop badgering him. He said he's never seen her." Clyde pushes Karl toward the backroom. "You're done here, Sheriff."

"What about you, Clyde? Have you seen her before?"

"No." Clyde points to the door. "It's time for you to go."

Laura stares at him.

He keeps pointing to the door.

"You're making a mistake, Clyde."

"Get out of here, Sheriff."

Laura feels she has no choice but to do what he asks.

Reluctantly, she leaves the store and climbs back in her SUV. She should've taken her own advice that she'd given to Joe about going easy on Karl, not confusing him. If only she could talk with him alone without Clyde interfering. It's possible Karl knew Kayleigh, but it's also possible he didn't know her. With Karl, she just can't tell.

It's dark by the time she pulls into her driveway. She makes her way into the house, turning on the lights as she walks toward the kitchen, pausing only to toss her keys onto the counter, before heading to the back door, where she finds a manila folder. She opens it, skims the autopsy report on Logan Mense, then drops it onto the kitchen table.

She doesn't like that Agent Ring has been to her home. It feels like an invasion of her privacy, an infringement of her personal space, and she starts to wonder how far he's willing to go with whatever game he's playing with her. Surely, he wouldn't break into her house, rummage through her drawers, trying to dig up something on her. She has to assume he knows plenty about her life already.

But he's with the FBI, and they don't always play by the rules.

Crossing her arms, leaning against the counter, she listens for any unusual sounds in the house. The air conditioner kicks on, but other than that it's quiet. If someone has been here, she'd know it. Wouldn't she?

Quietly, she moves through the living room, flicking on more lights, checking the recently vacuumed carpet for footprints. The tracks in the hallway are hers or Joe's, but whose print is that? It's just hers. Her bare feet from this morning.

She heads straight to the spare room. Nothing on the desk looks disturbed. The charts are where she left them. The map hangs front and center, covered in pushpins of all the places she and Pop have searched. She wonders what Agent Ring would think if he saw this. Would he think she was obsessed with Kayleigh's case? Or would he think what Joe does, that she's just someone who cares?

The photo in her pocket weighs heavily on her chest, and she touches Pop's picture, the one of him in his sheriff's uniform.

Laura leaves the spare bedroom and checks the bathroom, taking a quick peek behind the shower curtain. The shower's empty.

She stands outside of Charlotte's room. There's not a single footprint on the carpet.

Laura heads to her bedroom. Everything looks the same as she'd left it that morning. The bed is made. The drawer where she keeps her firearm is open, but only because she forgot to close it. Nothing in her closet is out of place.

Satisfied Agent Ring had dropped off the autopsy report and left, she heads back down the hallway, but something about Charlotte's room isn't right. Pausing in the doorway, she leans against the doorjamb, arms folded, and stares at the empty bed with its crisp, tucked sheets and perfectly smoothed comforter.

It's the bed.

Charlotte never made her bed. She'd always leave the sheets crumpled, comforter half on the floor no matter how many times Laura had told her about it.

Laura walks into the room now. Before she realizes it, she's kicking off her shoes, removing her firearm, laying it on the nightstand, and climbing under the covers. Rolling to her side, she brings the sheets to her nose, searching for her daughter's scent. But Laura's washed the bedding since her daughter was last home at the start of summer, remaking it with hospital corners, centering the comforter perfectly over the mattress.

Rolling to her other side, she pulls the sheets and comforter with her. Then she kicks her legs, feels the sheet at the bottom become untucked. She kicks her legs harder. And harder still. Before she knows it, she's rolling from side to side, flipping around until the sheets are crumpled and twisted, and the comforter is dragging on the floor.

Slightly out of breath, she gets up, tugs on her shoes, holsters her firearm, smooths the front of her uniform. Composed once again, she walks out of the room.

In the kitchen, she sits at the table and opens the folder.

Logan Mense died of asphyxiation from blunt force trauma to the larynx and trachea, which is consistent with hanging. However, the ME believes the trauma occurred prior to the rope being tied around the victim's neck. The lividity, the settling and pooling of blood, on the victim's back was fixed. Meaning the body was set in one position for more than eight hours. When this occurs, it can't be shifted by changing the body's position. It suggests the victim died on his back. Signs of rigor mortis had started prior to the hanging, and curiously, the victim's left leg was broken.

When you look at all the physical evidence, one could reasonably assume the victim was dead prior to being hung in the tree, and suicide can be ruled out.

All this means is that the scene was staged, as they'd suspected.

Laura continues reading the section on blunt force trauma to the throat. It could've been caused by an object or quite possibly a fist. A throat punch is uncommon but not unheard of. Derrick could certainly deliver that kind of blow. He's tough, physical, from years of playing a rough sport like ice hockey. Karl could probably exert enough force to cause similar damage.

Laura can sit here and speculate all she wants about who killed Logan, but it's not who killed him that concerns her. It's the time of his death. Based on the medical examiner's finding, Logan Mense was dead almost eight to twelve hours *before* Derrick was shot in the head.

Logan couldn't have killed Derrick. And if Logan didn't do it, then someone else did. And that someone is still out there.

Clyde and Karl know this.

It's why they were dressed in hunting gear and wearing war paint.

It's the reason they were in the woods.

CHAPTER
THIRTY

Karl isn't aware his lip is curled over his teeth or that it's been that way ever since the sheriff left. He doesn't like that bitch. She pretends to be on his side, smiling and talking all slow-like to him. She acts like she cares, but she doesn't. No one cares about what happened to Derrick, not as much as he does.

Clyde grabs him by the collar of his T-shirt and shoves him against the wall. His dad is three inches shorter, wiry, and as strong as a freight train, and yet, Karl could take him down if he wanted to. He's got fifty pounds on his dad, easy, but he's a good son. He was raised to respect his dad and take whatever his dad shelled out.

"What the hell was that about?" Clyde's face is two inches from Karl's. He can smell the shot of whiskey on his dad's breath that he'd downed moments before the sheriff had walked through the door.

"I don't know," Karl says, because he isn't sure what his dad is talking about.

"Why did she ask if you were at the cabin?"

Karl thinks about that. Usually Derrick handles any questions that come up about the cabin. Karl's not sure how to answer his dad.

"What girls, Karl? What's she talking about?"

"I don't know. Ask—ask Derrick." He doesn't know what to say. Derrick has been speaking for him for so long, it's as though he's forgotten how to speak for himself. Derrick has a way of explaining things to him so he understands them. He makes the things they do okay even though deep down Karl knows they're not. How can he say this to his dad without messing it up?

"What did you boys get yourselves into? What's going on? Answer me!" Clyde pulls his hand away from Karl's T-shirt and takes a step back.

His dad looks older than he did just two days ago. The skin on his face and neck looks gray, and it's not from the paint. It's a skeletal gray. His eyes are red and glassy. His dad has cried more in the last forty-eight hours than Karl has ever seen him cry in his twenty-four years. He wonders if his dad would've cried this much if it was Karl who had taken a bullet to the head. Thinking about how his cousin was shot makes him angry all over again.

Clyde is talking, and Karl is trying to keep up.

"I should've paid more attention to what you boys were up to. He was just so proud to buy us all that stuff. I shouldn't have looked the other way." His dad rambles on, something about Derrick selling drugs and if Karl was involved.

"Drugs? No. No way."

His dad rubs his brow. "If not drugs, then what?"

"Then nothing. We didn't do anything." Karl never knew how to tell his cousin he didn't want to do the things they were doing. He struggles talking about his feelings, and he didn't want to disappoint his cousin. Ever.

"It's that son of a bitch who shot him who's to blame," Karl says. Clyde stares at him, studies him.

"I swear, Dad. It's the truth."

"What about this guy in the tree? Do you know who he was?"

Karl did know him. He came to the cabin sometimes with the girls. They partied, drank some beers, had fun, an all-around good time. It's what Derrick used to say. *Didn't we have fun, cous? An all-around good time.*

Karl's never been any good at lying, especially to his dad, but something tells him now isn't the right time to be honest. Tears fill his eyes and he tries to hold them back. One escapes, and he wipes it away with a fist. He recognizes the tightness in his chest and the hanging of his head. It's a familiar feeling and one he has often after spending time in the cabin. Karl didn't have the courage to stop the things Derrick was doing, and he didn't have the strength to tell Derrick no when he wanted Karl to do them, too. Karl would do whatever his cousin asked of him. He loved him. He's family.

Karl closes his eyes briefly, then he opens them. His lashes are wet. "I don't know who the guy in the tree is. I never saw him before in my life. I swear," he says, as convincingly as he possibly can. He punches his thigh over and over again.

"What about the girl in the picture? Who is she?"

He continues punching his leg. "I—I don't know." He didn't recognize the girl in the photo. Or he doesn't think he did. He doesn't remember Derrick bringing a girl around who was so young.

Clyde takes Karl's hand, and he stops Karl from hammering it against his thigh. "It's okay, son. It doesn't matter. What matters now is that we have a plan."

The woods were crowded with cops for a while, because of that guy in the tree. Karl and his dad were careful not to be seen. They were sneaky enough not to be noticed by anyone in law enforcement and that included the sheriff.

They hunkered down not far from the crime scene in a thicket of hardwood saplings. Only when the woods were quiet and its peaceful energy restored did Karl feel a sense of calm and familiarity. Once they were on the move again, it didn't take him long to pick up the bleached-blond guy's scent.

Karl and his dad followed an overgrown path, where they found signs someone had been there recently. To an untrained eye, the snapped twig, the single drop of blood on a fallen leaf would go unnoticed, and the guy's pretty scent would be lost on the average nose. But Karl saw and smelled all of these things, as if someone held a magnifying glass up to his face and a bar of fancy soap under those big, special glands in his nostrils, and he didn't even have to slow his pace to do it. If he had a gift for anything, it was understanding the woods and its creatures, its sights and smells, seeing nature as it's intended to be seen.

They followed the trail for some distance, stopping when they reached the witch's cottage that sits far back in the woods in the middle of a small clearing. The cottage has always given Karl the creeps, and growing up, while the other kids egged the stone walls and dared each other to knock on the front door, taunting the woman inside, he made a point of staying away. The kids talked about how the witch would steal babies and eat them. Those same kids said that on windy nights a person could hear the ghosts of crying children blowing through the branches of trees.

Karl shivers at the thought. He doesn't like messing with anything supernatural, mostly because it's one of the things Derrick wasn't able to explain to him. But the guy who shot Derrick is holed up inside her cottage. They tracked him there, and they know he's in there with at least two or three other people. They heard voices. One was definitely female, probably the witch herself. It was getting dark, and they couldn't see inside the cottage clearly. They decided to wait, to come back later, after they had a plan.

Now, his dad is talking about that plan, but Karl's not listening. He's picturing the guy on the security camera with the bleached-blond hair putting a gun to his cousin's head.

Boom!

Karl pokes the spot between his eyebrows where the bullet entered Derrick's brain. "Right here, Dad. That's where he shot him. Right here."

Clyde isn't looking at him. He's staring at something over Karl's shoulder.

"He did it like it was nothing. Like Derrick was nothing." Karl is crying hard. It's the first time he lets the tears flow without trying to stop them. They roll down his face and mix with the snot coming out of his nose. "He can't get away with it. We can't let him." Whatever his cousin has done, he didn't deserve this.

When Karl's cried out, he wipes his eyes and nose with the back of his arm. Then he reaches into his pocket for the snuff. A dip is what he needs to calm himself down, but he can't find the can of cool spearmint chewing tobacco he always keeps with him. He feels around his pockets. He must've dropped it somewhere in the woods. He'll just have to grab a new can from the shelf. Karl's been helping himself to snuff and snacks and sodas from the store's shelves his whole life. His dad doesn't say anything, but what Karl doesn't know is that his dad has been secretly deducting whatever Karl helps himself to from his small paycheck every week.

Clyde snaps back from wherever it is he has drifted. He talks about ambushing the cottage. "We have to be careful who we shoot. I'm not surprised this guy ended up at Hester's. I know Hester and criminals like to hang out together. He probably sniffed her out like the animal he is, but she didn't take part in what happened to Derrick."

"She's a witch, Dad."

"I don't buy that crap. She's got problems. I'm not saying she doesn't, but let's not worry about her. We'll stick to the plan. We'll ambush him. We'll take him down."

It's a simple enough plan. It's a good plan. "We ambush him. We take him down."

CHAPTER
THIRTY-ONE

Noah stands over Fen's body. He reaches down and picks up Fen's nine-millimeter from the floor. Then he shoves it in the waistband of his jeans. He feels good about shooting Fen. It serves Shot right for sending other men to do his business for him.

It was a fine shot to the forehead, almost dead center. Bull's-eye! Noah doesn't see an exit wound. The bullet is lodged somewhere in Fen's brain. The blood from the entrance wound drips down the side of Fen's face and onto the hardwood floor.

Noah's trying hard to wrap his head around the fact that Shot didn't think his business with Noah was important enough to handle himself. The absolute nerve of the guy. Shot has screwed up every aspect of this job, putting Noah's reputation on the line, his entire business. He supposes Shot still expects to get his half of the money, but there's no way Noah's going to give him even one cent of it.

Not now.

Not ever.

Noah's going to have to kill the little prick once and for all.

The girl stands next to him. She's small, barely reaching his shoulder. He smells the salty, sour sweat of her skin.

"Is he dead?" she asks.

"He's dead."

She breathes out what Noah takes as a sigh of relief. The girl was afraid of Fen. Noah could see the fear in her eyes and hear it in her voice. It's the reason he took her advice seriously. *Shoot him or we're all dead.*

But how did this Fenton guy even find them?

It has to be the girl. She must have a tracking device on her somewhere. The clothes she's wearing are different from the ones she was wearing that first night in the woods. The device probably isn't sewn in them. Then Noah notices her sneakers. If he were a gambling man, he'd bet she doesn't even know what's been placed inside her shoe.

"Let's make a deal," Witch says. She's standing by the couch, rocking the baby, who has woken up from the sound of Noah's gun going off.

"What kind of deal?" he asks.

The girl lingers over Fen's body, peering closer at his corpse, but not too close, as though she's afraid he's going to come back to life and grab her.

"I told you he's dead," Noah says, and he switches his attention back to the witch. "Go on, let's hear it. What do you have in mind?"

"You promise to leave the girl and the baby with me, and I'll tell you where your money is."

"I promise. Now where's the money?" He has no intention of going through with any such promise, but what's she going to do about it?

"Before I tell you where it is, he needs to get off my living room floor."

Ah, there's always a catch, he thinks.

The witch continues. "You help me bury him in the woods out there and then you'll get your money."

The girl bends over Fen's body. She's braver now, checking the man's pockets.

"Get away from him." Noah grabs her arm and flings her over by the couch, where the witch is rocking the baby.

"Do we have a deal?" Witch asks.

The girl hasn't said anything about what the witch is proposing. He wonders why. Maybe she's waiting to hear how this plays out. He can't imagine the girl wants to stay here with the witch, but maybe she's had a change of heart due to recent events.

Noah glances out the window. It's already dark outside. His clients are just going to have to be patient a little while longer. Once the baby is in their arms, he's certain they'll forgive him for taking so long to deliver her. He considers the witch's offer. He really doesn't want this guy's corpse hanging around. It scrapes at his nerve endings, which are already raw from the insult he's suffered from this guy's boss.

He turns to the witch, deciding he has some time before Shot shows up, and that it's one less body he'll have to dispose of later when all this is over.

"How do you suggest we move him?" He touches his shoulder. It hurts like a bitch. It's possible it's infected. He'll definitely need to see a doctor as soon as he gets back to the city. *Fuck, can bears have rabies?*

"I got a chain saw out there," Witch says. "It's fancy. Real quiet. We can cut him up and move him in pieces."

The girl's jaw drops.

The witch is out of her mind. Or maybe she's playing with him. Maybe she wants to turn the chain saw on him. "You can't be serious?"

"I didn't say *I* was going to cut him up. I figured you're a twisted fuck. You could do it."

"Not me," Noah says. "Do you know how messy that would be? Blood and guts everywhere. I'm not doing it."

They both look at the girl.

"Don't look at me. I'm not doing it, either. Not that the bastard doesn't deserve it."

"Then what do you propose?" the witch asks. "We've got to get rid of him. What are we going to do if my cousin, the *sheriff*, drops by? You going to let her in with a dead man on the floor? She stops by unannounced all the time. Just ask Girl." The witch continues rocking the baby.

"She's right," Girl says.

The witch doesn't have a clue that Noah actually agrees with her. "What if we use your wheels out there?"

"Good luck finding the keys." It's the way Witch smiles at him that he's now certain she's hidden the damn keys, too.

He glances at the girl's sneakers again. He really doesn't care about the keys, because he has no intention of going anywhere. It's only a matter of time before Shot's going to come for the girl and the money himself. It's what Noah would do in Shot's position, and once he shows up, Noah's going to blow the motherfucker's brains out.

"Fine," he says to the witch. "We have a deal."

CHAPTER
THIRTY-TWO

Laura pushes the autopsy report on Logan Mense aside. She considers going back to Fisher's Market and begging Clyde not to go looking for trouble or to do anything stupid. Clyde is hurting over losing Derrick, and at the same time, he's trying to protect Karl. He's not thinking clearly.

He could get himself and his son killed.

Laura should've said all of this to him, but she's not sure it would've made a difference. You cross a Fisher, you wrong one of their kin, they're not going to let it go, and she realizes there's nothing she can say or do that's going to change their minds.

There's a knock at her door, and she thinks about reaching for her gun, but if Clyde or one of the other Fishers was coming for her, they wouldn't knock first. There wouldn't be any warning. But of course, she's being silly. The Fishers have no reason to hurt her.

The front door opens.

"Laura," Joe calls.

"In the kitchen."

"Hey," he says when he enters. He leans against the counter. "What's this?" He points to the folder on the table with the autopsy report.

"It's nothing." She stands and tosses the folder on the countertop. The last thing she wants is to argue about Agent Ring and the case. "Do you want a beer?" She opens the fridge.

"I'm still on duty."

"Right. Forgot." She grabs a beer for herself, twists off the cap, and takes a long swallow.

"I stopped to let you know Hester's power is back."

Shit. With everything else going on, she forgot to call the power company for Hester. "How do you know?"

"I called to make sure they didn't forget about her."

"Oh, well, thank you. You didn't have to do that."

He's never made her feel embarrassed about her cousin, accepting Hester as a part of her life, even going out of his way to help Hester on occasion like he did just now.

Her cell phone rings, set to the sound of an old rotary phone, a ringtone specifically chosen so she knows it's her daughter calling. Before she answers she turns to Joe.

"It's Charlotte. I don't want her to know you're here."

"Fine, whatever."

It's a sensitive subject between them, and Laura puts her back to him before she says hello. Her heart already feels lighter just hearing her daughter's voice.

"I'm sorry I forgot to call yesterday," Charlotte says. "I know how you get around this time."

"Well, I'm not sure what you mean by how I get, but it's okay."

"You know exactly what I mean. You get all sad and then you fixate on that missing girl like she could bring Pop back if you found her or something."

"Whoa, okay. I don't think that's quite true, but you're right I get sad and working Pop's case does make me feel close to him."

Laura has always been careful not to let her daughter know how finding the girl is as much about Charlotte as it is about Pop. By not giving her daughter too much information, she's protecting her, keeping the specifics about the case and Laura's job to herself.

Joe comes up behind her, quietly puts a hand on her shoulder when he notices how she's struggling to keep the emotion from her voice. Eventually, the conversation turns away from Pop and the case and jumps to Charlotte's internship.

By the time Laura hangs up, Joe has stepped away. He's leaning against the counter again, next to the folder with the autopsy report the agent had left at her back door. He puts his finger on top of it.

"Are you ever going to tell me what you and Agent Ring were talking about?"

"He asked me not to."

"Why?"

"That's a good question."

"I don't like it when you keep secrets from me."

"I'm not keeping secrets from you. I'm doing my job, and if I'm keeping something from you, it's because it's my job to keep it from you."

"Yeah, your job. You seem to forget it's my job, too." His radio goes off. He glances at it, reluctantly takes the call about assisting on a domestic. "I gotta go. You going to be okay?"

She nods.

Before he leaves, he says, "One of these days you're going to have to tell Charlotte about us. You know that, don't you?"

She doesn't answer, but maybe he's right. Charlotte is old enough now to know about her and Joe and whatever it is they're doing. If Laura's honest, it's what she wants. *He's* what she wants.

She downs her beer in several large gulps, wipes her mouth with the back of her arm, and tosses the bottle in the recycling bin. Picking up the folder on Logan Mense, she carries it to the spare bedroom, where she drops it on the desk with the charts she keeps on Kayleigh.

She stares at the map on the wall. She doesn't want to do it, but she has to put her personal feelings aside, including her pride, and ask for Agent Ring's help. He has access to tools and information that she's not able to get through her own channels.

Grabbing her laptop, she sends him copies of the files she and Pop have amassed in the last five years, along with a copy of Kayleigh's photo. She's taking the agent up on his offer and then some, she thinks, and hits send.

Her phone buzzes: a text from Agent Ring. *This just came in.*

There's an attachment in the text, and Laura opens it. He's sent her the autopsy report on the young woman they found dead by the dumpster in the alleyway. If he's seen the files on Kayleigh she just sent to him, he doesn't mention it.

She scans the document. The victim is between twenty and twenty-five-years-old. Not much older than Charlotte. The woman's identity is still unknown. The cause of death was ruled to be a fentanyl overdose, like the agent had said.

Laura continues reading, pauses, rereads it again to be sure. Then she's texting Agent Ring back, frantically pressing the small letters on her phone.

CHAPTER
THIRTY-THREE

"What do you do for a bump on the head?" Hillary asks.

"I'm not sure. Let me look it up on the internet." Emeril pulls his phone out.

"No." She covers his hand. "We don't want any incriminating evidence in the search history."

"Right. Hmm. What about ice? For the swelling?"

They're standing in the kitchen waiting for the angel's call. It's going to be anytime now. Hillary can feel it. She opens the commercial-size refrigerator, grabs some ice from the freezer, and wraps them in a tea towel.

"Maybe I should do it," Emeril says.

"No. She's clearly angry with you. You're the one who locked her in her room, remember?"

"You hit her on the head with a vase."

"Chalk and cheese." She waves him off, and she heads for the staircase at the back of the kitchen.

On the third floor, she pauses outside the nanny's bedroom door. She doesn't hear any sounds coming from the other side. They'd confiscated the nanny's phone and computer. A necessary precaution. They'd even removed the TV.

Quietly, Hillary unlocks the door and steps inside.

Rachel's in bed, sleeping, but her eyes open when she senses Hillary's presence. The nanny pulls herself up and clambers backward, pinning herself against the headboard. The sandwich on the tray that Hillary and Emeril left for her has been nibbled on and the water glass is empty.

Hillary walks up to the bed, sits on the mattress next to the girl. She holds up the tea towel. "Ice for your head." She puts it on the area where the bump would be.

Rachel's body is rigid. Her eyes wide, scared.

"I'm sorry about this," Hillary says. "I really am. It'll all be over soon. Then when you're feeling better, you can come downstairs and help me with Elsie. I still need your help, Rachel."

Rachel's eyes grow wider. Is it fear or shock? Hillary isn't sure. Maybe both. She wishes the girl would stop looking at her like that.

"Ma'am. Elsie is—"

"No, Rachel. She's not. You hit your head. You're confused."

"But ma'am—"

"No. You're confused. The baby is just fine." Hillary hears someone at the front door, voices in the foyer.

"But ma'am, I didn't hit my head. You—"

"Shush," Hillary says, and listens. She recognizes her mum's lilting tone. What's her mum doing here? She rarely comes to visit, and she's not the type of person who drops by unannounced. Everything her mum does is meticulously scheduled, planning her days down to the minutes. Two minutes to call a patient about test results. Five minutes if she's delivering bad news. Such is the life of a general surgeon. When Hillary was little and she wanted her mum to come around, she didn't, so what's she doing here now? How is she going to get rid of her?

Hillary turns to Rachel.

"Not a word. Do you hear me? Not a peep."

"But ma'am—"

She covers Rachel's mouth. "Not a word. Do you understand?"

Rachel nods.

"Good. I'd hate to have to give you another bump on that head of yours."

Hillary rushes from the room and locks the door behind her. Oh my god, she can't believe she's just threatened the nanny. *Who is she?* She runs down the long hall in her bare feet, down the steps to the second floor. Then she races down another long hall and stops at the top of the split staircase, clutching the railing, peering down at her mum and Emeril. Clarice is wearing slacks and little ballet flats. Her shirt is neatly tucked. A solitary diamond pendant hangs around her neck, a gift from Hillary's father when Hillary was born. She looks up at Hillary.

"What are you doing here?" Hillary asks.

"Is that any way to greet your mother?" Clarice says.

"Sorry. It's just that it's not like you to pop in without any notice. Is everything okay?"

"It is with me. I'm here because I was worried about you. You sounded—oh, I don't know—so *depressed* the last time we talked. I thought I should come and see for myself how you and the baby are holding up. Maybe there's something I can do to help."

Her mum is referring to the little pills she'd prescribed to Hillary in the days after Hillary had given birth. "Mommy's little helpers," Clarice had called them. Something to stave off the baby blues and tie Hillary over until her hormones had a chance to set themselves right. Hillary has been known to struggle with minor bouts of depression in the past, especially when things don't go her way. In the last few days, Hillary has stopped taking the little pills. Probably a mistake.

For a brief moment, Hillary considers confiding to her mum about what has happened to Elsie, because honestly she could use someone like her mum in her corner. Someone who is logical, if nothing else. Hillary would gladly take all the sensibleness she can get, but she dismisses the idea almost immediately. Clarice would not understand their situation, not with her strict ethical codes: one to practicing medicine and the other to having morals. This is the difference between Hillary's family and Emeril's. Even if her mum would entertain the idea of buying a baby (moral issues aside), she couldn't afford it. Not really. When a person has millions, dare she say billions, well, you rethink everything you once thought about the world you live in and what it can do for you. This is something Clarice could never grasp.

Emeril stands behind Clarice, a drink in his hand—scotch on the rocks—and silently he says to Hillary, *what do you want me to do?* Hillary's not sure, but he has to do something. Her mum cannot be here now. They both know she will not support their decision.

"Is the baby sleeping?" Clarice starts for the stairs.

Ma'am! Please!

"Is that the nanny?" Clarice pauses with her foot on the bottom step.

Hillary doesn't know what to do, what to say. "I—"

Emeril drops the scotch glass. It shatters on the black-and-white checkered tile floor. He falls to his knees. Before Clarice turns around, he slices his palm open on a large shard of glass.

"What is going on?" Clarice rushes over to Emeril.

His blood drips onto the perfectly polished tiles.

"Ow. Ow." He glances up at Hillary, trying to coax something out of her.

"Oh, dear, Em, are you okay?" She pauses at the top of the stairs as though she's going to come down, her mind racing, trying to figure out what Emeril is up to. The nanny calls for her again.

Ma'am!

Rachel isn't as scared of Hillary as she originally thought.

"You're going to need stitches," Clarice says. "I didn't bring my bag with me."

It takes Hillary a second, but she suddenly understands what Emeril's asking of her, what he's done. He's injured himself to get her mum out of the house, giving them more time to wait for the angel's call and to shut the nanny up.

"Mum, can you take Em to see Dr. Reginald? The baby is crying, and the nanny is calling for me. I should really go check on them."

The little lie hurts. There is no Elsie, no crying baby. Just Rachel, that cow. Dr. Reginald is the private physician they use whenever they spend time at the chateau. He's hired to be on call around the clock if they should need him.

"I'll let Reg know you're coming. Wait—" She runs to the nursery, grabs a muslin cloth from the closet and returns to the staircase. "Here." She tosses the cloth down to Clarice.

Her mum wraps it around Emeril's hand, and she leads him to the front door.

"Ohhh, ow." He pushes his mother-in-law out the door ahead of him. While her back is turned, he spins around and quickly tosses the burner phone up to Hillary. He seems to be saying he's done all he can, and their future is now in her hands. She's going to have to take the angel's call, confirm the time and place for the exchange, and calm the nanny down.

But his toss is short.

The burner phone seems to hang in midair just out of Hillary's reach. It can't drop. It will shatter like the scotch glass, and then how will the angel get in touch with them?

Hillary leans over the railing, stretching, tossing her arms into the open space below the crystal chandelier where not long ago she entertained the idea of dropping it on Emeril's head. She flings her body into the open space, her ankles hook onto a baluster, and she's flying, soaring through the air at the exact moment the front door closes, and her mum and Emeril disappear outside.

Months of taking aerial silks classes before the pregnancy have proven to be more rewarding than she could have ever hoped. Her body is limber, her arms and legs shaped into perfectly elongated muscle like an acrobat's—minus the soft, pillow belly. Forget about what the classes have done for her and Emeril's sex life. It's become clear the private lessons at the club with Phoebe, her personal instructor and fitness trainer, where Hillary has perspired all over the divine, smooth fabric, has served a bigger purpose.

Reaching, stretching, flying. The phone miraculously lands in her hand. She grips it in her palm as she dangles by her feet high above the foyer floor.

What a catch!

The blood rushes to her head as she hangs upside down and tries to catch her breath.

Ma'am!

Won't that girl ever be quiet?

She ignores the nanny. It's going to be hard to pull herself up. On the count of three. Using her arms, clutching the phone tightly in her grip, she swings her body, but she doesn't swing high enough to grab the baluster, and she finds herself dangling once again. If she falls from this height, she'll surely crack her head open, and what a mess that will make on the beautiful checkered floor.

Trying again. She summons all her strength, all of her determination, and sheer force of will. Once more on the count of three. This time she rocks back and forth, picking up momentum on each swing, faster and faster, higher and higher, imagining she is an acrobat under a big circus tent instead of a chandelier. She can almost feel the silky fabric cupping her bottom, cradling her, supporting her, lifting her, sliding between her legs as she reaches the railing.

The imaginary fabric glides through her thighs as she slips through the balusters. The silky material drifts away, floating to the floor below.

She's done it!

What a performance!

Bloody brilliant!

Ma'am!

Lying on her back in the hallway, staring at the extravagant circus tent chandelier, the burner phone covered in Emeril's blood pressed to her pounding heart, she smiles.

She couldn't have picked a better man.

CHAPTER
THIRTY-FOUR

Hester doesn't trust the cowboy. He says he agrees to the deal, but they're just words. At least she's bought herself a couple of hours, another night with Baby Ivy. In the meantime, she'll have to figure out how to make sure the cowboy keeps his promise after she tells him where the money is. *If* she tells him. Maybe Eve will come up with something.

One of them has to.

He is not going to steal the baby.

Hester is not going to let that happen.

Swaying gently, she rocks Ivy in her arms. Ivy gazes up at her. Hester wonders what she sees, if the baby mistakes Hester for her mother. Hester could be, she longs to tell her. If only Ivy was old enough to make the choice herself.

Ivy pulls her legs to her stomach and then she kicks. She does it several times before farting. Even the baby's flatulence is cute. Hester could gobble her up. She's such a lovable bundle of joy, but there will be time for snuggles and cuddles later.

Hester turns her focus to Fen, the dead guy, on her living room floor. "If we're not going to cut him up, how do you suggest we move him?"

The cowboy's rubbing his temple. In his other hand, the gun points to the floor. It's the first time it's not aimed at her or Eve. She isn't relieved by any means that he's relaxed his stance and points the barrel downward. Hester has seen how fast he pulls the trigger. He really is like a cowboy from one of them western movies she watches on TV, the ones with quick draws. He must practice an awful lot of target shooting.

Her rifle is lying on the floor underneath the chair he sits in. Unloaded. A lot of good it's going to do her there. Hester is a decent shot herself, but nowhere near his skills.

"I'm going to carry the baby," he says.

Hester immediately starts to protest, but she stops when he raises the gun.

"I'm going to carry the baby. You two will carry the body."

Hester is strong, and she knows despite Eve's size, she's strong, too. The dead asshole on the floor isn't big for a man. He's thin and kind of short. They could do it. They could lift him. Leave it to the women to do the heavy work. Isn't it always the way?

"I'll get his legs," Eve says.

"Now hold on." Hester hates to do it, but she doesn't see another way around it. She kisses Ivy's forehead, and she says to Eve, "Take the baby." Then she says to the cowboy, "I have something to help you. It's a front baby carrier. You strap it to your chest. I don't want you dropping her in the woods. It's going to be awfully dark out there. You're going to have to be extra careful."

Hester heads toward the hallway and back bedroom.

"Where are you going?" he asks.

"It's back here where I keep the baby stuff." She finds the front car-rier in the closet underneath a pile of pink footie sleepers. Ivy should be wearing something more than a diaper, and she pulls a pink onesie from the shelf. It should fit since she bought actual baby clothes for a real live baby even though she was only using them on the doll.

She returns to the living room. "Let's put the baby in some clothes, and then we'll get you strapped into this thing." She tosses the front carrier at the cowboy.

He catches it, grimacing when he raises his left arm, where the cuts on his shoulder bleed. The cowboy's injury is always in the back of her mind. It could be useful to her later.

Once the baby is clothed, Hester helps him put the front carrier on, and then she places the baby inside it.

"I'll get his legs." Eve squats near Fen's feet.

"Yeah, fine." Hester doesn't see what the big deal is. She slips her hands underneath the guy's armpits and lifts. Eve grabs his ankles. The two of them maneuver him out the front door. He's heavier than Hes-ter expected. She's already out of breath, and they haven't even left the porch.

The cowboy waits for them at the bottom of the steps. The stars flicker and shine against the night sky. The half-moon thinly illumi-nates the patch of yard creating small pockets of soft light and dark shadows.

Eve walks down the steps first, but she's moving too fast, and Hester starts to lose her grip.

"Slow down," she says, but it's too late. Her hands slip out from underneath Fen's arms, and she drops him.

Eve continues dragging him down the steps. His head smacks against each stair.

Thump. Thump. Thump.

"Well, shit," Hester says, but it's not like he can feel it.

She grabs him under the arms again, and they carry him across the small yard. They drop him on the ground next to the toolshed. The cowboy opens the door.

"I can't see anything. We should've brought the lantern."

"Get out of the way." Hester pushes him aside. She doesn't need to see. When you live alone, you know where you put things, and they don't move unless you move them.

Reaching into the shed, she feels for the hooks on the wall, counts four across. *Found them.* She grabs the two shovels: a square digger and a pointed digger. The square digger she uses for edging and moving small bushes. The pointed digger is for cutting through roots and removing rocks. On the other side of the shed, closer to her feet, is the fancy chain saw.

"Last chance to use the chain saw."

No one says anything.

"Kidding. Geez. Where's your sense of humor?"

The cowboy carries the shovels. The two women pick up Fen, and they make their way toward the trees.

"How are we going to see?" the cowboy asks. "Are you sure we're not going to get lost?"

"I know my way," Hester says. "Just follow me. I know a perfect spot. And be quiet."

The trio leave the yard and enter the cover of trees. The woods have a personality all their own. Hester listens, searching for the familiar sounds of the creatures, sniffing the air for the scent of maple and pine. She's lived here long enough to have learned what noises the woods make, the sounds of the seasons, and the animals who accompany them. The woods are like a parent and the animals her children, and both have adopted Hester as one of their own. They have revealed to her their secrets, where the soil is soft, less rocky, and good places to dig.

The night has grown darker under the trees. The branches throw shadows as black as pitch along the ground. A light breeze rustles the leaves. The cool air dries the sweat on Hester's brow. The cowboy's body heat will keep the baby from catching a chill. She can't say the same for Eve. Hester swears she can hear the girl's teeth chattering.

"You're not from around here, are you?" Hester asks her.

"I'm from nowhere," Eve says.

"No talking," the cowboy says. "I thought we were supposed to be quiet." He's walking behind Eve. Baby Ivy seems content in the carrier.

Hester ignores him. "Nights get cool this far north, even in the summer and especially under these trees."

"I'll remember to pack warmer clothes on my next visit," Eve says. "How much farther?"

"We're almost there." Hester's leading them in the opposite direction of where the guy was hanging in the tree, away from the lake, and deeper into the woods.

They bump along slowly, noisily. It's not easy moving a body through the brush and maze of saplings. It doesn't help that Fen gets heavier with each step. Hester watches where she puts her feet as best she can in the dark. Every now and again, she catches a glimpse of the gun in the cowboy's hand, the shiny barrel reflecting off a sliver of moonlight.

Eve stumbles and falls, landing on top of Fen's legs. She lies on top of him, breathing heavily. "I need to rest."

Hester releases his upper body, letting his shoulders and head hit the ground.

Thunk.

Screw setting him down gently. Her arms are tired from carrying his heavy ass around. Besides, he doesn't deserve kindness from her even in death. If he had his way, he would've killed her. He would've killed all of them. Hester plops down next to him, trying to catch her breath. The front of her pants is wet with his blood.

The cowboy leans against a nearby tree.

"Do you smell something?" he asks.

"No," she says.

He opens his arms, the gun in one hand, the shovels in the other. "I think she took a shit," he says of Baby Ivy.

"Yeah, well, I didn't bring another diaper with me so deal with it."

The cowboy steps away from the tree, waves his arms around, as if he's trying to air out the smell, as if he can get away from it.

"Watch where you swing those shovels."

Not far from where she's sitting, in a patch of small plants, something bluish reflects off that same slice of moonbeam. Probably trash. She reaches for it; she'll toss it in the garbage when she gets home.

It's a can of chewing tobacco. It doesn't look like it's been out in the elements long, and she opens it, sniffs it. It smells fresh and minty.

Finders keepers, she thinks, and she sticks it in her back pocket.

While the cowboy is distracted by the pooping baby, Eve has been rustling around Fen's legs. The girl is looking for something. Whatever it is, Eve has shoved it into the back of her shorts.

"Break's over," the cowboy says. "Are you sure you don't smell that?"

"Stop your bellyaching." Hester pulls herself up.

Eve grabs Fen's ankles. Hester slips her hands underneath his arms, and they're moving again.

For the next fifteen minutes, they shuffle along, Hester walking backwards, leading the way. On occasion, her back strikes the trunk of a tree. The third time it happens, it starts to hurt.

"You could warn me, you know," she says to the cowboy. He has a better view of the direction they're heading, since he's not burdened with carrying a dead body.

"I can't see a damn thing. I told you we should've brought the lantern."

"Oh, yeah, like that wouldn't draw attention to what we're doing."

"Who's going to see us out here?"

"Would you two shut up," Eve says. "You bicker like an old married couple."

The cowboy scoffs at that, and Hester chuckles. How absurd. Married couple. Hester is twice his age. She may be a lot of things, but she's no cougar. She bets fancy pants here is very particular about the women he dates. They're probably all models, rich girls who spend a fortune on their looks.

Finally, at the edge of a knoll, they stop. The ground underneath her feet is soft and spongy.

"This is it."

They drop Fen's body.

"About fucking time." The cowboy tosses the shovels on the ground in front of them. "Get digging."

"Why do we even have to bury him? Can't we just leave him here?" Eve asks.

"No." Hester picks up the shovels and hands one to Eve. Hester wants to bury him. It will give her more time to figure out what she's going to do about the cowboy, and how she's going to get rid of him.

Hester and Eve get to work. It's not easy digging a hole big enough for a dead man, even a small one like Fen. It would've been much easier if he was in pieces. They could've carried him in garbage bags, dug a couple small holes here and there, easy peasy. Digging a full-size grave is a grueling job. Surprisingly, Eve isn't complaining. The girl seems to take to the work. It's something they have in common.

It takes them two hours to dig the hole deep enough before they can throw the body in. The work goes much quicker when they toss the dirt on top. They don't talk while they work.

When they're finished, the cowboy snatches the shovels from Hester's and Eve's hands, as if he's afraid they'll hit him with them. They wouldn't dare with the baby strapped to his chest. The cowboy must know that. It's probably why he insisted on carrying the baby in the first place.

"Get us out of here," he says.

Hester leads them back the way they came. The new sweat on her back dries in the cool air, giving her chills. She must have seven layers of sweat on her, collecting in rows on her skin. Eve's teeth are back to chattering by the time they reach the cottage. They sit on the steps of the porch, dirty and tired. Burying a body is hard work. No one tells you that up front, do they? It's something you find out only when you have to.

The cowboy leans on one of the shovels. For a moment, it almost feels as if they're coworkers, taking a break after a long night on the job. Or maybe they're a family. Eve and the cowboy and their baby, visiting Hester, their mother, helping her plant a garden.

Hester allows herself these little daydreams. She's been alone for such a long time, she relies on them for entertainment. She glances at Eve sitting beside her, and then at the cowboy and Baby Ivy, who's asleep in a diaper full of shit. Hester has forgotten how nice it is to have company. Even the killing kind.

The can of chewing tobacco in her back pocket pokes her in the butt. Her hand is sore and her shoulder aches when she reaches behind her to pull it out. Then she tucks a pinch of chew inside her bottom lip. It's quite refreshing.

"That's disgusting," the cowboy says.

The revolted look on his face makes her smile. She hands the can to Eve to see if she wants in on the action.

"Don't do it," he says to Eve. "You'll look as vulgar as she does."

Eve tucks a wad of chew inside her bottom lip.

Atta girl, Hester thinks. She guesses Eve does it to prove a point or to show a kind of camaraderie with Hester. They're on the same side, at least for now, anyway.

Hester spits on the ground near the cowboy's feet.

He jumps to get out of the way, but not before placing a protective hand on the baby strapped to his chest. "Watch the shoes."

Hester and Eve laugh. Then Eve spits near his feet, and he dances out of the way again.

"That's not funny."

They continue laughing at him, spitting at his feet, watching him dance.

"Stop it. I mean it. Enough already." The cowboy looks at Hester. "You really need to change this diaper."

Hester's feeling the lightness of the moment and she says, "Let her mom, here, change that one." She bumps Eve's shoulder playfully.

The mood shifts suddenly, swiftly. All of the fun of a second ago has been sucked out of the air. No one moves.

"What did I say?"

The cowboy looks her over. His face gets clearer with each passing moment, because as the moon sets, the sun rises, the sky slowly brightening in the early dawn.

He laughs. "Girl's not the baby's mother."

231

CHAPTER
THIRTY-FIVE

Y ou're not her mother?" Hester asks.

"No. Why would you think that?"

Although Eve has an idea why Hester would assume that she's Baby Ivy's mom. Eve did show up at her door in the middle of the night with Ivy in her arms. Eve supposes on some level she's allowed Hester to believe what she wanted to believe, and she used it to her advantage to get Hester to take her in. But after Fen showed up, she just assumed Hester had caught on to what was really going on and to what Eve's involved in.

Hester jumps up from the porch step. "You lying bitch!" She storms into the cottage.

"Go, go, go, follow her." The cowboy waves his gun at Eve to get moving.

Eve spits the wad of chew from her mouth, and she drags herself from the step. A disgusted look crosses the cowboy's face. *Good.* There's satisfaction in repulsing him, and an unexpected bonus—the chew tobacco didn't taste half bad.

She crosses the porch and enters the cottage. Her body is sore and bruised. All that shoveling didn't help. Her arms hang at her sides: her biceps like wilting leaves, her bones like splintered limbs. Any movement on her part and her arms might just fall off.

Hester's storming around the cottage, slamming the windows closed as though she needs to bang something to release her anger, and then she turns on them, hands on her hips. "Shoot her," she says to the cowboy.

"What the hell, old woman?" Eve says.

"You lied to me. You're not the baby's mother any more than I am." Hester looks to the cowboy. "Shoot her, and then you and I can make a new deal."

"What kind of new deal?" the cowboy asks.

"Hold on a second," Eve says.

"Shut up." The cowboy makes a point of aiming the gun in her direction. "Go on," he says to Hester.

"I'll tell you where your money is if I can keep the baby. Then you can go on your merry way like this whole thing never happened."

"I can't do that. I promised my clients a baby. *This* baby. I have a reputation to uphold."

Eve crosses her arms, feeling smug. There's no bargaining with him. Why hasn't Hester figured this out already?

"Fine, have it your way. Now, give me the baby so I can change her, or do you like the smell of shit under your nose?" Hester waves her hands at the cowboy, motioning for him to give her the child.

While the two of them fuss with getting Ivy out of the front carrier, Eve sits on the couch, but first, she turns off the fan. Hot and cold. Dry and wet. She hasn't been comfortable since she got here, and yet, it's the most comfortable she's ever been. Eve has lived in her own filth enough times to not let it bother her. She's sat in her own urine, in

233

other people's urine, laid on a mattress soaked with all kinds of bodily fluids. If the last few days have shown her anything, it's that her circumstances have improved.

And still it's not enough.

The remnants of the minty chew tobacco can't hide the taste of freedom that's been on her tongue ever since the stormy night in the woods. She'll never be able to get rid of it. It's embedded in her mouth. It's filled her lungs and swelled her heart. Once a person breathes it in, it becomes a part of them that they can't live without. They'll fight for it even if it kills them.

Fen's ice pick jabs her side. The point digs into her flesh. Neither Hester nor the cowboy knows she removed it from Fen's calf when they were in the woods.

The cowboy sits in his favorite chair, pointing his favorite gun at them. The front baby carrier is strapped to his bare chest on one side. The other side flaps open where Hester has removed the baby.

Hester changes Ivy's diaper on the floor at Eve's feet, but she's put her back to her, as if she can't stand to look at her.

"Well, now I know why you're not breastfeeding," Hester says. "It's because you can't."

"I never said I was her mother."

"You let me think you were and that's the same as lying."

"I needed your help. The baby needed your help. *Needs* your help. You're really good with her, you know."

"You think so?" Hester looks over her shoulder at Eve.

"Yeah, I do. You're a really good mom."

Instincts have taught Eve to say the right thing under the right circumstances. It's how she's stayed alive in the underbelly of the world. Tell them what they want to hear, and they won't hurt you. Give them want they want, and they won't beat you. Do as you're told, and they won't kill you.

Eve has come to understand that Hester has never cared about helping her. It's always been about the baby. Hester protected Eve, because she believed Eve was the mother. It was the only reason, and now that Hester knows the truth, everything has changed.

If Eve had figured this out sooner, say on that very first night with Hester, she could've gotten the money and been long gone by now. Eve is typically quicker, sharper, in these types of situations, but this newfound opportunity for a chance at freedom has not only surprised her, but it's also knocked her around, and somehow, she's lost her edge.

Maybe it's not too late to make her own kind of deal with Hester. The cowboy seems content for the time being to let the women battle this out on their own. Or is he just tired from the long night in the woods? His skin seems paler than usual and beads of sweat are covering his bare chest.

"Tell me where the money is," Eve says. "And I'll let you keep the baby."

Hester stares at Eve. "You'd let me keep her?"

"She's an orphan, and she needs a good home. I think you'd give her one."

Hester hitches her thumb in the direction of the cowboy. "But what do we do about him?"

"We kill him."

"Let me get this straight," Hester says. "We kill him, and then I tell you where the money is and you leave, but the baby stays here with me?"

"Yes."

Hester nods. "Okay. I'm in."

They both look at the cowboy.

He's shaking his head. "You seem to have forgotten something." He raises the gun to make his point.

Hester turns back to Eve. "That is a problem." She picks up the baby and goes to the kitchen.

"What're you doing?" the cowboy asks.

"She's hungry. I'm getting her a bottle."

While Hester bangs around in the kitchen, trying to prepare a bottle with one hand while holding the baby with the other, Eve senses an opportunity.

"Why don't you take that baby carrier off? You look ridiculous with it hanging on you." If she can get close to him, she can better assess what's going on with him, if he's weakening possibly from exhaustion or from the loss of blood from his shoulder wound.

"That would require using both my hands, and I'm not about to put my gun down."

"Suit yourself. It was worth a shot."

"You have to take them when you can."

"Do you want me to help you get it off?"

"No."

"My word, you're paranoid. Look." She holds up her hands. "I'm unarmed. You can point the gun at me the whole time."

He looks past her shoulder at Hester in the kitchen.

"She's holding the baby. There's no way she's going to do anything, especially with the baby in her arms."

The cowboy seems to consider Eve's offer. He has to be uncomfortable with the strap cutting crossing his injured shoulder. He's definitely tired. They all are. Hester continues fiddling around in the kitchen, heating up the bottle.

"Fine," he says. "But get up slowly and keep your hands raised." He stands from the chair.

Eve does exactly what he asks. She stops in front of him, hands raised. Hester is standing by the stove, watching them. Eve can feel the woman's eyes on her back.

"Are you sure you know how to take this off? Maybe the witch should do it."

"Stop whining." Eve lowers her arms. "I'm going to unclip the strap at the bottom where it's hooked, and then I'm going to slip it over your shoulder. You shouldn't have to lift your arm. Just don't shoot me if it hurts, okay?"

She takes a step closer. This is the closest she's ever been to him without his hands squeezing her upper arms, tossing her around as if she's some kind of rag doll. What she notices are the dark roots of his hair. They're almost black compared to the rest of his bleached-blond head. Dark stubble covers his cheeks and chin. He's in need of a shave. When she meets his gaze, she notices the green flecks in his eyes and something else—the lack of trust.

He puts the barrel of the gun between her eyebrows. "Don't try anything stupid."

Sweat breaks out on her forehead, stings the open wound where she was cut with Logan's knife. More sweat drips down her back. It's not the first time she's had a gun pressed against her skin. Shot wielded his nine-millimeter like a toy, probing and prodding. It was his own sick, twisted form of foreplay, terrorizing her with his weapon, while the other girls in the stable performed for him.

The only difference now is that this is not a game. This is life or death. Honestly, she can't decide which is worse.

The cowboy searches her face, probably looking for fear in her eyes. Maybe that's what gets him off. He wouldn't be the first bastard who gets their kicks from scaring women, but something tells her it's not what drives him. He kills cleanly, free from emotion. He doesn't like to mess around with his victims, taking his one shot and ending their life as quickly as he can.

"I swear I won't try anything stupid."

She's weak from the night's exertions, but her adrenaline is kicking in. She has to take her chance now, because she might not get another opportunity. She takes a small step away from the gun, and she waits for the explosion to go off inside her head, but he doesn't pull the trigger. Positioning herself on his left side, where the clip on the strap is located, she leans over and unfastens it. Then she looks him in the eyes, makes sure it's all right for her to continue.

He nods and lowers the gun so it's no longer aimed at her head but rather at her torso.

She moves the strap down, sliding it over his wounded shoulder with her left hand a careful inch at a time. The scratches on his skin are deep and oozing pus. The pungent smell tells her they're infected.

This is a good sign. An infection could weaken him further.

Her right hand reaches behind her back.

Her heart is pumping wildly in her chest.

Easy.

She finds the handle of the ice pick that she's tucked in her shorts. It feels cool in her sweaty palm.

"Almost off." She glides the strap over his elbow.

With one swift motion, she pulls the ice pick from her shorts. She sees the whites of the cowboy's eyes as she plunges the pick deep into his side with every last bit of strength she has left.

"You fucking bitch!"

The gun goes off.

She stumbles backward.

Bits and pieces of ceiling rain down on her.

Is she shot?

She doesn't feel pain anywhere.

The baby is crying.

Somewhere behind her Hester is hollering, but she can't make out what the woman is saying. The handle of the ice pick sticks out of the cowboy's side. Drops of blood dot his taut stomach. The front baby carrier hangs off his forearm, soaking up more blood, before dripping it onto the floor next to the chair. He stares at her as though he's in disbelief. He touches his side, then looks at the blood on his hand.

Eve steps farther away from him, bumps into something, some kind of furniture.

The couch.

She's disoriented.

It's as though everything is happening in some kind of alternate universe.

Eve has never stabbed someone before. She's never been the aggressor, if she doesn't count attacking him with a rock or punching Hester with her fists. Eve has always been the victim until now, and she has certainly never tried to kill someone.

She's not sure how she feels about sinking an ice pick into the cowboy's flesh. She thought she'd feel elated to stick it to him. Finally, she could get some satisfaction—revenge—on the bastards who have stuck their fingers in her, starved her, raped her, and treated her as though she was a piece of property. They did what they wanted with her without any regard to the fact that she was a human being.

Take that, asshole, she thinks, but she feels no satisfaction in what she's done. She's no better than he is. She's sunk to his level, fallen to the depths of hell alongside all her other captors.

It's not what she expected.

And still, she wants him dead.

CHAPTER
THIRTY-SIX

Laura has been up all night checking her phone, waiting for Agent Ring to get back to her. He hasn't responded to her texts about the possibility that the young woman behind the dumpster could have a baby out there somewhere. According to the autopsy report, the girl's uterus had been slightly enlarged and her breasts had been engorged. Both signs that she'd had a baby as recently as a couple of weeks ago.

Laura has already called several hospitals in the Burgh. There's no record of a young woman delivering a baby who fits the description Laura has given them. It's possible the woman had the baby in another city, another hospital, or maybe she didn't go to a hospital at all.

Laura makes a list of clinics and shelters in the area around the alleyway. Then she checks her phone, puts it down. Agent Ring not only hasn't texted her back, but he also hasn't responded to her email and the files on Kayleigh that she sent to him.

Maybe it's time she learns more about the agent's case.

Sipping her third cup of coffee, she pulls up Logan Mense's arrest history on her laptop. He's a colorful guy for someone so young. A couple stints in the penitentiary for minor drug offenses, carrying while on probation, and breaking and entering. Nothing that warrants the attention of the FBI.

She stumbles onto Logan's older brother: a Norman "Shot" Mense. He doesn't have quite the rainbow of a record like his younger brother. There's mention of two arrests, though, both for charges of sex trafficking, but they haven't been able to make either of them stick. It seems he gets arrested and twenty-four hours later he's a free man. No wonder Agent Ring is protective of his case. He doesn't want to let this guy walk free for a third time. Laura imagines the agent's reputation is on the line. A dangerous place for any cop to be.

She spends the next thirty minutes reading about the dark web where the Norman "Shot" Menses of the world do business. It's where sex trafficking and human trafficking sets up its roots, and those roots run deep into the underground. Laura isn't sure how to access them even now that she's found the tree. She's savvy enough around computers to get by, though, and after a couple of clicks on obscure links, she pulls up several images she wishes she didn't see. There are so many sites to sift through. It feels like an impossible task to see if Kayleigh's image comes up on one of them.

When Laura's stomach can't take much more, she shuts the computer down, checks her phone yet again. Agent Ring still hasn't responded.

She stretches, rubs her eyes, and finishes the rest of her coffee. Rays from the early morning sun cut across her desk. There's finally enough light for her to check the one place she's been dreading all night. She's waited long enough for the agent to get back to her. She'll just have to find out for herself if the alley (but really, she's thinking of the dumpster) has been thoroughly searched.

Grabbing her car keys, she heads to her SUV and drives to the Burgh. She doesn't bother checking in at the office, going straight to the alley, blocking the entrance with her vehicle.

Before she heads to the dumpster, she steps into the coffee shop. It's locally owned and has a hippie vibe going for it with its far-out colors of yellows and oranges. Several small tables are scattered about the space. The seats next to the large windows are the coveted spots.

Heads turn when she walks in and just as quickly drop back to their phones and computer screens. Everyone's paranoid they're doing something wrong. Maybe some of them should be worried if they're sexting, watching porn, or surfing the dark web using Tor.

"Hi," Laura says to the barista, whose name tag reads Chloe, with a big smiley face in the center of the o. "I wonder if you can tell me the last time the dumpster was emptied?"

"Oh, right, well they were supposed to empty it yesterday, but well, you guys were in the alley most of the day, and they couldn't get back there. So, it hasn't been emptied since last week. I'm not sure when they'll be back to pick it up. Maybe not until next week. Is there a problem?"

"No problem. I'm going to take a look, though, so hold off on sending any more trash out there for a little while."

"Yeah, sure. Do you want an iced mocha latte to cool you off some? I hear it's going to be another hot one today. It's on the house." Chloe gives Laura a big, bright smile.

"No, thanks. It's against policy, but I appreciate the offer." If she drinks any more caffeine, she thinks, her hands will start to shake. They're shaking enough as it is.

Laura exits the shop and heads to the alley, slipping on latex gloves. The large metal dumpster huddles near the coffee shop's brick wall. She stands in front of it, questioning whether she really wants to do this. She doesn't have to do it. Let the FBI handle it.

She sighs. Because of the kind of person she is, the kind of *mother* she is, she won't be able to rest until she knows for certain whether there's any chance that there's a baby inside. She feels she owes it to the young woman to look.

Lifting the dumpster's lid, she pushes it against the wall. The smell that drifts out of the open container crinkles her nose: a week's worth of moldy food and sour-milk lattes shoved in plastic garbage bags. There are other odors, too, of rotten eggs and ass. The smells seem to get worse with each bag she opens.

The one thing she's not getting a whiff of—a corpse.

After searching the last bag, she's relieved the whole dirty process is over. There's hope the young woman's baby is still out there somewhere, alive and well, swaddled in someone's arms. Laura's thoughts jump to Hester, but her cousin always comes to mind whenever there's any mention of babies. It's hard to separate the two given Hester's history.

She tosses the bags back into the metal container, along with the latex gloves, and closes the lid. Then she climbs into the SUV, catching the end of a call on the radio from dispatch.

Joe jumps on. "I'm on my way."

Denise gives him the address.

Hearing his voice, a deep baritone that seems to come straight from his chest, has a way of reaching down and softening Laura's insides. It's exactly what she's been trying to avoid all this time. These types of feelings have no place on the job.

"Say again." Laura releases the button, waiting for his reply, but the radio is silent.

Fine. I'll just meet you there, she thinks. Then Denise jumps on, repeating the information to Laura.

Someone called in about an abandoned black sport utility vehicle with an out of state license plate. It was spotted by a couple of concerned citizens. They said it's been sitting at the edge of the parking lot for several days at the southern end of the lake.

CHAPTER
THIRTY-SEVEN

For the second time, the girl surprises Noah.

He presses his hand to his side. His fingers straddle the object that's lodged in his torso. It's not a knife. The part of the metal that hasn't been shoved into his flesh feels round between his fingers. It's some kind of poker or perhaps it's a kind of pick. Where did she get it? It could've come from Fen. It was too dark in the woods when she was carrying Fen's body to keep track of her every move. Maybe she lifted it off the dead man when Noah wasn't looking.

"Fuck! It hurts!"

He should've patted Fen down and searched for any other weapons outside of the nine-millimeter before he allowed the women to move the guy.

It's Noah's mistake.

His fault.

He shot a bullet into the ceiling when he could've easily put it in the girl's head. It took a behemoth amount of restraint on his part. She has no idea how lucky she is to be alive. It's an improvement in his self-control. He gets another gold star for his performance. Although, it may be premature, because he's aiming the gun at her. His finger is on the trigger. Any second, he could pull it and show the little pissant who's boss. He's shaking with rage, but no matter. Even shaking, he's an excellent shot.

"Please, don't shoot me," Girl says. "You need me to cross the border. Remember? You still need me."

Noah knows that. Otherwise, she'd already be dead.

"Sit," he says, and the girl drops onto the couch. "You, too," he says to the witch.

The baby has stopped crying now that she has a bottle in her mouth. The witch joins the girl on the couch.

Noah slumps in the chair. Sweat drips in his eyes and he blinks it away.

"Neither one of you makes a move unless I say so. You even flinch and I'll blow your fucking heads off."

A stream of light from the window cuts across the living room floor, shining on the coagulating blood that oozed from the hole in Fen's head during last night's adventure. Noah can smell the sharp tanginess of it. The metallic taste is in his mouth and on his tongue. Come to think of it, maybe it's his own blood he's eating.

As long as he leaves the pick in, he shouldn't bleed to death, but how is he going to meet with his clients looking like he does? The clothes he shoved into a leather bag in the back of the SUV are slim fitting. Noah likes his T-shirts snugging his chest and arms. His abs. He has a good physique. Scratch that. He has a *great* physique, and he's worked hard for it, spending long hours at the athletic club just a few blocks from his apartment in the city. Noah has been a loyal member for the last five years.

He'll never be able to hide the bloody pick sticking out of his side underneath the shirt he's packed, but he can't let his clients see him like this. It will frighten them. They may not want to go through with the transaction. Part of how his business operates successfully is his capacity to understand his clients' needs and their unwavering belief in appearances above all else. Noah shows up polished and pressed with whatever they've requested from him, in this case a baby, and they buy into it. They don't see the dirty parts of the business. The blood and guts, the thugs and whores. *And witches.* Noah protects them from it, and he does it willingly. He would even say happily.

He tries to think of some way to conceal the wooden handle poking out of his side, but he's not coming up with anything. He should've packed a sport coat. He'll just have to worry about it later. Right now, he has to stay focused, alert, while he waits for Shot. The only way for Noah to keep all of the money is if Shot is dead. Sooner or later the guy is going to turn up. Once he does, Noah's going to put a bullet between his eyebrows for the insult and for fucking with his business. When he's through with Shot, then he'll proceed to rip the witch's fingernails off one at a time, until she tells him where she's hidden *his fucking money!*

He leans into the pain searing his side. Getting worked up only makes it hurt more. The switchblade in his pocket jabs his groin. He pulls it out with some difficulty and hides it in the palm of his hand. Somewhere in the back of his mind a little voice whispers, telling him that he doesn't need the girl after all. All he really needs is her sneakers. He can get by without her. The witch can take care of the baby for him until he meets with his clients. She can pretend to be his mother or mother-in-law in the eyes of border patrol. With his connections, he should be able to sort out a passport for her without too much difficulty. It could work. Damn straight it could. He doesn't have to wait until he's across the border to kill the girl. He can shoot her right now for stabbing him.

But what fun would that be?

"Come here," he says to her.

"No."

"If you don't come here, I'll shoot you, because guess what? I just realized something. I don't need you anymore."

"Yes, you do."

"No, I don't. I have Witch, here. She'll come with me and the baby."

"Like hell I will," Witch says.

"Then I'll shoot you instead of Girl. I only need one of you. So, which is it? Make up your minds. I don't have all day."

He's lying, of course, because he really only needs the witch now that he has a new plan. He can kill the witch easily enough after he crosses the border. Then he'll deliver the baby to his clients and return to the cottage to look for the rest of his money, but only after he gets his shoulder and side stitched up. Eventually, he'll find the money, every last one-hundred-dollar bill, because he's lucky that way. He wonders why he didn't think of this sooner? Perhaps because his head doesn't feel right. It's possible he has a fever.

The witch and the girl are looking at each other as though they're trying to decide their next move. Noah's tired of waiting, and he fires a warning shot over the girl's shoulder to scare her into doing what he asks.

"What did you go ahead and do that for?" Witch says.

Noah ignores the witch, and he says to the girl, "The next bullet will be in your head. Now, come here."

"If I do, do you promise not to shoot me?"

Noah considers her request and thinks, why the hell not? He has other plans for her, anyway.

"Absolutely. You have my word."

"Pfft," Witch says. "Your word. That's laughable."

The girl stands.

The witch grabs the girl's forearm and shakes her head, warning her not to go. "You should've stabbed him in the neck," Witch says.

The girl yanks her arm away. Slowly, she walks over to where he's sitting, and she stops in front of him. "What do you want?"

"Come a little closer."

She glances over her shoulder at the witch. The witch shakes her head again. Then the girl takes another small step. Her knees almost brush against his.

"Closer."

She hesitates. Her gaze goes to the gun in his hand.

Noah points the barrel away from her. "This is between us. It's about the money, and I don't want the witch to hear what I have to say."

The girl is staring at his face, looking in his eyes, trying to get a read on him. He has no idea what she sees, but she doesn't seem all that afraid of him—and she should be.

She takes another tiny step toward him, leans in to hear his secret.

Noah presses the button on the handle of the switchblade. The knife springs out, and he shoves it deep into her side. It takes less than a second for the blade to slide into her flesh. She gasps. Now she is the one who is surprised.

"Tit for tat," he says in her ear.

CHAPTER
THIRTY-EIGHT

K arl squats behind a stack of firewood: a double-barrel shotgun in his hands. The sun is on his back. The shadows from the trees sway on the ground in front of him. He's sweating, dressed in full camouflage gear from his head to his toes. The twigs and leaves he's stuck in his trucker hat are itchy. He sticks a finger underneath the cap and scratches his scalp.

Karl and his dad left their house at the break of dawn. It's taken them a couple of hours to move through the woods as quietly and cautiously as they could. They've finally reached their destination: the witch's cottage.

The muscles in Karl's arm and back twitch. Even one of his eyelids is twitching. He doesn't know why his nerves are jumping and jerking around. So far, everything is going as planned. He knows the woods and he knows the sounds that make up the space. He didn't hear anything unusual as they sneaked their way here. Nothing to cause alarm. The birds haven't shut up all morning. A good sign. It's when the birds are silent that you have to worry. Even now, they're chattering. It's giving him a headache.

"Shake it off, Karl," he says into the dewy air, and then he stretches his arm, flexes the muscle, and rubs his eye. He has a clear view of the side of the cottage and window, and he doesn't see any movement inside.

His dad is making his way to the front of the yard. Karl can just make him out between the trees and brush. Occasionally, a twig snaps underneath his father's boot. Karl cringes. What his dad lacks in stealth, he makes up for in brains. His dad is the smartest man he knows. Derrick always used to say, "You may not have a lot of smarts and I may have some, but your dad is the smartest man I know."

Karl takes comfort in his cousin's words, and he trusts that his dad knows what he's doing. Karl's in good hands with his dad at the helm. Although, at the moment, he's torn. He's not supposed to leave his position but the noise his dad is making is causing him concern. He decides the best thing for him to do is to take a peek at his dad's progress. He has his dad's back if something goes awry.

He crawls on his hands and knees through a patch of thistle, then lies on the dirt floor. His shirt rides up and debris sticks to his skin. The ground feels cool in the shady spots and warm where the sun's rays graze the earth. The shotgun shells on his belt press into his hips. Twenty-five shells are a bit much, but they give him a sense of security. He stayed up late into the night practicing loading and unloading the shotgun. Karl needs to be able to do it quickly if he's going to have any chance against this guy. He saw how fast the guy pulled his gun and put it to Derrick's forehead. Karl doesn't even remember having time to blink.

From his belly, he spies his dad standing behind a splintered tree. From the scar on the bark, it looks as if it's been struck by lightning. One of its thick branches is missing. It explains the freshly cut wood on top of the stack of old firewood he's supposed to be crouching behind for cover. His dad steps away from the tree, rifle aimed and ready to shoot. He's also dressed in head-to-toe camouflage. His dad scurries through the small patch of yard, if you can call it a yard. It's mostly stiltgrass with the odd wild bush. Several ferns fan out alongside the porch. Moss grows on the stone walls. There's an energy to the place that gives Karl the creeps.

Voices are coming from inside.

A shot is fired.

His dad races toward the cottage and presses his back against the stone wall.

Someone is yelling.

It sounds like a female.

It could be the witch.

"What did you go ahead and do that for?" the voice says.

Karl doesn't hear a reply. It's good if they're arguing. Even better if they're trying to kill one another. They'll be distracted. Karl pulls himself up. He doesn't see his dad anymore, and he wonders if he's made it onto the porch.

Creeping back to his position behind the firewood, he decides to wait a few more seconds to make sure his dad is set. This is the part of their plan that's a little dicey. Karl can't see from his position at the side of the cottage whether his dad has made it to the front door. It's not going to work if his dad's not in position, waiting to burst inside.

Karl counts—one Mississippi, two Mississippi, three Mississippi— he raises the shotgun. Four Mississippi, Five Mississippi—

He thinks about Derrick, the hole between his cousin's eyebrows. It shakes the nerves right out of him—six Mississippi, seven Mississippi—the muscles in his arm and back have stopped twitching—eight Mississippi. His eyes are clear, unblinking—nine Mississippi—

He lines up his shot, aiming for one of the living room windows.

Ten Mississippi.

"This is for you, Derrick."

CHAPTER
THIRTY-NINE

Eve stumbles backward and falls onto the floor in front of the couch, hitting her ass hard when she goes down. She touches her side where Logan's switchblade hangs out of her. The living room window has shattered, spraying glass all over the floor, cutting her shins and thighs. Blood soaks her shirt, or rather Hester's shirt. The one Eve borrowed after her only shower on that first day here, after she showed up in the middle of the night at this wretched cottage.

The front door bursts open. A man in full camouflage gear enters, aiming a rifle at Eve, then at Hester, and then he stops on the cowboy. The man's face is painted. Eve is feeling a little disoriented and lightheaded. She wonders if she's somehow entered into some kind of fucked-up war zone. One thing she's certain of, he's not a cop, and he's not here to help. If he was a cop, there would be a team of them, yelling for them to drop their weapons, raise their hands. Of course, she doesn't have a weapon, unless she pulls the knife out of her side.

In the next second, another man enters through the front door. He's also dressed in camouflage, and his face is painted. Twigs and leaves stick out of his trucker hat. It looks ridiculous. He's pointing a shotgun at the cowboy. Stupid hat guy kicks the front door closed with his heavy boot.

For a fleeting moment, she thinks they're here for her. Some of Shot's soldiers perhaps. But it's becoming clear, they have no interest in her. They're both concentrating on the cowboy, who hasn't moved or said a word, although he's now aiming his gun at the camo guys and not at Hester and Eve.

Hester is the first one to speak up. The baby cries in her arms.

"Are you fucking crazy shooting out my window? You could've hit the baby!"

"Sorry about that," the first camo man who entered the cottage says. "How are you, Hester?"

"No names," the cowboy says. "She goes by Witch."

"Yeah, that's good," the second guy in the stupid hat says. "She is a witch. She eats babies."

His voice is familiar, Eve thinks. Where has she heard it before?

"Keep your mouth shut, Karl," the first guy says to the second guy.

Eve recognizes the guy's name as well as the voice. She presses her hand firmly against her side, trying to stop the bleeding, and eyes up this Karl guy. He's hiding behind face paint, but she knows exactly who he is now. He's one of the monsters from the hunting cabin.

Eve has a long history in that shack.

It's where she was taken to be seasoned by Logan, before she could be considered part of Shot's stable. Logan was joined by this man standing here now, along with one other guy she tries hard to obliterate from her mind. But she can't forget Karl, not while he's here in front of her, and she's once again on the floor. What she remembers about Karl was how different he was from the other two, how he was reluctant to go along with them. He needed to be persuaded. It's amazing how far one will go with a little peer pressure, because Karl not only aimed his urine at her, but with some prodding, he also mounted her from behind like the coward he is. He wasn't able to look at her face while he violated her and the other two cheered him on. When he finished, he collapsed on top of her, pinning her down with his enormous body. Then he whispered in her ear, *I'm sorry*, right before he got up and left the room, leaving her shackled to the wall.

Eve should've saved the ice pick for him.

The cabin was also the location Logan chose to wait with her and the baby before their rendezvous with the cowboy. The transaction wasn't supposed to take place until dark. Logan's excuse was that they had some time and he wanted to lie low, but he was a mean son of a bitch. He brought her to the cabin to relive his fantasies and evoke fear in her, because, of course, she recognized the permanently stained throw rug where the monsters had circled her.

"Brings back good memories, doesn't it?" Logan had asked her.

Bitterness rises in the back of her throat from remembering the sincerity in his voice, and how she'd clung to the baby at the time. They couldn't hurt her while she was holding Ivy. Shot would've killed them if they'd harmed the child and fucked up the exchange. Karl and the other guy from her original seasoning were eying her up, maybe hoping for another round with her, all the while spitting chew tobacco into a cup.

Logan had noticed the two idiots leering and laughed. "You can't touch her," he'd said. "She's a bottom girl now. Hands off Shot's merchandise." They talked about her as though she were a shiny new car they weren't allowed to drive.

Eve doesn't recognize the first guy who entered the cottage. He seems much older than the other guy who was with Karl at the hunting cabin. It's possible the old guy's a john. Those men are wiped clean from her mind.

"Is that you, Clyde?" Hester gently rocks the baby in her arms, trying to soothe her and stop her from crying. "It's hard to tell with all that paint on your face."

"It's been a long time," Clyde says.

"It certainly has. What are you doing here?"

"This pretty boy killed my nephew."

Hester turns and looks at the cowboy. "You shot Derrick? The town's big hockey star?"

"If Derrick is the loudmouth camo guy—then yeah, I shot him right between the eyebrows. I fed a hungry bear in the process, too, I might add."

The cowboy seems pleased with himself for the last part. Eve feels a little pleased herself, learning the camo guy who the cowboy shot is the other guy from the cabin. Good, she thinks. Derrick got what he deserved.

"A bear, you say?" Hester asks. "Is that how you got those scratches on your shoulder?"

The cowboy shrugs.

"Can I shoot him, now, Dad?" Karl asks.

Eve notices the vein bulging in Karl's neck, and how the sweat is dripping from his brow, streaking the paint on his face.

"No. Take up a position over there," Clyde says.

Karl seems to hesitate.

"Go on, son, I got your back."

The father and son duo want to separate so they're not standing next to each other, giving the cowboy a tougher time at hitting both of them.

"Be careful, Clyde. He's a real good shot," Hester says of the cowboy.

The cowboy keeps his gun pointed at Clyde as Karl skirts behind the couch and crosses to the other side of the living room. Eve finds she can't sit up. It causes too much pressure in her gut, as if the blade is pressing and pinching her organs. She slides her back down the bottom of the couch so just her head is propped up. A piece of glass from the shattered window wedges itself into her calf.

"I know you," she says to Karl.

"I don't think so," Karl says.

"Yes, I do. Maybe you should tell everybody here how I know you. I'm sure they'd be very interested to know what you're doing to young, innocent girls. Ones like me. Or maybe you're ashamed to tell them?"

"I don't know what you're talking about."

"What's going on, Karl?" Clyde asks.

"Nothing. She's lying."

"You don't know?" she asks Clyde. "Well, I'll tell you. He rapes girls. Don't you, Karl?"

Karl aims the shotgun at her. "Keep talking and I swear I'll fill you with holes."

"Karl! What's she talking about?" Clyde asks.

"It wasn't me. I swear! She has me confused with someone else. It wasn't me!"

Eve can almost hear it when Karl swallows what she imagines is the knot in his throat.

"Calm down now, son. I need you to focus."

Karl swings the shotgun back at the cowboy, who has grown quiet along with Hester. Even the baby isn't making any noise.

"Why do you always do what everybody tells you to do, Karl? Can't you think for yourself?" Eve finds herself asking him what she's wanted to ask him back when she was chained to the bedroom wall. If only he would've stuck up for himself, and her, but he didn't, and she loathes him for it.

"I'm a human being. You had no right to do the things you did to me." She shimmies herself to a sitting position, finding strength in anger.

The room is uncomfortably silent.

Hester is looking at Eve. There's something different about the woman's gaze, something a little softer, kinder.

The silence lingers. No one seems to know what to say. The only sound is the steady drip of the cowboy's blood striking the floor. Then Clyde motions to the cowboy. "Looks like someone got to you first."

Eve raises her left hand as best she can, propping her elbow up on the floor. "That would be me." Her right hand grips the handle of the switchblade that's slick with her blood.

"Well, darling, maybe you did us a favor. It will be my pleasure to sit here and watch this young man die a nice, slow death."

"Let me shoot him, Dad."

"Change of plans. I think we should let him suffer a little while. That's if you don't mind having us?" he asks Hester.

"Since when does what I mind count? You going to pay for blowing up my window?" Hester spits the chew tobacco at Karl. Eve can't believe it's been in Hester's mouth this entire time. The wad lands on the top of his boot. "Eat babies, my ass."

The cowboy laughs, shakes his head. Eve also finds herself smiling, as she slides the blade from her gut. It's not as painful as it sounds. It's a numb kind of feeling, like pulling out an earring from your earlobe. The only difference is the blood. There's so much of it, but she barely notices. When pain becomes so great, the mind has a way of protecting itself. It becomes impervious to it in order to survive. Eve is not only planning on surviving, but she's also going to get the bag full of money along with her freedom.

She may not have the ice pick at her disposal, but she has the switchblade, and it's time one of these bastards pays for what they've done to her. Years of suppressed rage tornadoes through her, overtakes her, silencing the pain and giving violence a voice.

This time, it's *her* voice.

Eve springs from the floor, screaming, the knife raised in the air. She charges at Karl, prepared to sink the blade into his cold, dead heart.

There's a loud popping noise.

Before she registers what's happened, she crashes to the floor. Her knees hit first, then her elbows and chin. The knife flies from her hand. A new red stain soaks the front of her shirt. No, that's not right, it's Hester's shirt. Eve's ears are ringing. Her head feels fuzzy. She gazes at a blurry Karl fumbling with the shotgun and the shells on his belt.

This was not the plan.

This was never the plan.

"Shoot him," Eve says to the cowboy as saliva mixed with blood bubbles up in her throat, dribbles from her lips.

"Which one?" the cowboy asks.

"Shoot him in his goddamn head like you did the other one."

Several shots are fired by the time she finishes her sentence. From her position where her cheek is pressed to the wood, she isn't sure who shot whom. Blood rushes to her head, or maybe it's rushing out. Her hands are sticky with some kind of gooey substance. Sounds reverberate around her. There's not one, but two loud thuds.

Two bodies hitting the floor.

CHAPTER
FORTY

Laura pulls up behind Joe's vehicle and parks. He's standing in the middle of the lot talking to two women. The women are dressed in baseball caps and workout gear, probably out for a walk on the myriad of trails around the lake. Their heads are tilted, looking up at Joe's face. They're smiling, and their ponytails swing when they talk.

Laura exits her SUV. The sun warms her shoulders and face. A gentle breeze blows off the water. Billowy clouds glide across blue skies.

The stranded vehicle is parked at the edge of the lot. Two of its wheels are pressed up against the woods. It's not exactly a parking space. She can see why the women called it in, especially if they noticed it sitting there for several days.

Joe finishes talking with the women and he makes his way over to Laura. Together they head toward the black SUV. Keeping their eyes straight ahead, they avoid looking at each other directly.

"What did you find out?" she asks.

"The two women I was talking with called it in. They noticed the vehicle when they take their daily walks. They thought it was strange given where it's parked, how it hasn't moved in the last three days, and how no one seemed to be around."

They stop next to the black SUV. It's a newer model with Connecticut plates.

"I already called it in. I'll see what came back." Joe heads to his car.

Laura walks around the front of the vehicle and looks through the driver's side window. It's got nice leather seats and seems to be pretty clean. There isn't any trash on the floor or dust on the dash. There's a black bag and an infant car seat in the back. A pink blanket is draped over the car seat. There's no way to tell whether there's an infant inside or not.

Shit.

"Joe!"

She runs back to her SUV. Opening the trunk, she pushes the fire extinguisher and first-aid kit aside, along with her rifle. Then she pulls out a black duffel bag and searches for a slim jim, trying not to think about what it will mean if a baby has been locked inside the car for three long days.

Laura rushes back to the stranded vehicle.

Joe jumps out of his car and joins her.

"There could be a baby inside."

She shimmies the slim jim down between the window and door frame, finding the lock and opening it. Laura doesn't need a search warrant in cases of an emergency, and this qualifies as an emergency if there ever was one. She pulls the rear passenger-side door open. The first thing she notices is the stale air and the absence of the smell of a decomposing body.

Laura lifts the blanket from the car seat. There isn't an infant inside, and she breathes a big sigh of relief. Then she brings the blanket to her nose, searching for the child's scent the way mothers sometimes do when they're longing for the days when their own children were babies. The blanket has a never-been-washed, brand-new smell.

Joe is staring at her.

"What?"

"Nothing. I didn't say anything."

"It's a new blanket and crazy soft. Expensive, too. The label is from a couture baby designer." Laura watches entertainment news about celebrities and the superrich when there's nothing else on TV. Who doesn't fantasize about living a life of luxury?

"It's a rental," Joe says about the vehicle. "The guy gave the rental company a fake driver's license. I say that's probable cause to peek around further." He slips on latex gloves. "Let's see if we can find out what's going on."

Joe circles around to the driver's side. He grabs the black leather bag from the back seat. Laura tugs on a spare pair of latex gloves that she keeps in her pocket. There's a box of them in her SUV. She always carries at least two pairs on her person. She used the first pair of gloves digging around in the dumpster earlier this morning.

Opening the glove box, she finds a nice pair of designer sunglasses, a burner phone, a phone charger, and three passports. One passport is for a John Smith. A generic name. She glances at the names on the other two passports. One is for Eve Smith, and the third one is for an infant named Ivy Smith.

"What name did the guy give to the rental agency?" she asks.

"John Smith," Joe says.

"What do you bet these are fake, too?" She holds up the passports. If they are fake, someone has paid a lot of money for them because even to a trained eye, they'd pass as authentic.

She sifts through the photos again. Something about Eve's passport gives her pause. It's the shape of the girl's face. The girl in the photo appears sickly thin with hollowed-out cheeks and sunken eyes, and yet, there's something familiar about her.

Joe's digging through the bag, giving Laura a laundry list of its contents.

"Looks like a change of clothes. Black T-shirt, super soft. Designer jeans. Not something you'd buy at Walmart, that's for sure."

She's not really listening, unable to tear herself away from Eve Smith's picture. She isn't sure what she's seeing, but the girl has similar features as Kayleigh. Is she imagining it? Is she delusional, experiencing some kind of false hope?

Joe returns the clothes to the bag and moves to the back of the SUV, opens the cargo area.

"Nothing but a pair of men's sneakers in here." He proceeds to give her a description. "Size ten. White or off-white. They're pretty snazzy actually."

"Snazzy?" she says absently.

He smiles. "That's about it. So what have we learned? We know John Smith likes fancy clothes, but where are the woman's things? And the baby's? You don't go anywhere with an infant without packing half the house. Am I right?"

Laura barely registers what he's saying. She can't take her eyes off of Eve Smith's photo. "Joe, look at this passport."

He takes it from her.

"I'm not crazy, right? There's a resemblance?"

He brings the photo close to his face and then holds it out at arm's length. "Yeah, I think you could be right. There's a resemblance."

Her heart lurches, racing and stumbling at the same time. She looks at the passports again. John Smith is completely foreign to her. She peers at the baby's ID. *Ivy.* Where has she heard that name before? Then she stares at Eve's photo.

"But you agree with me? This could be her, right? We have to do something."

"Let's take a moment here, okay, and think things through." He pauses and takes a second before speaking again. "We don't know for certain it's her. We only know there's a resemblance to the girl on the passport. I think the first thing we need to do is get a search team out here and check out these trails and surrounding woods."

"Right, of course. I'll call it in." Laura rushes to her vehicle, stopping halfway there. She remembers where she's heard the baby's name before.

Ivy is the name Hester called the doll.

Laura's not an alarmist, but right now every muscle fiber in her body is on high alert. This is more than an abandoned vehicle and a passport of a woman who may or may not be Kayleigh. This involves the FBI and sex trafficking. The SUV is somehow related to the woman's body they'd found in the alleyway by the dumpster and the woman's baby. The Burgh is only twelve to fifteen miles from here. The guy in the tree was close to Hester's cottage. She called the doll Ivy. There are too many coincidences for them not to be connected.

Laura takes her phone out to text Agent Ring, but she hesitates.

Joe walks up behind her. "What's the matter?"

"They were going to try to cross the border."

"Who? This John Smith guy?"

"Yes, but I have a feeling Hester has somehow stopped them."

"I'm not following you. What does she have to do with it? Would you please tell me what's going on?"

"It's sex trafficking, Joe. It's why the FBI are involved. And now I think maybe Kayleigh is a part of it. And a baby. A baby is missing. And I think—" *Dear God, is she really going to say it?* "I think my cousin has something to do with that."

"You think she's kidnapped the baby?"

"She's done it before, hasn't she? She kidnapped Priscilla when she was an infant. I think at this point, anything is possible."

Laura remembers it as if it were yesterday: her parents' hushed voices in the next room, whispering about Hester, how she'd stolen the information on the adopting parents from the hospital, and how she'd always been a resourceful girl. Hester had checked herself out of the maternity ward, driven straight to the couple's home. No one knows how long she'd been sitting outside their house, but she'd figured out where the nursery was, crawled through a window, and snatched Priscilla from her crib. For three days they'd searched for her and the baby. Eventually, they'd found her hiding out right here in the woods. They'd arrested her for kidnapping and thrown her into the juvenile detention center for girls.

Laura shoves her phone back in her pocket. "Do me a favor and have the vehicle towed to the station."

"What about a search party?"

"If I'm right, we won't need one."

"Where are you going?"

"To my cousin's." Laura rushes to her SUV and she climbs inside.

Joe is right behind her. "I'm coming with you."

"No. Stay here and wait for the tow truck."

"I don't think you should go alone."

"I'll be fine."

"You sure?"

"I'm sure. You'll need to bag and tag the evidence while you wait for the tow. I'll radio you as soon as I know something."

Laura starts the engine and throws it in drive. Then she pulls out of the parking lot, heading in the direction of the northern end of the lake.

Oh, Hester, she thinks, what have you done now?

CHAPTER
FORTY-ONE

Hester holds Ivy close to her chest. The gunshots are horribly loud. They probably hurt Ivy's little ears. Hester doesn't know what to do other than to keep herself and the baby out of the line of fire.

She huddles with Ivy on the floor near the couch. There's a strange man standing in the doorway. She never even heard him come in. He's wearing an oversized T-shirt, jean shorts that come down past his knees, and big, flashy sneakers. His head is shaved and the only way she can describe the look on his face is *menacing*.

She really needs to start locking her door.

Clyde and Karl lie on the floor not far from where she's crouching. Clyde is dead from a single gunshot wound to his neck. By the looks of it, the bullet hit his jugular. He died seconds after collapsing to the floor. She guesses the shot must've come from the cowboy. Although he seems to favor a headshot, she supposes either one is just as effective. She has to give it to the cowboy; he doesn't waste a single bullet. There are three holes in Karl's chest, though. They must've come from the new buckaroo standing in the doorway with a nine-millimeter in his hand.

A wet, gurgling sound comes from Karl's throat that not even the crying baby can drown out. Karl is still alive, but Hester regrets she'll hear his last breath. I'm so sorry, Clyde, she thinks, but at least he won't be around to see both his nephew's and his son's funerals.

"You must be Shot," the cowboy says to the man standing in Hester's doorway.

The buckaroo nods. "And you must be the angel."

While the two idiots point their weapons at each other, Hester scoots across the floor with the baby in her arms to where Eve is lying next to the box of diapers.

"Is he dead?" Eve asks.

"Who?"

"Karl."

"Not yet, but he will be soon."

"Am I dead?"

"No."

But what Hester doesn't tell the girl is how she's close to it. That is, unless Hester can stop the bleeding. She doesn't see how she can stop it, not entirely anyway, but she does have an idea about how she might be able to slow it down. Hester cradles the baby in one arm and with her free hand she starts pulling diapers from the box and packing them on Eve's wounds.

"This will help with the bleeding," she tells her.

Eve has taken a bullet to the chest from Karl's double-barrel shotgun (the first bullet blew out the window). And, of course, there's the knife wound from the switchblade that Eve has foolishly pulled out of her side. *Stupid girl.* It's the knife wound that's causing so much blood loss. If Eve would've left the blade in, it would've continued blocking the severed vessels. Pull it out and there's nothing preventing them from spilling their contents.

Karl releases one last gurgling breath. Hester knows it's his last because there's not another one that follows it.

"He's dead," she says to Eve.

A small smile crosses Eve's lips. The diapers are already soaked through with the girl's blood. Hester packs more of them on Eve's wounds, but in no time, the blood saturates these new diapers, too. In all the years Hester has worked in the hospital, she's never seen this much blood. She's going to have to invest in several bottles of bleach if she ever stands a chance of getting the stains off her floor.

"You've got to kill Shot and the cowboy," Eve says. "Get the gun and kill them both."

Hester looks around. "What gun?"

"Over there." Eve motions to Karl's body. The double-barrel shotgun lies inches from his hand. "Kill them and give me the money so I can get out of here. Can you do that for me, Hester? Can you kill them and give me the money?"

Hester considers how she can kill the cowboy and the buckaroo and give Eve what she wants and protect the baby at the same time. She doesn't see how, not without using both her hands, but she refuses to put the baby down. The child won't ever leave her arms again, not if she can help it. But how can she refuse the girl's dying wish? She can't, not really. Hester sees herself in the girl, a younger version of herself anyway, when she was vulnerable and in need of help. Her parents had turned their backs on her, forcing her to give up her baby, kicking her out of the house when she was in trouble with the law. And for what? For taking back what was rightfully hers to begin with. Hester won't turn her back on Eve even though the girl's death is most likely imminent. So much blood.

Another thought crosses Hester's mind, a wicked thought, and one that concerns the bag full of money. It could be Hester's now. She could run with the baby, so much farther than she'd run before, and leave these woods for good. With all that money, she could take the baby and never look back. But where would they go? Anywhere. Anywhere far, far away where no one knows her, where people will mind their own business, assume the baby is hers and she's caring for her granddaughter. The money gives her a second chance to be the kind of mother she always knew she could be.

"Okay." She lets the girl believe she'll do it for her. She'll kill the two idiots, when really, she's doing it for herself. What harm can a little lie do when it's doubtful the girl's going to make it, anyway?

"So, you'll do it?" Eve asks. "You'll give me the money?"

Hester takes a deep breath and checks that the cowboy and buckaroo across the room aren't paying attention to them. "Yes. Consider it done."

There's so much relief on Eve's face; Hester swears she hears the girl say *thank you*. The poor thing. She has no idea how bad of shape she's in. After glancing at the two idiots one more time, making sure they're still enamored with each other, Hester takes another deep breath, then shuffles on her knees as quietly as she can over to Karl's body.

"Where's Fen?" Shot asks.

"Dead," the cowboy says.

Hester pauses next to the double-barrel shotgun. Karl fired two shots. She's going to have to reload it. Carefully, she lays the baby on her thighs. Ivy stops crying and doesn't make another sound, as though she understands what's at stake. Hester picks up the shotgun and pushes the lever, opening the break-action, discarding the spent casings, making sure the barrel is pointed away from her and the child. There's extra ammunition on Karl's belt, and she reaches for it, pausing midway when the cowboy says, "Don't even think about it, Witch."

The cowboy's gun isn't aimed at her, but she can feel the bucka-roo's eyes on her back, and it's enough to know that his nine-millimeter is. Slowly, reluctantly, she has no other choice but to put the shotgun down. There has to be another way, though, because she's not giving up that easily.

She glances at Eve. The girl's shoulders rise and fall.

Hester considers crawling to Clyde's rifle. He never got a shot off so it has to be loaded and ready. All she needs to do is pick it up and fire away, but the buckaroo's practically standing on top of it with his big, flashy sneakers. Then Hester notices the switchblade underneath the kitchen chair. It's within reach and her only other option.

A voice coming from outside the cottage explodes from a mega-phone, filling up every inch of space in the room. "This is Special Agent Ring."

The fucking feds.

Who the hell invited them she wants to know? Quickly she picks up the baby off her lap and holds her close to her bosom with both arms. When she was a young girl, she was frightened of the cops, the way their flashlights cut through the trees like laser beams, their search dogs barking, pulling at their leashes to get at her. After three days in the woods, hiding with her baby, it had left her tired and weary and defenseless. A woman in plain clothes had marched right up to where Hester had been feeding Priscilla from her breast, and she'd plucked Priscilla from Hester's arms.

Please, give me back my baby, she'd begged. But in the '70s, closed adoptions were the norm and the birth mother's rights—Hester's rights—were never considered.

Hester didn't do anything wrong then, at least not in her mind. But it feels as though the same thing is happening all over again. The cops, *the feds*, want to take Ivy from her, inserting their presence where it doesn't belong, bringing with them the long arm of painful memories. She holds onto the baby a little tighter.

"I know you're in there, Shot," Agent Ring says. "I need you to come out with your hands raised."

"You brought the feds with you?" the cowboy asks.

"Fuck," Shot says. "I was fucking *careful.*"

"Well, apparently you weren't careful enough."

"We've got the place surrounded," Agent Ring says. "Now, we can do this the easy way or we can do this the hard way. It's up to you how this plays out."

Shot fidgets, transferring his weight from one sneakered foot to the other. "All right, listen, don't worry about them. I'm like fucking Teflon, man. Nothing sticks. Unless you're a snitch?"

"I'm not a snitch," the cowboy says.

"Well, I ain't no snitch either."

"That's just great," Hester says. "It's all settled then. Neither one of you is a snitch. Now get out of here. Both of you. Go on."

"Shut up!" they say.

"Geez, I'm just trying to help."

When they turn their eyes away, she shimmies closer to the kitchen chair and stretches out her arm, reaching with her fingers for the switchblade, deciding any weapon is better than no weapon. She hits her head on one of the chair legs, but she's able to pick up the knife. The handle is sticky, and the blade drips with the girl's blood.

"What do you say, Shot?" Agent Ring asks. "Are you coming out? Or are we coming in?"

Shot says to the cowboy, "You know I can't walk out of here without killing you first. You killed my baby brother. I can't let you get away with that."

"I take offense to the fact that you sent your brother in the first place," the cowboy says. "You should've dealt with me directly. If you had, we wouldn't be in this position."

"That's what this is all about? You take *offense* that I wasn't there to do the exchange myself?"

The cowboy shrugs. Hester knows him by now. His calm demeanor belies the hurricane hidden on his insides. His pupils contract. He's trying hard to tamp down his temper, but he's worked up, and she knows what's going to happen next. The ice pick in his side has stopped bleeding. He's one lucky bastard if it didn't nick an organ.

"What did my brother do?" Shot asks.

"He pulled a knife on me. I might've overreacted."

Agent Ring's voice breaks in. "I'm done waiting, Shot. Last chance to come out with your hands up."

Shot mumbles something Hester can't hear. Then he says, "Where's my money?"

"Your money? *Your* money?" the cowboy says. "I don't think so."

Hester doesn't see the cowboy pull the trigger, just the bullet hole in Shot's head, but not before Shot gets a round off. She drops the knife, covers the baby as best she can with her arms.

More shots are fired. They're coming from outside.

The fucking feds are shooting at them, too.

A spray of bullets penetrates the stone walls of the cottage, sending pieces of masonry flying. The glass in the remaining two windows shatters. Hester curls her body around the baby, using her flesh as a protective shield as best she can.

The baby cries in Hester's ear. Ivy's face is red and angry. Her little fists flail near Hester's face. *I'm trying, little one. I'm really trying.*

Pieces of plaster from the ceiling fall on them. Debris whizzes by and smoke fills Hester's nostrils. They need some kind of cover, and she starts to crawl across the floor to hide behind the couch, the baby tucked in the pouch of her belly.

Her knees scrape against the floorboards. Tiny shards of glass embed in her skin. She passes Eve along the way, smearing the girl's blood that lies in puddles. Eve has been shot again, but this time she's been hit in the shoulder and thigh. Another bullet hits the floor, splintering the wood near Eve's face, but the girl doesn't flinch. Instead, she stares at Hester, watching her with lifeless eyes.

CHAPTER
FORTY-TWO

The sun's warmth penetrates the windshield of Laura's SUV. She cracks the window. The wind blows across the top of her head. She's driving fast, in a hurry to get to Hester's cottage. While she watches the road, she thinks about Kayleigh and the young woman who was found behind the dumpster, the autopsy report confirming she'd given birth recently. It occurs to Laura how Agent Ring might've known all along who the young woman is, but would he lie to her about not recognizing Kayleigh? If he did, why? Does he know about the baby?

Laura has a pretty good idea where the child ended up. The guy in the tree, Logan Mense, was found not far from Hester's cottage. Of course, Hester would take Ivy in, provide a place of refuge for the infant and whoever accompanied her. It's what her cousin has wanted all these years, a baby to love and care for, to make up for the one her parents had forced her to give up for adoption.

Laura wonders where this John Smith fits into all of this. Another thought crosses her mind, one much darker than the others. Could

Hester somehow be responsible for killing the man hanging in the tree? And if so, did she do it so she could steal the baby?

Laura's not paying attention to the road, and she has to slam on the breaks, almost missing the turn onto the dirt driveway. Stones kick up from the tires. The shocks work hard as the SUV bounces over potholes. Her radio goes off, Joe telling her that the tow truck is on the scene. They're getting ready to tow the stranded vehicle with the Connecticut plates.

"Copy that."

She's not halfway to the cottage when she hears the sound of gunfire.

No, no, no.

She presses hard on the accelerator. The wheels spin out when she goes around the bend. Another SUV is blocking the road. She stands on the brake pedal to avoid hitting it. When she comes to a stop, it takes her a second to register what's happening, what she's hearing.

More shooting.

It's the FBI.

Agent Ring.

Laura flies out of the SUV and she races toward the cottage. At the same time, two agents appear out of nowhere, flanking her, blocking her from getting any closer. They grip her upper arms.

"What do you think you're doing? Let go of me!"

They wrestle her out of harm's way, under cover behind another vehicle that's parked on the shoulder of the road. She struggles to fight them off, but all it does is make them squeeze her arms tighter.

"Get your hands off me!" She tries to yank her arms free. "You don't understand!"

The crying she heard in Hester's cottage was not the cries of a doll. Hester was hiding a real live baby somewhere in one of the back rooms.

The agent on her left releases her. "We've got the sheriff here," he says into a radio.

The other agent hangs onto her right bicep.

"Is that Agent Ring?" She grabs the radio. "Agent Ring, tell your men to stop shooting!" She's trying hard to be heard over the gunfire. "There's a woman and baby inside!"

All the while the rounds continue, blowing apart the stone walls, the steps, the porch, until all she can see of the cottage is dust and debris.

CHAPTER
FORTY-THREE

Hester continues to use her body as a shield to protect Ivy. The first bullet strikes Hester near the kidney. It feels as if something has jumped up and taken a bite out of her. The second bullet hits lower, closer to her tailbone. Two more bullets enter her back by her thoracic spine. The fifth bullet lodges in her shoulder blade.

Hester imagines the pictures she used to draw when she was a child, the ones where you connected the numbers, teaching you to count. When you finished connecting the dots, assuming you counted correctly, you had a completed picture of a dog or a horse or a pig. Instead of numbers on Hester's back she has bullet holes, and the picture they will make is a dead witch.

The couch blows apart, sending the foam cushions into the air. One of the cushions hits Hester in the head on its way down. Another cushion drops onto the floor near the baby doll in the corner by the fireplace where Eve flung the toy after Laura had left the cottage two days earlier. It seems like forever ago, a happier time when it was just Hester, Eve, and Ivy. She wonders where it all went wrong. Nothing is clear, not when her head feels cloudy and her thoughts hazy. The frame of the couch breaks, collapses in a heap.

Shot lies in the doorway not far from Clyde's body. Neither man moves. Clyde wears a viscous scarf around his neck made of his own blood. There's a gaping hole in Shot's forehead. A shard of glass sticks out of his forearm. He's not wearing the big, flashy sneakers anymore. They've been blown right off his feet. Hester thinks of every war movie she's ever seen, the bits and pieces of men's bodies strewn across battlefields. But it is nothing, *nothing*, compared to the massacre taking place in her cottage and now lying on her living room floor.

And then there's the cowboy.

He's also lying on the floor. The chair he was sitting on has tipped over. The legs splintered and chewed with bullet holes. The Magnum that hasn't left his hand in three days is far from his fingers. The wooden handle of the ice pick has snapped off, leaving the metal poker embedded in his torso. Hester can't see his face because his back is to her, revealing the expanse of his shoulders and the rippling muscles underneath his taut, smooth skin. The inked wings decorate his deltoids, expand over his trapezius muscles, covering his shoulder blades. The feathers cascade down his lower back, where the tips touch the swell of his buttocks.

The image is beautiful, elegant, angelic.

Through the haze of dust and debris, she almost swears the feathers are fanning out into the open air around him, hovering over him, fluttering as though at any moment he could fly away. But there are bullet holes in the delicate wings of his picture.

The angel isn't flying anywhere, anymore.

Hester doesn't feel the pain of her own injuries and for that she's grateful, but what she doesn't know is that one of the bullets has severed her spinal cord. All she knows is that her body feels numb, like her face sometimes does after getting a tooth filled.

There's another explosion, several more rounds being fired. The sound echoes inside her head like popcorn popping in slow motion, the kernels moving through a thick layer of mud. Somewhere far away, the baby is crying.

Shhh. Shhh. It's going to be okay.

Hester can feel the words on her tongue. They roll around her mouth like marbles. But she's unable to hear her voice or feel its vibrations in her chest.

Somehow, miraculously, she keeps the weight of her body from crushing Ivy. She imagines she's made of armor.

Her flesh absorbs lead.

Her bones deflect slugs.

Nothing can penetrate her to get to the baby. This is what mothers do, protect their children at all cost. It's innate, an instinct inside of them revealed the second their child leaves their bodies. Hester has felt this basic instinct, this need to care for and protect a child that never should've been taken from her in the first place.

Hester will not let anyone or anything harm Baby Ivy.

She thinks of Priscilla and her little boys, and she thinks of Sophie—the granddaughter she'll never get to meet.

All Hester ever wanted in this life was a chance to prove what a good mother she would be.

CHAPTER
FORTY-FOUR

"T ake her to Ring," the agent who has taken back his radio says.

The other agent, who's gripping Laura's right arm, leads her through the woods. He pushes her forward as they dodge branches that seem to jump out in front of them from nowhere. She trips over weeds tangling around her ankles. His strong grip on her upper arm prevents her from falling.

They approach an area designated as central command. There are no more than four agents perched between trees, weapons aimed at the cottage, but not one of them is shooting. Most of the gunshots come from their left. The team is strategically located throughout the dense woods to prevent any potential crossfire.

"Are you trying to get yourself killed?" Agent Ring walks toward them, heavily suited in a bulletproof vest.

Laura pulls her arm away from the guy holding her. "Tell your men to hold their fire! There's a woman and baby inside the cottage!"

Agent Ring stares at her as though he's trying to get a read on her intentions.

"The woman we found by the dumpster. The autopsy report confirmed she delivered a baby in the last few weeks. I believe *that* baby is inside *that* cottage." She's pointing, hoping he understands. She can't even hear her own voice over the shooting.

Agent Ring continues looking at her when he says into the radio, "Hold your fire."

In another second, the firing stops. Her ears ring in the sudden silence. Laura pushes the agent aside, the one who was forcibly holding onto her arm, and she runs to the cottage.

Several other agents emerge from the trees all camoed up—like a goddamn wet team.

They enter the structure ahead of her where the front door used to be. Their weapons are raised. They keep her from following.

Laura waits, standing in a patch of ferns, the leaves covered in bits and pieces of stone and masonry broken from the porch and steps. Hester's El Camino looks as if it's been used for target practice. A wad of chewing tobacco lies in a clump of dirt near Laura's feet. She closes her eyes, tries to prepare herself for who it came from and what it means.

"All clear," one of the agents says.

Laura opens her eyes and steps through the rubble. There's so much dirt and grit that it's hard to tell what she's looking at. Dust floats through the rays of sunlight poking through the holes in what's left of the walls, but it's the quietness of the scene that makes her uneasy. It's as though she's stepped onto a movie set for some action thriller, because this can't be all that remains of her cousin's cottage.

Somewhere in the debris she hears the faint cries of a baby, but where is the sound coming from? It's only then she notices the bodies on the floor.

Laura steps over a young male in shorts and socked feet. She squats next to a second male. *Clyde.* Across the room where the couch is torn apart, she recognizes Karl's body. She wants to holler at them for acting so stupidly. She tried to warn them, and she has to stop herself from grabbing Clyde's shoulders and shaking him. If only he and Karl had listened to her.

Laura tears herself away from Clyde. She counts two more bodies— another male, shirtless, a large tattoo covering his back, and a young girl riddled with holes and stuffed with bloody diapers. *Dear God.*

She makes her way over to the girl. She recognizes the hollow cheeks and sunken eyes from Eve Smith's passport. But there's so much more about her: a familiarity only Laura can see after years of staring at this same heart-shaped face and lightly colored eyes.

Oh, Kayleigh, it is you. It's you. I'm so sorry.

Laura has always understood finding the girl alive was unlikely, but to be so close, within minutes of saving her—it's hard to make sense of it.

Maybe there's no sense to make of it at all.

The baby's cries get louder. Laura's ears are opening up and the ringing is subsiding. She pulls herself away from Kayleigh. Behind what's left of the couch, she finds Hester's body curled around the child.

Laura drops to her knees and scoops up the baby. She's wearing a pink onesie. A little girl. *Ivy.* Her face is dirty and streaked with tears. Her arms flail and her legs kick. She's covered in blood, but she appears unharmed. The blood must belong to Hester or possibly someone else. Perhaps it's blood from Kayleigh, whose body is packed with diapers.

Laura holds Ivy close to her chest. "You're going to be okay. I got you. You're safe now." She looks down at Hester. There are so many bullet holes in Hester's back, but somehow her cousin is still breathing.

"You did it, Hester. The baby is alive. You saved her."

Hester blinks once, slowly, as if it hurts to move her eyelids. Then she says, "Firewood."

"What? I don't understand."

Hester takes a shaky breath, struggling to get the words out.

Laura bends closer to Hester's face. "What is it? What are you trying to tell me?"

"Firewood."

Another word escapes Hester's lips. It sounds like dig. Laura wonders if she's somehow misunderstood her.

An agent comes to stand by Laura's side. She coaxes Ivy from Laura's arms.

"Hester," Laura says. "What does that mean?" But she's too late. Hester's mouth is slack, and her eyes are empty, staring at something only the dead see.

Oh, Hester, no.

She smooths the hair from Hester's forehead. "I'm so sorry I didn't get here in time. I'm so sorry for everything."

The growing pressure inside Laura's chest, the ache, is too much to bear, and she rushes out the back of the cottage through a large hole in the kitchen wall. She falls to her knees in the patch of yard, and she presses the back of her hand to her mouth to control the sobs collecting in her throat.

Inside the cottage, the agents are talking, parceling out orders, organizing the scene. Laura feels someone come up behind her. Agent Ring. He squats next to her.

She wipes her eyes and nose, pulls herself together. "You fed me information, but you wouldn't let me get too close and now it's too late. Why?" she asks. "Why?"

"I thought you might be able to get what I needed a lot quicker than if I used one of my own men. You already had the trust of the people here, and you had the information I needed whether you knew it or not. Let's just say I wanted to see what you'd do and where you'd lead me. And you did great. You led us to the hunting cabin, which led us closer to Shot, and eventually, it led us right here where we are today."

"You used me."

"I wouldn't put it that way, and I'm sorry if that's how you feel, but I won't apologize for doing my job or for using every resource available at my disposal. All I did was feed you the right information at the right time. You did the rest."

"You're an asshole."

"Sometimes, yes, when I have to be."

"Did you know about the baby?"

"No. That I didn't know."

"And the girl? Kayleigh? Did you know it was her?"

"Not until now." He hands her a photo of Kayleigh, one which was altered by the FBI's age progression software. "The goal was always to take Shot out and put an end to his trafficking ring. We did that today, and you should feel proud about that."

Laura gazes at the ground. *Proud?* All she feels is an overwhelming sorrow at the loss of so many lives, and how she was too late to save them. She doesn't say this to him. He doesn't deserve to know how she feels. She doesn't say anything. He stays with her for a few more seconds, until one of his men calls him back inside, into what's left of Hester's cottage.

The birds are singing. The insects hum and the gnats buzz around her ears. The leaves rustle in the warm, summer breeze. The bright, sunny day only makes her feel nauseous, like someone has kicked her in the gut. Laura lifts her head and wipes her cheeks. She looks around, realizing she's searching for something.

And then she finds it.

Next to the toolshed.

The stack of firewood.

CHAPTER
FORTY-FIVE

The angel didn't come and they let the nanny go.

It was a mistake.

Hillary sits in front of a mirror, touches the single strand of pearls around her neck. Her eyes are puffy, glassy. Her gaze is filled with the pain of an empty promise. She gives her head a little shake to get rid of the sullen thoughts attempting to invade her mind. Now is not the time to slip into the darkness that's been threatening to overtake her every minute of every day since Elsie's death.

Clarice walks into the room. She touches Hillary's cheek. "You should've told me about Elsie."

Oh, mum, you don't know the half of it, Hillary longs to say, but she swallows the nasty business with the nanny and angel, along with a pill. Hillary picks up the black fascinator, pins it in place, and adjusts the small veil that covers much of her face.

Clarice leaves the room when Emeril walks in. He comes up behind Hillary. He's wearing his funeral suit, the one he had custom-made when his uncle had passed unexpectedly of a heart attack last autumn. She meets his gaze in the mirror.

"Ready?" His bottom lip trembles.

Somewhere in the background, not far from the chateau, is the sound of sirens.

Hillary begs him silently, *please be strong for me today*. She doesn't think she can get through the service if he can't hold it together. She's counting on him for one day, this day, to be the one to stand upright, to be the statue of composure, for both of them. Soon enough, they'll have to carry it off alone.

Hillary stands. He takes her hand. The white bandage on his palm has been replaced with a more appropriate black one. He holds her hand as they walk down the stairs, and he continues to hold it as they make their way to the chapel in the north wing.

The sirens are getting louder.

A dozen people have gathered, those closest to them, every one of them family. Hillary and Emeril know many people, hundreds in fact, in their social circle. Their wedding alone had over five hundred guests. Most of whom she can't recall without looking at the list. Who are their friends really, she wonders now? You find out when a tragedy knocks on your door. You learn who you want to let in, who you want to stand by you, and who you want to stay away. She's discovered in the last twenty-four hours how to notice the difference between the three, and how to know who is who. She's received text messages, of course, from numerous socialites from past and present, expressing deep sorrow for her loss, but to have them here, in her home in the chapel, on the hardest day of her life? Hillary wouldn't put that kind of pressure on any friendship. It's unseemly and borderline boorish.

There are standards for family as well, but if family teaches us one thing, it's that they stick together. Her brother and sister-in-law are here. Her parents, and, of course, her in-laws, as well as Emeril's two sisters and their husbands. Emeril's cousin and closest mate is here with his wife. Children are noticeably absent, off with their nannies, ignorant of the family's loss. It's exactly how it should be. They'll learn one day of their dead cousin, Elsie, only to be talked about in hushed corners of darkened rooms.

Emeril escorts Hillary to the chairs in front of the vicar, who nods at their approach. Hillary sits, folding her black-gloved hands in her lap, and she stares at the impossibly small coffin. There's something innately wrong about its size. Something horribly unnatural.

They agreed to an autopsy. Any hint of foul play was ruled out. A final, *legal*, diagnosis of SIDS was written on the death certificate. The doctors assure Hillary that no one is to blame. Sometimes these things happen. Her obstetrician believes she shouldn't have any trouble conceiving again.

As for the FBI—

It's not their sirens they're hearing.

Hillary and Emeril won't be receiving a visit from them. Their name won't be found anywhere in the investigation. A senator and friend of the family has taken measures, precautions, and a substantial sum of cash to make certain their names are left out of all inquiries. But the senator's reach stops short of the Canadian border.

Rachel is Canadian.

And their sirens are quite loud.

The vicar looks around, concerned. Hillary's father-in-law stands, pulling out his phone as he rushes down the aisle, calling the family's lawyers. The service is cut short. Hillary and Emeril and the family gather in the formal dining room.

The sirens stop, a series of small chirps, car doors slamming.

Hillary and Emeril are arrested, charged with assault and kidnapping the nanny.

The rest of the family goes on to eat a light meal served on bone china dinnerware and polished silver flatware. It's all very polite, civilized, and morose in many ways.

As for the angel—

Sometimes he visits her in her dreams. He's human-like in form, floating above her, the wings on his back giving off a celestial glow. He carries a baby in his arms. It isn't Elsie, but she looks a lot like Elsie, close enough to fool anyone around her. Hillary reaches out to take the child from him and he gladly hands her over. She holds her tightly and silently weeps.

In reality, the news of the angel's death ripples through the walls of mansions and castles and chateaus alike. From Los Angeles to New York and back again. The ocean waves carry the gossip across the pond. *What a shame*, they say. *What a waste.*

They talk in hushed whispers, phones off and stored away: a safety precaution against anyone who might be listening. All the while, inquiries are being made and arrangements are being discussed.

A search for a new angel.

CHAPTER
FORTY-SIX

Three Months Later

Laura packs up the desk in the spare bedroom, puts the last of the charts and pushpins into the box. She takes the map off the wall, folds it, and places it in the box before closing the lid.

If only she would've found the girl sooner. If only she would've gotten to the cottage quicker. If only she would've beaten the FBI there. If only, if only, if only.

It's not the outcome she wanted, but she takes some comfort in knowing, at least in the end, Kayleigh wasn't alone. She was with Hester, with someone in Laura's and Pop's family. It's not much, but it's something.

There's only one thing left to do, Pop.

Laura kisses her fingers, touches the framed picture of him in his sheriff's uniform. Then she picks up Kayleigh's photo, the one where she's fourteen years old, and slides it in her back pocket. Heading to the kitchen, she sits at the table to finish what's left of her coffee.

The toilet flushes in the hallway bathroom. She hears the water running, Joe washing his hands. They've been living together for a couple of months now. He moved in soon after what the locals ended up calling the *witch's cottage massacre*. What Laura realized from the tragedy of that day is how short life really is, and if you're lucky enough to find someone you want to spend your life with, you better make the most of your time with them while you still can.

Laura is still Joe's boss, and after some minor adjustments at work, the transition to a public relationship has been somewhat smoother than she expected. The move didn't come without some complications and compromises. She doesn't see herself ever getting married again, being someone's wife. Laura had tried that once and it didn't work out too well for her.

It's taking Joe some time to come around to the idea of cohabiting. They enjoy all the benefits of being married without an official document stating they are man and wife. So far, it seems to be working out. They're mostly happy. Yes, she would say they're very happy.

Charlotte wasn't surprised when Laura had finally told her about their relationship. Her daughter had said something to the effect of "about time you two got together."

Laura gets a text from Charlotte letting her know she will see her later today. She's coming home for the weekend. Laura is excited to see her. Her daughter is finished with her internship and she's started a new semester at college.

Priscilla, Adam, and the kids will be joining them for a family picnic. Priscilla has softened some where Hester is concerned. She's even found some empathy for her after hearing how she'd saved Baby Ivy's life. Laura is hopeful that one day Priscilla will come to the realization that Hester wasn't such a bad mother after all. And maybe, just maybe, Priscilla will come to that conclusion on her own.

Joe saunters into the kitchen, bends over to give the top of Laura's head a kiss. Then he pours himself a cup of coffee and leans against the counter.

"I thought I'd clean up the boat and get it ready for the kids this weekend. Maybe even take it out for a spin around the lake before they get here. Do you want to join me?"

"No, that's okay. Go ahead without me. I have some errands to run."

"You sure? We'll be back long before they get here."

"I'm sure. I'll see you later." She stands and sets her cup in the sink and then she grabs her keys from the counter.

Laura drives up the windy road to the northern end of the lake. She almost misses the turn for the dirt driveway. The vegetation is overgrown, blocking the view from those passing by. If a person didn't know it was here, they'd miss it altogether.

She bumps along the narrow road, the tires of the blue pickup truck kicking up dust. She's not on the clock so she leaves her sheriff's SUV behind.

Laura takes her time navigating the potholes. The deeper she plunges into the woods, the thicker the foliage, the branches dense with autumn leaves.

At the end of the long driveway, she finds the remains of Hester's stone cottage. The roof has collapsed and shrubs have started growing inside where the floors used to be. Parts of the walls are still standing, moss creeping up the stones, much like they did when Hester lived here.

There's graffiti painted on some of the fallen rocks. The word "witch," of course, and "massacre." The local teenagers continue to harass poor Hester even in death. Laura has heard the cottage has become a favorite site for paranormal investigators looking to capture an image of the witch and record the sounds of a baby crying. Some even bring toy dolls with them in an attempt to lure Hester's ghost out. When Laura hears about such goings on, she hightails it to the cottage and chases the intruders away. What she tried to do for Hester in life but she wasn't always successful, she's still doing for her in death. She's sticking up for her cousin.

Laura sits in her truck and continues staring at the rubble. Time has a way of dulling memories, smudging the sharp edges of tragedy, smoothing out the vivid images in order for a person to go on living. She supposes what she's feeling now, sitting here, is a kind of quiet reflection. It doesn't mean she forgets the sacrifices that were made or the lives that were lost. She often thinks of Kayleigh, and she thinks of Baby Ivy, whom Hester saved, and how a nice family from Maine has adopted her.

Laura is slowly moving on, yet, every couple of weeks, she finds herself here, staring at what's left of the stone structure. She gazes at the spot where the toolshed once stood. It has since been knocked down. The pile of firewood has toppled over. Some of it has started to rot, becoming a part of the woods' floor.

After Agent Ring and his team removed the bodies and all the evidence, they cleared the premises. It wasn't until they'd gone that Laura returned later that night armed with a lantern and shovel. She moved the fresh cut pieces of firewood that were on top of the pile, as well as the older pieces underneath, stacked them off to the side, and started digging.

She smiles when she thinks back to that night when she pulled the black bag out of the hole and found all that money inside. *Damn, Hester.*

Laura remembers looking around, how paranoid she was, wondering if Agent Ring was still following her. She recalls how quickly she filled the hole with dirt and restacked the firewood exactly how she'd found it, in case the feds came back for another sweep of the place. It was wrong of her not to tell Agent Ring what she'd found. It was evidence, a part of an ongoing investigation, but at the time, she considered it payback. She owed the feds nothing for how they treated her and the people in this town.

For days, she kept the money hidden in a lockbox in her closet, but after a couple weeks went by and Agent Ring and the feds weren't showing up at her door looking for it, she decided it was time she got rid of it. She found herself thinking about all the things she could do with it: pay off the mortgage and Charlotte's student loans, take that vacation to the Hawaiian Islands with Joe, or buy a new boat.

In the end, it didn't feel right to keep it, so instead, she made an anonymous donation to a nonprofit organization in the Burgh, one that works with runaways and pregnant teenagers.

It was the right thing to do, honoring Hester and Kayleigh in this way.

Laura gets out of the truck, walks up to a pile of rocks where the porch steps used to be. Reaching in her back pocket, she pulls out Kayleigh's photo and props it up against a large boulder.

It's time she lets go.

Then she gets back in the pickup, puts it in reverse and turns it around, exits the way she came, bumping along the long dirt road. The remains of the lonely stone cottage deep in the woods grows smaller and smaller in her rearview mirror.

ABOUT THE AUTHOR

Karen Katchur is the Amazon Charts–bestselling author of *River Bodies*, the first book in her Northampton County series. She holds a bachelor of science degree in criminal justice and a master's degree in education. Katchur lives in eastern Pennsylvania with her husband and two daughters. *The Greedy Three* is her most recent novel. For more information, visit www.karenkatchur.com.

DISCOVER
STORIES UNBOUND

PodiumAudio.com

CPSIA information can be obtained
at www.ICGtesting.com
Printed in the USA
BVHW032319140223
658501BV00004B/29